Praise for *Summer on the Blac*

Not for the faint of heart, Jennifer Odom's debut novel, *Summer on the Black Suwannee,* is a stark reminder of the spiritual forces at work around us. A must-read for those who enjoy a page-turning thriller that will leave readers looking nervously over their own shoulders.

Marian Rizzo
Bestselling author of
Angela's Treasures and *In Search of the Beloved.*

Jennifer Odom has crafted an amazing story of betrayal, intrigue, and the power of faith. *Summer on the Black Suwanee* is a must-read and will keep you turning pages well into the night.

Mark Mynheir
author of *The Corruptible*

Jennifer Odom has a fresh, innovative voice that captivated this writer's soul. A reader cannot help but to be enthralled with the power of Jennifer's dynamic command of the elements of storytelling. Her characters come to life on the page and capture the imagination and the heart of those turning the page.

Fay Lamb
author of *Everybody's Broken* and *Stalking Willow*

Summer on the Black Suwanee is a captivating, fascinating, suspenseful tale geared for teenagers navigating the complexities of life.

Sonja Lonadier,
Missionary

I could not put *Summer on the Black Suwanee* down! The words flowed as if I was standing right there beside the old black river itself. All the characters were well defined and the setting was so well described that I could almost hear the flow of the river and see the faces of each person, whether they portrayed good, bad or evil itself. I hardly ever make time to read a book in one day. *Summer on the Black Suwanee* was an exception!

Cheryl Cannon
elementary education teacher, retired
multi-year recipient of Teacher of the Year

This jaw dropping, emotional roller coaster will surely touch your heart. Not only does it teach you the value of friendship and family, *Summer on the Black Suwannee* radiates the awareness of God and His presence, as well as exemplifying that no matter what circumstances you may face He will always be with you through the trials of life.

Abigail Lonadier
Reader
15 years old

Summer on the Black Suwanee is not only a thrill ride of a story for young people, but it also addresses very real issues of spiritual warfare, occult practices, demonic activity, and the power of prayer. It is at once enlightening and encouraging without skirting around the issues of consequences of making ill-advised decisions.

Dr. Ricky Roberts
Senior Pastor, True Light Ministries

SUMMER ON THE BLACK SUWANNEE

Summer
on the
BLACK SUWANNEE

a novel of suspense

JENNIFER ODOM

WordCrafts

Dedication

To Pastor Ricky Roberts who reminded me that God didn't give me the idea for someone else to write; *it was for me to do.*

Prologue

Something large and wicked rippled under the Black Suwannee. It stirred the pickerel weeds and jostled the floating spatterdock. A low fog, the color and stink of rotten eggs, curled above the disturbance. It slithered between mid-river and the cypress knees along the shore.

Owls fluffed and widened their eyes. The familiar thumping, like beating sails, echoed over the river. His presence was near. Then in unison across the river rose a flurry and flutter heavy wings, and *floof! floof! floof!* the owls and nighthawks disappeared.

All fell quiet except for the bubbling and quaking half of the river.

A swell rose at its center and the reptilian beast slowly emerged. He stood tall on two legs. Large obsidian eyes, as black and round as billiard balls, scanned the shore. Water drained off his snake-like jaw and ragged amber teeth. It streamed from the V of his loose scaly neck. He stepped to where the dead tree, straight and smooth, stuck out straight from the shore. Its roots stretched tall like a spider web against the woods. He straightened, all proud and steamy, and swung his reptilian leg across the log. And there he perched, his breathy "Haaaaaaaaaaaaaah" rattling the trees.

His thin, lizardy fingers gave a commanding snap. The creatures hidden in the shadows peeked and blinked in response.

"You will not fail me, you idiots," he rasped. "Carry out the plan. They are coming." His laughter ricocheted across the water. "And they are mine. To curry any favor you will give them to me."

That was all. He clapped a dismissal. The shadows darkened.

He slouched with his knees apart and morphed into a beautiful olive-skinned man in a pristine white suit.

With a snort he mocked the Creator who couldn't stop him now. Not with all his prior successes. He was fearless. Fearless. "I am, I am, I am. See, I can say it, too. Your people are here in my place now. And unlike You I have come to steal, kill, and destroy. Which I will do. I will. Watch me."

The disturbance in mid-river settled. But the thunderstorm came.

Torrents thundered over the river. It boiled up like a black cauldron beneath the log and Lucas' dangling feet. He dipped the toe of his shoe in the churning surface.

Upriver, a light flickered between the trees.

He squinted into the night. Had to be their headlights, that girl and her mother.

Or lightning bugs.

Worthless things.

Another puff. Smoke curled briefly from his nose and disappeared as rain's rhythm slowed.

The lights reappeared playing faintly through the black myrtles of the shoreline. A minute ticked by, and the headlights glimmered brighter through the leaves. They rounded the bend, lighting up the rain like broken shards of glass.

He should write a song about that. He loved sharp cutting things.

With a snicker he stirred to rise, but his hand touched a wet mound. Well, well, look at that. A turtle. His fingers curled around its slippery hardness as the reptile's legs scrambled inside for safety.

Lucas crushed it over the water like a tomato and snorted. Its blood drained into the Suwannee. He flicked aside the crusty mess then wiped his fingers on his still dry pants.

The thundering, louder now, filled the deep night of the woods. Lucas closed his eyes, punched his fist toward heaven, and roared with all his might.

The river's churning drowned him out.

He took another drag on his cigar, laughed, then spewed smoke from his nose. "*I'm* the roaring lion!"

But the rain hammered his voice back down.

After Lucas stretched, he extracted the cigar. It was still dry despite the rain, and he turned a languid smirk toward the sky. "You'll see."

A gator, as long as Lucas was tall, slithered toward the bank, and Lucas kicked in its direction. Missed. Too bad. Could have destroyed with that one, too.

Lucas rose on sure feet and strode up the slanting log to where its roots rose as high as the windows of his cabin. The headlights drew near and glanced across him. He checked his clothes and grinned at his own wonder. The starched white pants, unaffected by the rain, showed no sign of blood, turtle or otherwise.

Leopard-like, he dropped between the cypress knees and slipped through the dripping palmettos toward the cabin.

Time to get to work.

Chapter 1

Emily leaned her cheek against the passenger window, letting its coolness saturate her skin. As if a fire hose had been turned on in the dark void above, the rain's battering and blowing began anew, pelting the outside of the thin glass. Rivulets turned into the raging underside of a waterfall.

"Almost there," Mom said.

Yeah, right. There was no end to this road. Emily flipped on the interior light.

She unrolled the snapshot curled in her hand, a photo of her and her friends that only existed because of the Citra Fish Camp lady. While shooting nature pics out on her dock, she'd taken one of the friends fishing and volunteered to email it to Emily.

As Emily examined the four faces in the dim light, the corner of Dad's picture slid from behind the photo. She studied his features for several minutes.

If she and Dad could just be together again.

She turned the light off and pressed the pictures between her hands, a photo-hug. With a sigh, she laid them in the glove compartment.

The dirt road made a sharp right, and Mom's headlights swung around too, across a deep puddle of floating weeds and a short wooden sign. "This is it," Mom said, stomping on the brakes. She backed up until the headlights glimmered through the raindrops and lit up two rotten boards. A crust of curling gray lichens camouflaged the carved letters.

We-com- to E-rth M-ther A-res
Wh-r- Sh-tter-d L-ves are He-l-d.

Great. And this was supposed to be some kind of nice retreat?

The sign ought to say *Welcome to Cruel Mother Acres, Where Great Summers are Interrupted.*

Emily pursed her lips and glared at the dash. A white square of paper on the console caught her attention. Even in the dark she knew it was Tony's phone number in Gaskille. The one he'd handed to her in the driveway. She snatched the paper up and stuffed it in with the photos.

Tony was a nice guy and all. But no friend could replace her buddies in Citra. No sense in starting up a new friendship in Gaskille, the very place she wanted to leave.

Emily sighed. Speaking of leaving, maybe Mom would realize this retreat place was a mistake and they'd leave. Right now would be fine. Even in this storm. Emily would be more than happy to backtrack through the miles of slashing myrtles and mud-filled ruts again, past the incessant, ratcheting frogs—the ones she'd absolutely love under other circumstances. Emily could take all of it, even the mud drubbing under the car, a racket that still vibrated in her ears. If Mom would just forget the retreat and go back.

But nothing had slowed Mom down. The little Honda Civic burrowed deeper and deeper into the black doom of the woods. No matter what, Mom was dead-set on getting to the end.

And here they were. Maybe Mom was happy now.

Emily glanced at the glove compartment and smiled at her fish camp memory. The friends, who were thirteen back then, had scraped together their coins that day and shared

5

a soda and pecan tart, then explored the woods on the way home. Even tried to make a campfire with a magnifying glass. Now, only two years later, the group had split and only three kids remained. A lump formed in her throat.

It was Mom's fault for moving away.

Mom leaned back and massaged her neck with both hands.

Emily closed her eyes. Mom was probably thinking, *Safe at last, thank you, Lord, we're finally here.*

Like Mom hadn't put them in harm's way herself. A limb could have crushed them. Pinned them down until they drowned and bears ripped the soggy flesh off their bones.

Mom shouted over the racket coming through the car's roof. "Pastor Mario was right, wasn't he? It's quite a retreat."

Emily shook her head at Mom's inappropriate happiness. She just didn't get it.

"A retreat should be just like this. Far away." She reached to straighten Emily's bangs, but Emily turned her face to her window. Lightning struck again, revealing the towering woods. To the right sat a wooden cabin, high enough on its rock supports to hide a deer.

"See, lights in the window. That must be the office." The tires spun as Mom pulled closer to the porch. "Got your umbrella?"

Emily reached under the seat for it. She wasn't spending the night outside in this typhoon.

"I know you don't want to be here," Mom said. "But see how you're clamming up on me? These people can help you."

"I don't need help. Or a retreat." Emily opened the nylon cover and slid out the umbrella. "You heard Grandma. It just takes time. And family."

"Grandma doesn't know everything." Mom turned off the

ignition and pointed the key at Emily's nose. "You remember that."

"She's right most of the time."

Mom arched her thin eyebrow.

"You never listen to her."

"We're living in a time when trained psychologists handle things like this. Your grandmother is old-school."

"I trust her more than your dumb old friends."

"My friends—"

"Please keep them out of my business."

"They only want to help."

"Stop yelling, Mom."

"At this place, you'll get the help you need. Whether Grandma Rene agrees or not."

"No wonder things turn out bad for us. You always listen to the wrong people."

"Don't talk back to me."

"You should have stayed with Dad."

"We're not going through that again."

Emily thumped the seat with the umbrella, her mind racing for another excuse. "This is a waste of money."

"Well, it isn't coming out of our pocket, is it?"

Lightning flickered again. Emily focused on the cascade falling over the cabin's roof. Suddenly a yellow bulb lit up behind it, illuminating the porch. A gypsy-skirted woman leaned toward the car, motioning for them to come up.

Emily opened the door, and the roar intensified. She jammed the umbrella between the door and frame, shot it open, then whirled around one last time. "I don't need this. Bill didn't do anything to me."

"He tried, didn't he?"

"You're the one who married him."

Before Mom could answer, Emily threw the wadded umbrella cover against the seat. "I'd rather die than spend my summer here."

Chapter 2

Emily plunged through ankle-deep water and gasped as the cold rain touched her skin. With no handrail to grip, Emily used the fingers of one hand to steady herself on the slippery steps. The tiny umbrella did little to keep her dry. Once on the porch she closed it and pulled her cold, wet shirt away from her skin.

The woman wrapped a large towel around Emily's shoulders. "Thanks."

"You've got to be Emily, Charlene's daughter," the woman said, giving her a squeeze and a smile. "This rain is enough to drown the bullfrogs. I'm Maria, by the way." She lifted a corner of the towel toward Emily's face.

"It's alright. I can do it." Emily drew back and pressed the corner against her face.

"I bet the lightning made you a little nervous."

Emily shrugged and nodded as Maria set the umbrella aside.

"When your mom comes up, I've got something warm for you to eat."

Mom appeared at the bottom of the steps. Good. Let *her* do the talking. Emily had nothing to discuss with these people.

Mom climbed the steps with the two overnight bags. Rain splattered off the top of her head and dripped form the ends of her hair.

"Charlene?" Maria took a bag and extended her hand. "Welcome to Earth Mother Acres. Maria Barber, owner and head counselor. We chatted online. So pleased to meet you."

Mom smiled and grasped Maria's hand. "It's very nice to meet you, too."

Maria handed Mom a towel from off her shoulder. "Here, wrap yourself up, and let's get you girls inside."

Mom scraped her feet on the worn-out mat and dried her face. She squeezed out her hair. "I had no idea a June rain could be so cold. It's amazing how much those clouds hold."

"That's just good old Florida for you." The screen door groaned as Maria jerked it open. She yelled inside, "John, our newest guests are here. Charlene and Emily."

After they entered, the screen door slapped against its frame. Maria latched it and switched off the porch light. A rain-chilled breeze followed them through the hall's dim interior.

Emily inhaled the piney scent of the walls. This place reminded her of Grandma's. Sort of. And it did beat the soggy outdoors.

In the living room, a gaunt, middle-aged man rose from the shadows. He smiled and shoved one hand toward Mom while pushing his wire-rimmed glasses back up on his nose with the other.

"I'm John Barber. We're pleased to have you here and so glad Faithful Disciples referred you for therapy." He motioned to the black couch with its cracked leather seat before nestling back into his own sagging chair. "Please, sit down. Make yourselves at home. No need to be shy."

He grinned at Emily and nodded toward the rocking chair. "Sit there if you like."

She followed his lead then glanced around the room. The ancient furniture must have belonged to the man's own grandmother.

"Thank you, John. It's such a relief to get out of the car and come indoors," Mom said.

"You and the young lady are going to get help here," John said. "You certainly are. Anyone who has been through something like she has needs a retreat."

Emily chewed the inside of her cheek. Over-reactors. Just like Mom. Nothing had happened, and she was okay, for goodness' sake. She didn't need to waste a good summer with a couple of weird strangers.

In the doorway, Maria held up a finger. "Before we get better acquainted, may I get you some hot cocoa and fresh blueberry cobbler? The bushes are loaded this year."

John cocked an eyebrow toward Emily. "What do you say?"

She wasn't about to smile, so she shrugged and nodded.

"I'm sorry, John," Mom said. "Emily hasn't been herself for a while now."

"You're here to fix things, remember?" He slapped his leg and stood. "I'll go help Maria. You folks hang on a minute."

Yeah, with that old gray ponytail and Nehru shirt, Mom probably thought he was pretty charming, all groovy and retro. Maybe they'd have a VW Bug in the backyard for her, all covered with flower-power stickers like Mom said her Jesus friends had back in the sixties.

Emily leaned against the arm of the chair. If she could just wake up from the unending nightmare. The move to Gaskille, Mom's marriage to Bill. His attack on her, and now this place.

Across the room Mom traced her finger over the stiff leather of the couch. Emily studied the smile pasted across mom's mascara-streaked face. Probably thinking back to those late night prayer meetings with her college buddies.

11

She'd described a place just like this once. Maybe she wanted to share her hippie days with Emily.

No, thank you. That *peace, brother* talk hadn't improved the quality of Mom's poor life-decisions.

Mom sat up when John returned and handed out napkins. "Maria will be right in with the dessert."

"John, this is so lovely," Mom said.

"Well, we're here for you. The best therapy you could ever find, and we'll do whatever it takes to get your daughter back to her old self."

"Thank you, John. I believe that."

Maria entered with a tray. Steam rose from hot cocoa and large portions of blueberry cobbler. "Here you are, something nice and warm." She placed her own plate next to Emily's on the coffee table.

Oh brother, here she was again, up close. With more questions, probably.

"John, Maria, thank you for taking us in." Mom unfolded her napkin. "I just have a good feeling about this."

Emily glared at her. Way. Too. Bubbly.

Mom barely took a breath. "I confess, I never really needed to pray about this move."

Emily furrowed her brow and sank back in her chair.

She hadn't even prayed about it?

Really?

"The pieces fit right together, and I knew in my heart it must be a God-thing. It was all so perfect." Mom took a sip and dabbed her lips. "This just feels so right."

Emily could say the same thing about her plan to run away and go back to Citra—go back to Dad's. It was all so perfect.

Live with him instead of staying in Gaskille.

"May I say something else?" Mom picked up her fork and poked at her cobbler. "Sitting here in your home is like putting on my favorite slippers. It's such a strong peaceful impression. It hit me as soon as I walked in your door." She smiled broadly. "I'm really big on first impressions."

Yeah, like with Bill.

John scraped blueberry syrup from his plate. "Maria is one of the leading psychologists in the nation. She boasts a ninety percent success rate. But you already gleaned that from the website, I'm sure. The program is challenging, and a few clients give up before it's over. But if you stick it out, we guarantee success. Guarantee it."

Emily loaded her mouth with cobbler. At least the dessert tasted good.

"Of course, we'd never think of quitting." Mom glanced at her plate. "This cobbler is unbelievable, Maria. What a great cook you are."

"Experimental cook," John corrected. "She actually works up new dishes for gourmet restaurants. And since you two are lucky enough to stay in our cabin, you'll enjoy her recipes all the time."

Mom pressed her napkin against her lips. "You mean we're staying right here? How sweet. I can't wait to try her other experiments."

"We use organic food in our recipes since we have lots of it on hand." Maria traded a look with John. "It's our special feature."

"Let me explain," John said. "Our eighty acres house multiple charity enterprises. Residents grow organic produce which we donate to the poor. They should have the very best, don't you think? You and Emily will enjoy the produce, too."

Mom shook her head. "This is terrific."

Emily stared at her. Not terrific enough to waste her summer vacation on.

"Working quietly with your hands in solitude to God is the backbone of the program," Maria said. "You'll have scheduled reading and writing activities to challenge, heal, and enlighten your inner woman."

"The system is very organized," John added. "So you'll always know just what to do if Maria ever has to run to town. I'll be mostly in and out, tending the farm."

Emily winced. It sounded like schoolwork. "Mom, I'm supposed to be on summer break. This is not a vacation." She set her empty plate on the table.

Mom's gaze flickered toward her, but her focus returned to John.

Emily slumped back in her chair. Nobody cared what she thought.

"We hope you truly grasp the magnitude of being chosen for the retreat," John said, "especially with two hundred on the waiting list, all ready to pay full price."

"Oh, no. I do I do," Mom said. "We're just so honored to be part of this."

"Long ago we decided to only accept the clients we could help on a one-on-one basis."

"So why did you pick us?" Emily asked. "Somebody's got to need this more than me." Maybe John would kick them out, send them home right now.

He chuckled. "When a church like Faithful Disciples recommends someone and offers to pay all expenses, we take it seriously."

Emily blew air from her nose. Insane people.

14

John ignored her. "You realize that's what your church did, don't you, Charlene?"

Emily pushed back in the chair and drilled her eyes into Mom. "It wasn't our church."

"That's the curious part," Mom said, ignoring her look.

"How so?"

"Faithful Disciples isn't our home church. Emily's psychiatrist from the health department recommended it."

"Really? I've never heard of that happening."

"A few weeks after we met the pastor—"

Emily cleared her throat to get Mom's attention. She'd told Mom before that he was more freak than pastor.

Mom glared at her. "Everything clicked, John, and they offered to pay all our expenses, said this would really help. Brother Mario's offer felt so right, like God's guidance."

More like guidance from the Creature of the Black Lagoon.

"Dr. Mario's reputation is well-known. That's why we moved you up in priority."

Maria tipped her head and gave Mom a warm smile. "The holistic therapy will cleanse and free you both. But without dedication to the program, we offer the client nothing."

"Emily, could you bring that briefcase to me, please?" John asked. "There, under your chair?"

Wonderful, a chance to stretch. As Emily bent, a thick whiff of rotten sardines hit her nose. She sniffed again. Maybe it was her tennis shoes. Or something in the kitchen. She stood, unable to ignore the horrid odor, then blew air from her nostrils as she placed the satchel in John's hands. The smell lingered there, too. She glanced at Mom, who smiled away, totally oblivious to the gross fumes.

"This disturbing experience will all be faint memories soon,"

Mom said, reaching for Emily's hand. "No more nightmares, no more sitting and withdrawing into her own quiet world. I'll have my little Emily back again."

Emily sighed and studied the wall behind John. A dumb retreat couldn't turn her into an extrovert. Maybe this whole thing was just so Mom could fashion Emily into a clone of herself. But Emily was happy to be like Dad. Her real dad. She slipped her hand away and sat back down.

John snapped open the clasps of the briefcase as if he'd done this a thousand times. "I know you're tired, but before you get all tucked in for the night, we need to get the final paper signed. This won't take long."

"Final paper?" Mom asked.

"You've already taken care of most of the paperwork." He fumbled in the briefcase and pulled out a sheet of paper. The signature line had been marked with a yellow highlighter. "We need your signature releasing us from liability if you don't finish the program."

"Let me have that." Mom took in a determined breath, signed her name, and handed the sheet back to John.

He winked at Emily as Mom tackled the last bite on her plate.

Emily shifted in her seat. That was just the way her step-father used to wink.

Like a self-assured loan officer, John stacked and clipped the paper with the others. "Great. You'll be so glad you chose Earth Mother Acres. You discussed the $30,000 repayment fee with Dr. Mario, right?"

Emily held her breath. Mom didn't have that kind of money. Maybe they wouldn't be staying after all.

John arched a dark eyebrow. "He informed us that if you

quit the program, your contract requires you to repay the church in Gaskille so it won't incur a loss. Is that right?"

Mom covered her lips with the napkin and swallowed. This seemed to be a big fat surprise.

John snapped the briefcase shut, and Mom blinked. Dead give-away. She hadn't known.

How could they leave early now? This mega-mess of a summer was looking like a bunch of work—all tied up with money strings. They shouldn't even be here.

"No," Mom mumbled. "He didn't mention it."

"Most likely, he wasn't too concerned. That only shows his confidence in you and in the seriousness of your need." John stood and tucked the briefcase beneath his arm. "No need to worry about it. You don't plan to quit, do you?"

"Of course not," Mom stammered.

"I didn't think so. Now, I know it's late, but Maria has a small assignment for you. Good night, ladies."

Maria stood as he disappeared down the hallway. "Good night, John."

Emily bent to re-tie the loose string on her wet tennis shoe. What a nightmare. And getting worse by the hour.

Rain, all but invisible in the black night, bombarded the cabin's tin roof at Earth Mother Acres and poured over its edge like sheets of glass.

On the porch, an Australian Shepherd lay trembling under the dusty rocker. A crack of thunder and long blue vein of lightning split the sky, revealing the shiny top of the Civic below.

Beyond it a pale figure materialized from the dark woods.

The dog's sharp eyes latched onto the man as he opened the driver's door. The slim figure, with his face obscured, leaned inside and popped the hood. He circled the car and reached inside the cooling, crackling engine. Seconds later, the lid thumped quietly back into place and the door clicked shut.

Lightning flickered, illuminating the man's white suit as he wiped his hands together, turned, and disappeared into the dark.

A stench of decaying flesh slithered across the dog's nostrils, fetid and strong. The hairs rose along his back and he sneezed, spraying the clammy dust. In his throat a quiet whine rose, then curled into a low growl. After a time, he quieted and laid his chin on his paws. Only the sounds of the downpour thundered across the woods.

But the hairs on his back remained stiff and high as he stared, wide-eyed, into the dark.

Watching.

Chapter 3

Emily leaned away from Maria's jabbing fingertips. She could find her way down the hallway without someone poking her in the back. Touch, touch, touch.

Just like Bill, Emily's stepfather. She shuddered.

And way too talkative.

Emily gripped the red strap of her overnight case, letting it bump against her knees as Maria prattled on to Mom about her old recipe books.

Grandma's were the only recipes Emily cared about.

And forget the thirty thousand dollars. Their stay hadn't really started yet. So why couldn't they just get in the car and go back home? Maybe it wouldn't count yet.

Maria guided Emily to the door on the right and pushed it open. "I'll run you a nice bubble bath in a minute. But let's drop off your things in your room first. A little bird told me you'd like the pink room. Your favorite color."

A little bird? Emily wasn't six anymore.

She stepped across the matted Pepto-Bismol-colored rug with a grimace. At least the walls were white. She set the bag on the bed and shimmered the pale pink prisms on the desk lamp. Maybe she could stand one night in this place, but several weeks—too much to think about.

Behind her, Maria's overly-cheerful voice began to grate. "Charlene, I want to thank you for following directions. I can see by the two overnight cases, you ladies have left most of your things at home. Like the brochure says, we provide all your outfits. Except for tennis shoes and personal items, of course."

Maria wedged past Emily and pointed to the closet, "You'll find your clothes in there. And," she said, patting a drawer, "your nightie's in here. Just leave your case on the bed for now. The bathroom's around the corner."

Pushy, pushy.

As Maria escorted Mom from the room, Emily dropped her case on the bed and peeked outside between the curtains. Great. Nothing but a black hole out there.

By the time she caught up with the others in the bathroom, water was blasting from the tub's antique faucet. Maria poured a thick stream of pink bubble bath into the claw-foot tub and tested the water's temperature. She held the jug up for Emily to sniff.

Emily coughed and wiped her nose.

"Great rose scent, isn't it? Makes great suds." Maria set the jug on the floor, stirred the bubbles, and pointed to a shelf over the toilet. Water dripped from her hand. "Towels are there. This is your bathroom, Emily, so why don't you run along and take care of your things while I get your mom settled?"

Emily glanced at Mom, but she was in another world, staring into the tub.

Looked like they weren't going anywhere tonight.

Back in her room, Emily reached under the inverted glass bowl of the lamp and turned it on. Its light cast a pink crisscross pattern over the beadboard ceiling. Once again she shimmered the prisms, soothed by their light clatter.

With nothing to do but waste time she opened the dresser drawer. It was empty except for a pink seersucker nightgown which she held up to her shoulders. Good enough.

She dropped it back in and added the contents of her bag,

her toothpaste, deodorant and underwear—along with the forbidden journal.

Temporarily. While she convinced Mom to get them out of here.

No writing materials allowed, the brochure had said. When Emily first smuggled the notebook into her suitcase, Mom had pulled it out. But she neglected to recheck.

Emily had to have it. She would absolutely die without her journal.

Bam! From the front of the house came the sound of a screen door slamming, followed by a scrambling, sliding racket that tore down the hallway in Emily' direction. Before she could figure out what it could be, a long-haired dog barreled past her and dove under the bed. Its silver-plumed tail disappeared under Emily's eyelet dust-ruffle.

Maria rushed into Emily's room. Mom stepped in behind her with her mouth hanging open.

"Sorry, Emily." Maria dropped to her knees beside Emily's bed. "Whenever John leaves the front door unlatched, this mutt gets in. For some strange reason he loves this bedroom." She groped under the bed, her gauzy brown skirt puffed around her feet, and slid the animal out by his hips. "He just dives in here for no reason. I don't know what gets into him." She clamped her arms around him and stood as the dog tucked his tail between his legs and looked up at Maria with guilty eyes.

"Back in a minute."

Emily slipped into the bathroom and turned off the bath-water. It had nearly run over. She'd have to drain some out. She pictured Maria shoving the dog down the steps in the rain and him slinking away. He'd probably sleep under the house. Poor dog. Maybe it would be dry under there.

When Emily returned to her room, Mom gave her a hug and a kiss. "We'll have to say good night in a minute. I'll be right around the corner if you need me."

"Can't we just go home?"

Mom let her go. "We're doing this for you. It's all going to work out. Now be a sweetheart, and I'll see you in the morning."

Emily closed the bedroom door and took her empty bag to the closet. Two pink "retreat outfits" stared back from their plastic hangers. She swatted at them and kicked the doorframe. This was so unfair. Like being in prison. And she was the convict.

After stepping out of her tennis shoes, she tried to line them up with her foot but met resistance behind them.

She squatted and peered into the dark corner. There was a wad of fabric back there.

With two fingers she lifted out a pair of blue striped shorts. Whose were they? She pulled the light chain. A matching tank top dangled off the back end of a plastic hanger. She unhooked it and held it against her chest. A splotch of mustard marred its front.

A knock behind her rattled the bedroom door. She dropped the clothes in the back corner, snatched off the light, and nudged the closet door shut.

"Hi, honey." Maria walked in and reopened the closet. She retrieved a metal box form its top shelf. "This is for your mom's things. I'll bring it back later. Sweet dreams, and good night, now.

"Oh," she said, pausing at the door, "after your bath, please do today's little writing assignment to your grandmother. I left the directions beside the green stationery."

No sweat, writing was Emily's passion.

"It's simple. Just tell her how nice everything here is, okay? So she won't worry about you. But do it before you get too sleepy."

Emily nodded. "Thanks for the cobbler."

"Sure, honey. See you tomorrow."

"Night."

As soon as the door latched, Emily darted to the closet.

She held the shorts against her waist. Same size. Someone her own age, probably. With quick movements, she folded them again.

They needed a special place. She glanced at the furniture. No, not the dresser. She laid them back where she found them. Her little secret. Something to tell her friends back in Citra.

If she ever saw them again.

Chapter 4

Charlene kept pace with Maria's quick steps as she led her to another bedroom door leading off the kitchen. Such a sweet, old-timey place. So rambling.

Inside, Maria rubbed her palm over a paneled wall on the right. "This used to lead to Emily's hallway. Odd, I know, but old, remodeled houses can be like that. No rhyme or reason. You'll be right next to her, just the same."

Charlene gazed into the cozy room with its lavender bedspread and embroidered bolsters. Mints and a goblet of water sat on the desk. "You shouldn't apologize. This is adorable."

"On the other hand, you'll have lots of privacy, so please, make yourself at home. I'll warn you, there's no closet." She slipped into the room and pointed to a narrow door. "We turned it into a little bathroom. Peek inside."

Charlene stuck her head through the door. "Cute. My mother has one of these under her staircase. Not much room, but it's functional. That's what counts."

"You have these big nails to hang your things on," Maria added, touching the one by the bathroom door. "That's all you'll need. Just don't poke your eye out."

She held a gray metal box toward Charlene. A pink ribbon hung from the key in its keyhole. "Store your wallet and valuables in here, but if you don't mind, I'll take your car keys so John can move your vehicle tomorrow."

Charlene fished through her overnight case, which had doubled as her purse. When she passed over the cell phone, Maria held out her hand. "I mentioned we don't use telephones at the retreat, didn't I? If not, I apologize. It's in our statement of policy."

"I didn't really think you meant it. Who goes anywhere without a cell phone these days?"

"I'm sorry, but it's a rule we have to enforce. Dismissing clients because of phone issues became a headache. It ruined their therapy. They might as well not have come."

Maria couldn't possibly realize how hard this was, letting go of her phone. Now she couldn't even call her office. Or Mother. Well, Mother would probably be alright back in Gaskille. After all, she had Kaye next door. Charlene laid the phone in the gray box, severing her connection from the outside world. Something she hadn't planned on.

Maria smiled. "We'll keep the lockbox in Emily's room. She has a small closet, and I'll put it on the top shelf." Lowering her voice, she confided, "We have a maid who comes every day. It isn't that I don't trust her, but these days you just can't be too careful." Closing the box, she handed the key to Charlene.

"Right. Who would look for this in a child's room?"

"Absolutely. One more thing, I know it's getting late, but the first night's assignment is to write a letter to your mother. The object is to record your first impressions while they're fresh on your mind. You've been living at your mother's, right?"

"Yes." Charlene closed the overnight case and moved it to the floor. Mother was all the practical support she had left. "Emily and I moved in with her after my first divorce."

"What's her name again?"

"Rene Thompson."

"Oh, yes, I had forgotten. In your letter to Rene, and this is all part of the treatment, just tell her about your experience up to now and how happy you are to be here. No negative thoughts, though, which would be like taking poison after a vitamin. Whoops, I almost forgot." She rummaged through the dresser drawer. "Here are some little lavender slippers for you, some bath beads, soap, and a matching satin gown."

Charlene shook her head. "My goodness, you people are spoiling us. Bubble baths, silky nightgowns. Wow."

Maria let the gown flow across the bed and laid the bodice across the pillow. "Our welcome gift to you along with some violet-embossed stationery in the desk."

"I can't get over all this. Thank you for everything." God was so good to send them here. Tomorrow their healing would begin.

Chapter 5

Back in Gaskille, Rene shielded her eyes, watching across the hedges where Kaye pulled another weed. Dappled light played through the limbs of the sprawling oaks, creating lacy patterns over their two yards and the concrete bench where Rene sat.

Her own trimmers sat idle on top of the hedges. Ever since the rehab center, she hadn't quite regained her old steam. Some days it was a struggle to maintain her large Victorian home in Gaskille's historic district.

Time for tea. "Ready for a break, Kaye?" she hollered.

Kaye peeled off her cotton gloves and scraped sweat from beneath her ponytail.

"Come on over. Let's sit a spell." Rene gathered her equipment and placed it on the ground beside the orange extension cord.

Over the years, almost everything had been discussed from the rocking chairs on Rene's ample porch. And today she needed to run something by her friend.

The iron friendship gate squeaked as Kaye pushed it open. Built by Kaye's late husband, it sat smack in the center of the hedges dividing their properties. Kaye patted Rene's shoulder as they climbed the steps together.

Indoors, at the other end of the cool hallway, sunlight exploded through the tall kitchen windows, bouncing off the pale yellow walls. Off to the side the door to the screened utility room stood open. Fresh air flooded the room.

"Have a seat for a minute, Kaye. I'll get the tea." Talking

had to wait until they settled into the porch rocking chairs with their tea.

"Let me help."

"Silly rabbit, sit down." Rene busied herself at the counter.

At the table Kaye plopped into her usual ladderback chair and squished a random ant wandering near the sugar bowl.

"Here, take a teaspoon." Rene's strong pekoe tea required at least a half glass of water to dilute it and a heaping dose or two of sugar.

The clinking of their teaspoons mingled with the warbling of the mockingbirds in the pecan trees outside. There couldn't be any finer sound in the world than their lilting music, and no better taste than sweet ice tea. Sugar swirled to the bottom of her glass, and Rene stirred again. She laid the spoon down and grabbed a plate of deviled ham sandwiches out of the ancient Frigidaire. "Ready?"

On the way through the dining room, Rene motioned toward the yellow box of Whitman's chocolates off the buffet. "Could you snag that, Kaye?" A southern woman always offered sweets to her guest.

"Absolutely."

"I'm fresh out of pecan pie, so this will have to do. When Charlene and Emily get back home I can justify baking again."

Kaye hugged the box against her chest and opened the screen door. "I'm looking forward to their homecoming, too."

Around the corner, the two rocking chairs and side table gleamed in the sunlight, their fresh green paint courtesy of Bill.

Before he went to jail.

Once they sat down, Kaye touched Rene's arm. "You're worried about them, aren't you?"

"I can't get them off my mind. The whole thing's fishy. I just don't know why."

Kaye wrinkled her brow.

"I hesitate to criticize a church. I love church, and I love God's people. But Charlene didn't know these folks from Adam. She'd just met them. Why would complete strangers pay for an expensive therapy just like that?" She snapped her fingers in front of her face.

"Maybe they were just kind souls and wanted to help. They saw a sweet little fifteen-year-old who almost got assaulted, and their hearts went out to her."

"That's the way Charlene explained it." Rene tapped her fingertips on the armrest.

"But?"

"Something's nagging me. I can't even sleep at night. If I do go to sleep, I wake up with a start, almost like a panic attack, and can't go back to sleep."

"I thought you agreed with Charlene on all this."

A strong breeze snatched at Rene's napkin as she lifted her tea glass. She caught it before it flew away. "Ever have a feeling that something was wrong, even if the details seemed right?"

"Something giving you the creeps?"

Rene shrugged.

"If you're bothered, then we ought to pray for them. And leave it in God's hands, okay? We can't help much by worrying."

God had been there all along. When she asked Him to bring Charlene back home from a bad marriage and when Emily needed protection from it. And now this...

"I know, Kaye. He'll come through if we ask. I should trust Him more."

Chapter 6

The morning breeze at Earth Mother Acres wafted clear and fresh. Mockingbirds darted in and out among the branches of the hammock surrounding the Acres and chirped especially loud after the previous night's driving rain.

Charlene steadied her hot coffee mug in one hand and followed John around a golf-cart parked at the end of the cracked sidewalk. The dew from the foot-high grass quickly saturated her tennis shoes and soaked her feet.

"Sorry, need to get that mowed." Behind the cart, a mammoth puddle eclipsed the dirt drive.

"What a lake," she said, following him around it. "It's amazing how God held all this water up in the clouds before He let it go."

John said nothing. Maybe he hadn't heard her.

Near the workshop, he stopped in the road and lifted his cup. Steam fogged his glasses, obscuring his puffy eyes. His gray-streaked ponytail seemed to be uncombed from the day before. Poor man. Such a hard worker must need a little more sleep. He probably had to wake up early because of her.

He gulped a mouthful of coffee and smacked his lips. "May I call you Char?"

"Sure, I don't mind." She tried to cradle her cup, but its heat burned her fingers. How could John drink his?

John shaded his eyes and gazed toward the back of the property. "It's a big place, Char." She glanced in the same direction but winced as the sunlight blinded her. He pointed to the far end of the property. "If you look as far as you can, there's a white van parked in front of the office near those buildings."

She shielded her eyes. "In front of the trees?" Scattered palms, like pom-poms on tall sticks, poked out through a massive green wall of oaks behind the building.

"That's another branch of our charity work." He gestured to the left. "See the garage with the open door? Our mechanic takes care of all the vehicles. This twenty-acre section is one of four. A total of eighty acres in all."

He waved toward the north. "Over that way are three more sections like this one, with buildings around the back edge and a front area for farming. We take up a nice chunk of the river's edge. Like this one, each section is divided into numbered plots."

"Numbered?"

"Organized. We know exactly who's working where. Without a system it would be confusing."

"Who are the people riding around in the golf carts?"

"Clients. Like you. They work in organic produce and use the golf carts to carry their tools and vegetables. All gardeners have certain plots to tend and wear green outfits. We assign jobs depending on individual talents or abilities."

Nearby, a worker's tools clattered against her cart as she emptied a basket of sweet peppers into it. "It's a lot of produce, isn't it?"

"Sure is." John pointed toward the flowers behind her. "Those are Maria's."

"I'm impressed. Someone's got a green thumb. My marigolds and petunias don't look anything like these."

"She wanted a little color among the vegetables." He lifted his coffee cup toward the flower-covered arch. "She asked me

31

to plant blue morning glories. Pesky little vines. I'm always pulling them off the benches underneath."

"But so charming. And the wrought-iron benches. A grape-fruit tree. It's like a botanical park in here."

He smiled, clearly enjoying her praise. She sensed him watching her as she looked around.

"But it takes so much work. How do you possibly keep up with it?"

He chuckled. "There's a little waterfall under that oak tree. Would you like to see it?" He led her through a gap in a nine-foot hedge of azalea bushes.

On the other side, azaleas surrounded a large mowed room. At the far side, a waterfall trickled from a rock arrangement nearly as tall as John. Beneath it, a kidney-shaped pool caught the crystal water. Concrete benches formed a circle with the waterfall at one side.

Charlene turned slowly in the middle of the clearing. "What a gem," she whispered. "We were twenty feet away, and I had no idea this was here."

She walked to the pool. Large koi swam among the hairy hyacinth roots. Coins glimmered at the bottom. Each one must represent the wish of some poor soul who needed a healing. Just like Emily.

She knelt in front of the water and reached to touch the large sun-sculpture. Its curved rays almost touched the pool's surface. "It must be copper."

"Custom made."

"Serenity itself." She brushed her hands against her clothes. "This is one of your chapels, isn't it? The literature said you're a pastor."

"You could say that." He turned abruptly and tossed the rest

32

of his coffee into the ferns beside a bench. With no further comment he headed toward the opening.

She hustled to catch up. "I'm so glad you showed me this sweet place."

"Let's go over to the workshop and discuss your duties," he said, stepping through the opening.

She frowned as she followed. This was such a pretty place. What a shame to leave so quickly.

Away from the shade, the air thickened, filled with rising moisture from puddles and wet foliage. They passed the huge puddle again and approached a workshop. Its peeling paint revealed gray concrete blocks, and dingy windows dated back to the sixties. On the double front doors, blue veneer hung in ragged strips.

Strange that with so many clients working around the place no one had been assigned to fix up the workshop.

"You can see, Char, the shop door opens away from the house. That way I don't run over Maria's flowers when I drive my van up to get your boxes."

"My boxes? What will I be doing?"

"You sew, right? You'll be attaching labels and buttons to the clothing."

"Simple enough."

"Come on in. Let me show you." He opened one of the double doors.

Charlene followed him past the room's perimeter of long tables to a central cluster of tables. The first was piled high with folded stacks of clothing. On another, thread, scissors, and other sewing equipment surrounded the room's focal point, a lone sewing machine. At her elbow, filled boxes of clothing lined another. A huge roll of tape lay on top, apparently waiting to seal them off. A sewing machine sat on a small table surrounded by more boxes of folded garments.

Charlene reached into a box and lifted out a nubby wool jacket. She smoothed her hand over the satin lining and the perfect seams. "This is so well-made. You could get hundreds of dollars for this in a store."

"That's next winter's supply." He picked up a small carton. "The buttons, thread, and labels for these jackets are all in here."

Charlene fingered a label in the box. "If the clothes are for charity, why are we putting labels in them?"

"The same reason we only turn out high-quality clothing. Our goal is to give every recipient something of value. Then they feel better about themselves. The fine-looking garments leaving here would amaze you." John waved his stained cup. "Nothing plain or shabby. No, ma'am."

"I love that," she said, recalling the ragged coat she'd bought for Emily when she was four. The fake pride of the thrift-store woman, as if Charlene had landed a bargain. How humiliating. The coat was fit for rags, but Charlene patched it together at home. Something intact would have been a bargain. But not that horrid coat.

Thank goodness for the coins Charlene had found under the couch pillows. Poor Emily. Score one for the old boozer husband. And a big round of applause for the woman and her store.

"I wish more people believed and cared like you do."

"Once you finish with the buttons and labels, fold the jackets and put them back in these." He kicked an empty box. "You leave here at exactly 5:00 and return to the house for your before-dinner studies. At 5:05, I'll load up your boxes." He raised his eyebrows. "Easy enough?"

Charlene surveyed the new surroundings. "What about breaks?"

"You can come back to the house for a restroom break in the morning and another one in the afternoon. We'll bring your lunch to you."

"Just two breaks?"

"You think you'll need more?"

"Maybe." Charlene paused. "And when will I get to see my daughter?"

"Suppertime."

"That's it?"

"Those are the rules."

"Only once a day? Are you kidding?" Charlene frowned. "Emily's a long way from home, John. She needs me. We need each other."

A condescending smile creased his face as he stepped closer, and he lowered his voice as if she were a small child. "Char, Char, Char... remember, working in solitude." He patted her shoulder and headed toward the door.

Charlene crossed her arms and tried to keep the disappointment from showing in her voice. "Just so I understand. I won't get to see Emily at all during the day?"

He paused then turned with that same smile on his face. "I appreciate your uncertainty. It's the hardest part of the treatment. But remember this. You can socialize all you want at suppertime."

She swallowed. This was not going to fly with Emily. Why couldn't they empathize with what the child had been through?

On the other hand, experts like John and Maria knew what they were doing. Look at the website. The protocol worked. Clients improved over time.

Maybe Charlene should just put a lid on it. Go with the flow.

John stepped to the door. "Come on outside. I'll show you something."

Charlene followed him to the corner of the workshop facing the woods and stopped. Huge marigolds, like a wall of burning flames in the sun, lit up the side of the building.

John motioned for her to follow him around the corner. A fifteen-foot space separated the two buildings. He pointed to a back window.

"That's Emily's window. Knock on it. Wave at her. Blow her a kiss. Say hello. All that good stuff. Just a little secret for you." He removed his thick glasses, and cleaned them on his shirttail. "Think of it as summer camp with visiting privileges at suppertime. Just don't mention our little secret to Maria."

"Thanks, John."

"You're welcome."

This program was tougher than she imagined. But no way would Charlene skip out early. She and Emily needed this time of healing.

Besides, the payback was out of reach.

Hopefully, the time would pass quickly. For both of them. Before they knew it, they'd be driving down the highway, heading home and wondering where the time had gone.

"One more thing, John. Did you move my car?"

"Tried to this morning, but it wouldn't crank. I had the mechanic tow it up to the garage. He has your key."

"That's strange. It's usually so reliable, and—"

"Don't worry. It'll be up and running again before you leave. He's very good at what he does."

She picked her way through the sodden grass.

The engine had just been serviced a week ago.

Emily lingered over breakfast, toying with the scraps of her Mexican omelet. The painted leaves on the china plate camouflaged the pieces of bell pepper she had picked out of the eggs. No need to insult Maria.

The woman sat across the table from Emily. Her straight black hair, peppered with silver, was divided down the middle and hung like a tent over her shoulders. A tent with a head and two big eyes poking out from underneath.

It probably hadn't registered on Maria that she was wearing the same old clothes from last night. But, by tomorrow Emily would be in that same situation herself.

Only twenty-four hours ago, Emily had been in Grandma's kitchen choosing between Honey-Nut Cheerios and Frosted Flakes. She'd poured the cereal into her red glass bowl. Eaten it with her curlicued sterling silver spoon, the one she'd found in the back alley when she was three.

A knot rose in her throat. Why did they have to come here? After all, her stepfather was in jail. He couldn't hurt her.

"I'm sorry you don't like the food, honey." Maria fingered the rim of her coffee cup. "But it's okay. We'll try something else tomorrow, and maybe you'll like it better."

"I like it fine. I just don't care for green peppers."

Maria leaned her chin on her knuckles. "Before I pick up these dishes, let's talk about you and your time here."

"Where's my mom?"

"You'll see her at dinner."

Emily bit her lip. "I want to see her now. I need to talk to her."

"To start with, every day we have a schedule, and we stick to it very carefully. Do you understand?"

Oh, please, not a schedule. This was sounding more like school all the time. What a control freak. A washing machine kicked into a new cycle on the back porch, swallowing up Emily's mumbled words. "This isn't a jail, and I should be able to see my mom if I want to."

"Please speak plainly and a little louder for me. Do you understand about the schedule?" Maria held Emily's gaze with her eyes too wide-open. Like her lids were afraid to touch the contact lenses.

"Yes."

"Speak up so I can hear you, okay?"

Whatever. Owl eyes.

"After breakfast, you'll have creative time. Arts and crafts. Things like that. The next hour is your writing time, and then you get free time for an hour."

Maria lifted a tiny spiral pad and a pencil from beside the hen and rooster salt shakers. Emily blinked. Wow. The woman's nails were the longest she had ever seen. How did she miss that last night? She'd be easy to draw, a tent head with claws. Like a witch.

She placed the notebook near Emily. "You can write the schedule here so you won't forget."

"It's just an hour for art, an hour for writing."

"Write it down anyway so you don't forget. Nine o'clock and ten o'clock."

Emily slapped her hand over the pad and dragged it across the table. What a pain. Bending over the pad, she wrote out the schedule. The loud ticking of the kitchen clock and the way Maria's owl eyes bored into her made her skin crawl.

She shot a glance over her shoulder at the clock then couldn't tear her eyes away. Gag. The dusty clock, a black and white tuxedo cat, jerked its bug-eyes left and right with each passing second. Its curved plastic tail twitched along in time. The stuff of nightmares.

Maria bustled to the sink with the last of the dishes. "Good, honey. Nice handwriting, too. Just tear the page off and keep it. Would you like to see your creative activities?"

"Sure." Anything to stay busy.

Maria yanked open the broom closet and pulled out a large brown bag from Save-A-Bunch. Beginner paint-by-number sets poked out of the top. The clear sides of a sewing box peeked through the bag's split side revealing its contents of scissors and thread.

"Just go through these things. From what your mom told me, I know you'll like most everything in here. I'll get you a new bag, too."

"Thank you." Emily groaned inside as she rummaged through the bag.

Emily laid the paint sets on the table and the sewing box in her lap. In the dim kitchen light the pale blue transfers on several pillowcases were barely visible. A ruffled doily lay folded on top of a flowery tin box. She rubbed her index finger over its textured roses and violets, her favorite flowers. The lid came off easily. Inside were cards of needles, and a rainbow of embroidery thread.

Grandma had taught her a handful of stitches. Thank the Lord, as Grandma always said. This project should keep Emily from dying of boredom.

Underneath the pillowcases she found a small bag of pre-cut calico squares for quilting. Maybe she'd sew them together into a pillow. Grandma could use a new one for her back at night.

But then, come to think of it, Grandma would not approve of the way Emily was thinking about Maria. She'd probably call her unkind.

This woman was trying to find her something to do, for goodness' sake. Besides, Emily's summer imprisonment at this retreat was Mom's doing, not Maria's.

Sorry, Grandma. Sorry, Lord.

Maria laid the new bag on the table, interrupting her thoughts. "Your mother told me you both enjoy sewing and quilting. Like your grandmother."

Emily unfolded a pillowcase. "Sewing runs in the family. These are nice designs." She picked up the black velvet paint-by-number kits. One was a stupid picture of the moon and stars, and the other, even worse, a dragon with fire coming out of its nose. She shoved everything but the metal tin and doily into her new bag.

"I'll take the embroidery for now."

"That's fine. Carry it all to your room. This is your creative time."

Emily picked up the bag and headed to her room.

After closing her door, she climbed on her bed and unfolded the doily. Aha, what was this? A half-embroidered flower with pink loop stitches and yellow French knots adorned one end. A threaded needle poked through the fabric. Someone else's work.

She sat cross-legged in the middle of the bed, smoothed the doily over her lap, then pulled the needle from the fabric. She poked a strand of pink thread through the eye and knotted the end. Whoever started this doily deserved to have it finished.

The hour sped by as Emily concentrated on her stitches, the satin, petal, chain, and the hardest of all, the knotted stitch. The doorknob rattled and she jumped. Maria's head poked in.

"Hi, honey." She eased through the doorway and approached the bed. "Have you been sewing this whole time?" She reached for the work and admired it with an approving smile. "You're pretty good, aren't you?"

Emily shrugged. Embroidery was embroidery. "Whose doily was this? I mean, someone worked on it before me."

Maria hesitated. "Who knows? Someone who lost interest, that's all. Let's put it away now." She wove the needle back into the material and dropped it into the bag.

Emily gathered her thread and scissors and dropped them in too.

"Time for your writing assignment."

"When do I get to see my mom?"

Maria smiled stiffly. "Every evening at dinner time. Won't that be nice? Your mom is working hard in the shop, and you need to stick to your schedule. I also expect you to dust and sweep your room every day."

"That'll take about five minutes."

"Which will give you plenty of time for your most special project, typing recipes. I've developed wonderful recipes that need to be entered into the computer. Your mom said you're a really good writer and can type."

"But I never typed a recipe before."

"I'll help you get started. The biggest challenge will be reading my handwriting."

"When do I start the therapy?"

Maria arched an eyebrow. "This is the therapy, honey. You'll heal as you go along. Trust me."

41

Housework and typing. The church donated money for this?

Maria held up one finger. "During your free time, you can go outside, but stay close to the house. If I can't see you from the living room window, I'll worry."

"I'm not a two-year-old."

"This is for your protection, honey. Gators and moccasin snakes live beside rivers. Rattlesnakes and other wild animals hide in the palmettos. You must never open the door to leave without asking permission. Always, always, ask permission. Do you understand, honey?"

If this woman said *honey* one more time... Emily leaned her head back. "Yes ma'am."

"You're probably too old for it, but there's a rope swing hanging from the front yard tree."

Maria opened the desk drawer. "First, though, today's essay." She lifted a tablet of green fluorescent paper and smoothed her fingers over the pad as if it were an expensive gift. Her purple nails clashed like a cartoon against the tablet's bright hue. She pulled the desk drawer out a little further and poked her hand around inside.

Good thing Emily had hidden the journal between the mattresses.

"Here it is," Maria said, fluffing up a lime green plume. "Look at this cute feather pen."

"Why was it crammed way back in there?"

Maria shrugged and thrust it towards her. "I thought you'd prefer writing with something that matched your paper. Don't you like it?"

"Yes, I do." Actually, the pen was awesome. "Thanks."

"The essay topic is, 'For my own protection, I must be

careful to ask permission when I go out.' Explain how John and I protect you from danger. When you're done, I'll see if you're as good a writer as your mother says you are."

Emily stared down at the Pepto Bismol rug. This poor woman had no idea how Emily and her friends romped and stomped through the woods in Citra.

Maria turned as she walked out the door. "See you in a little bit."

Emily ground her teeth. Maybe she should write about her own topic. 'How I am just fine and need to go home.'

Chapter 7

Emily hung her elbow out the passenger window, trying hard not to bounce like a bull-rider.

Maria glanced sideways at her from the driver's seat. "Sorry, these seventies vans didn't come with seatbelts. Don't worry, the church isn't far."

It wasn't so bad, really. After a whole week, at least they were getting out of the house. Maybe she'd meet some other kids.

The vehicle hit another pothole and sent Emily airborne. She banged against the ripped seat.

"Worn-out springs. No AC," John said from the backseat. "She still runs, though."

It might be easier if the thing fell to pieces. They could walk to the church.

Mom, seated directly behind Emily, resumed the conversation she'd been carrying on with John about organic produce and fruit trees. Emily twisted around to catch a glimpse of her but gave up with a sigh.

Maria had promised Emily she could talk to Mom anytime they got together. So much for that.

And forget turning around and kneeling on the seat.

In the few hours she and Mom had spent together this week, John or Maria, sometimes both, had hovered nearby. She and Mom were never alone.

What she'd really like to say was, *Hey, Mom let me out of here, I'm dying of boredom, and these people are idiots.* Emily laughed to herself. Try that out for fun. Old Maria would run the van into the bushes.

As if she'd read her mind, Maria choked the steering wheel with both hands and dodged left and right like an old granny. She hit every pothole and sprayed mud across the ragweed that scratched and screeched over the van's chalky paint.

Emily tightened her grip on the window and filled her lungs with the humid air. Her hair whipped across her face, but the sting didn't matter. The peppery scents of the undergrowth reminded her of home. In Citra. Before they moved in with Grandma.

Not that living with Grandma was bad. In fact, living at her house and eating her cooking was awesome. But Grandma wanted a little too much of her time. On the other hand, she deserved much more time than she asked for.

Because of Grandma, Emily had met Tony. Just before school let out. He wasn't a bad friend, but she'd brushed him off. Kind of.

After she'd come up with the secret plan. If that had worked, Emily wouldn't have needed new friends. Not in Gaskille.

She took a deep breath. It was the little things, like the fragrance of these weeds, that brought back the memories of simpler times when she could hang out in the orange groves with her friends near Orange Lake.

A time when she had a real dad.

A time before Mom dumped him and married Bill. The creep.

Emily pushed out a deep breath and focused on the sandy ruts. She should quit torturing herself and concentrate on something else. If she could only make time go faster and get this Acres thing over with.

A tall weed swatted her side mirror. She dodged, imagining herself traveling through a South American jungle in a rag-top Jeep. Her Citra friends would love this weed-slapping ride. Maybe Tony would, too. Really, he was about as nice as the other kids in the group.

She should give him a call when she got home. See if he still wanted to hang out.

If he wasn't mad.

Emily squinted around the back of Maria's head. Diamonds glittered off the river between the passing trees. "What's the name of the river, Miss Maria?"

"Suwannee."

That's all she had to say? How about some little added factoid?

Dizzy from trying to focus, Emily turned to the right. Across the weeds lay another compound.

Surrounded by Earth Mother Prison.

She blinked at the harsh sun glinting off the tree-tops, a stark contrast to the pewter skies looming in the distance. Spanish moss hung in the trees like shredded gray curtains, and a jay screamed its loud alarm of "Leave, leave."

The van hit a huge washout and bounced violently. Emily flew up and dropped like a brick. But Maria's foot never slowed. It kept up its dance, the brake, the gas, the brake, the gas.

It was bad enough to sicken a stunt-pilot. Couldn't they fix the stupid holes? Throw in some dirt. Put in some concrete. Do something.

Maybe Emily should offer her help. She knew how to use a shovel. And so did her buddies. They could come up here and make quick work of this.

A ripple of sadness worked its way through her.

God, I miss them so bad.

Emily glanced up from Maria's dancing foot so she wouldn't puke. "Why are we in such a hurry, Miss Maria?"

"Well, Sweetheart," she said, lifting her index finger from the wheel. But instead of answering, her attention drifted away to her driving maneuvers.

Emily squinted at the new pentagram and rhinestone on Maria's fingernail. A shiver ran up her spine. Did the woman even know what that meant?

Maria shook her head and zoned back in. "We share the church building with other groups today. Each compound gets a turn."

Emily sighed and scooted back in the seat. She didn't really care who else used the church.

The van rounded a small bend, and the white-washed walls of a small frame church burst into view. Its leaning steeple, vivid against the steely sky, appeared as something out of a National Geographic magazine. "This place must be a hundred years old," Emily said. The limbs of a huge hickory tree spread over the front yard. A gust of wind stirred its lower limbs, whipping the leaves into a frenzy. It reached through the van and cooled her face. Rain was coming.

The van turned left and lurched to a stop beyond the tree. Maria opened her door. "Here we are. Everybody pile out."

Maria's brown skirt billowed, and her hair flew into a witchy dance. She slapped the skirt back down. "Welcome to The End of the Lane Church."

Stepping to the ground, Emily hung next to her mother. Twenty feet away, a dozen women in green uniforms disembarked from a similar van. With a few kids in tow, they trailed silently up the cracked steps of the church, like inmates from a penitentiary. A couple of men and women in regular clothes followed behind. Like guards.

Mom smiled and squeezed Emily's hand, probably oblivious to it all. "How quaint! Can't you just imagine a row of horses and buggies lined up out here?" Mom said.

John lifted his hand in greeting and caught the attention of a square-jawed man wearing cowboy boots. One of the "guards." John introduced him to Mom as Dr. Mike, the resident pediatrician. He extended his hand, much like a giant speckled frog, and it pretty much swallowed Mom's.

As Dr. Mike talked to her, his brow wrinkled just-so, as if Mom were an important person. "So you're Charlene. Welcome. It's a pleasure to meet you."

Mom returned the sentiments. Completely charmed, apparently.

Frog-hand hadn't spoken to Emily. So she'd ignore him, too.

He smiled too broadly then hurried up the steps with John.

Mom smiled at Emily. "Certainly reminds me of an old boyfriend of mine back in the day."

"Oh, please." If Mom could just for once forget all this "back in the day" stuff. It made Emily want to puke.

They entered the church, and another man, younger than Frog-hand, spoke to Mom. "Good morning, Charlene, I'm Brian. John's told us good things about you and Emily here. This is Donna, my wife."

Mom extended her hand. "Happy to meet you."

"We're counselors too. We work at the far end of your complex."

"Sorry, folks." John appeared beside them and bustled everyone toward the front. "We have to hurry. Tight schedule."

Emily edged toward the wooden pews, but Maria took her elbow, "No, honey, let's sit in the folding chairs up front. We don't have a big group today."

Couldn't she even sit where she wanted?

As they approached the circle of chairs, Maria singled one out. "Here, sweetie, take this spot next to your mom."

Emily flopped into the hard seat. Mom leaned close and gave her a hug. But Mom didn't deserve a smile, not after bringing them to this place. Though the affection was nice.

"It's all right, Emily. Things'll be better, and we'll be home soon. Remember, I'm right here, and you know I love you."

Emily kept her voice flat. "I love you, too, Mom."

In front of the circle, John tuned his guitar. The determined chords forced the drowsy group awake as he led the singing. "God is so good, God is so good, God is so goooood, he's so gooood to me."

Mom sang along and sighed at the end. Way too happy for these circumstances. She acted like they were on vacation. "John isn't much to look at, but he can sing," she whispered. "Hearing that guitar is like going back, back to the sixties. I'm so glad we could share this, Emily. It feels so wonderful." Tears welled up in Mom's eyes. "Thank you, Lord," she whispered.

Emily massaged her temples. Stop it already.

When the singing resumed, she lowered her hands and looked around. She didn't know the songs, but Mom nudged her to sing.

Why should Emily sing? People who sing should have something to sing about, and Emily didn't have anything good to report, except that a few days were already over with.

She turned away from Mom and searched for an interesting

way to pass the time. Over her shoulder, a stained glass window rose on the side wall, still bright with sunlight. It must have been 12 feet high.

Emily crossed her eyes and the colored glass mixed like in a kaleidoscope. She turned back, with her eyes still crossed, and concentrated on the width of the room. Both sides came into view at the same time.

How wide was this place, anyway? Probably five or six giant steps. Maybe eight. She rubbed her eyes. Forget doing that. Now her eyes ached.

How many folding chairs? Twenty-five. Subtract the four empty ones and there were twenty-one people here, along with a few kids who scooted behind their mothers, or glanced away every time she looked at them.

Too bad she couldn't take them outside and play tag or something.

Boredom.

Bore. Dumb.

Emily slid down in the chair and tapped the toes of her tennis shoes together in time with the music. This fake church service couldn't be less interesting.

Tony was probably in church. A real one with regular people. Then he'd probably swim in his pool this afternoon and have all kinds of fun.

In Gaskille.

If she could just get back to Grandma's. Call some friends. Practice her piano. Hang out with Tony at the farmer's market like he'd asked her to do in the first place. She shouldn't have told him she was busy.

Emily twisted around again. Donna, at the front door, nudged it open with her elbow and struggled in with a coffeepot.

Emily faced the front and tapped her feet together again. She studied her shoelaces.

Eventually, the gurgling of the coffeepot brought her out of her reverie. After a few more songs, tendrils of the coffee's nutty aroma found their way to the front of the room.

The music wound down, and Emily joined everyone else in the back for donuts and coffee. They brought the food back to the circle where John set up metal snack tables.

Someone brought him a coffee, and he paused to sip. After a few minutes, he smiled and raised his hand to get everyone's attention. A nice smile, actually. "All settled?"

Emily, the last one to take her seat, leaned back and sucked the cream out of her donut.

De. Licious.

Nearby, a girl of about six dropped hers on the floor. With one eye on Emily, she snatched it up and ate it anyway.

John cleared his throat. "You've come to this unique point in your lives, sisters, that proves you've given the ultimate sacrifice. You've given your time and your money for your children, the same way God gives time and gifts to us."

A speck of powdered sugar moved up and down on his moustache as he talked. "You've also come to share with the poor."

Emily tuned out John's monotonous voice as she took tiny bites and studied the building again. A cross behind the pulpit would be nice. Or flower arrangements on the stage. These people obviously needed decorating help.

She finished off the donut and swung her foot to stay awake. John droned on and on. "The sacrifice of your labor is given from a heart of love."

Lots of words. Words, words, words. He sounded like

Pastor Mario from the church that sent them here. Her old minister, Pastor William, now he had something to say.

"And love is all there is," John said. "From you to your fellow man, from God to you, from your sponsors to you. Without love we are nothing. Those who reap the benefit of your love will never know you, but your love will remain forever and bring you heavenward."

With her legs extended, Emily slumped in her seat, crossing her arms and then her ankles. She brushed powdered sugar off her shirt and wiped her mouth. Hopefully she'd gotten it all. Didn't want to look like John.

That voice of his could put anybody to sleep. Emily fanned herself, fighting a creeping drowsiness. It was so warm in here. She bent her head down and stretched her eyelids. If she could just stay awake.

A loud rumble jerked her out of her stupor. Thunder, low and strong, growled again. Another blast rattled the windows. Raindrops clattered over the roof like pebbles. Must be a tin roof. That had to be hail. Hell. This place was hell. Over her shoulder the window's stained-glass brilliance had faded to gray.

Emily sniffed. Dead animals again. She cupped her hands over her mouth and breathed. Nope, not her breath. Probably a mouse in the floorboards.

Suddenly, an earsplitting boom shook the boards under her feet. Women gasped as blue zaps of lightning danced through the room.

John laughed. "Whoa, that was close. Mother Nature is telling us to get back to the farm." He stood, ending the meeting. "God bless you every one, and have a good week. Move on out, everybody. Meeting's over."

Emily leaned against the wall while the others stuffed napkins into their Styrofoam cups and headed to the door, dropping trash into the wastebasket on the way out. Kids huddled next to their mothers, and before anyone could say scat, most of the group had disappeared. Maria lingered, wiping around the coffeepot and tidying up the area.

On the way out, Emily stopped at the stained glass window and studied its design. The reds, greens, and blues of the Garden of Eden had darkened to nearly black because of the storm.

In the center, Adam and Eve stood naked beside a tree. Of course, that's how they really were in the garden.

The snake, more like an iguana than a serpent, stood on its back legs. But even with the window darkened, a light seemed to glow behind his iridescent scales. Strange. There was no space behind the window for a light. Only the storm-darkened outdoors.

The snake's claws held leashes wrapped around Adam's and Eve's necks. That wasn't in the Bible.

As Emily studied the design, it seemed like the snake smiled at her.

She shuddered and hurried toward the door, glancing back one more time before stepping outside.

Too, too, too weird.

Behind the church Lucas peeked through the crack one more time and chuckled. Oh, yeah. Maria had noticed him all right. Nearly jumped out of her skin when she caught him standing near that back door. Her spastic hands unplugged the coffeepot as she glanced from the girl to him and back again, afraid the kid would see him. Part of the coffee grounds missed the trash can. He chuckled again as she cleaned it up.

Ooooh, he loved surprises. Loved how they messed people up. Surprises like this. Watching in secret from the back room, waiting till everyone walked out to make his presence known to the old hen. Yeah, just his style.

Things were moving along fine, yes, sir.

He pulled his eye away from the crack.

The peeling door eased shut, and he strolled away as torrents gushed from the black sky.

The kid couldn't see him, of course. But she had seen his picture in the stained glass window. Glanced at it twice. Plain trouble, that one. A little too clever.

He would take care of it. Maybe in a roundabout way, but he would take care of it.

Chapter 8

Rene climbed the restaurant steps in front of Kaye, passing the two concrete lions which had guarded the entrance to Benny's heavy glass door for the last 50 years. She pressed the brass bar and held the door for Kaye as icy air flowed over them. The chill was welcome after their brisk walk.

A rack of ancient postcards, featuring bikini-clad girls and clusters of oranges from the Sunshine State, stood on the counter. The antique register dinged, and the cashier placed yet another receipt on the barely visible nail. Bustling today.

"I'm craving some key-lime pie," Kaye said as they waited in the foyer.

A waitress passed by and Rene eyed the fizzy Cokes balanced on her tray. "Yeah. And something cold."

The hostess smiled as she approached and led them to Rene's favorite table by the front window. A sea of pink hibiscus lined the sidewalk below. The traffic, muted by the thick glass, seemed so close she could almost reach out and touch the cars.

Rene fingered the paper placemat with its map of Florida. "This always brings back my youth."

"Hey, we're still young. What are you talking about?"

She had to laugh at that. "If I had a second chance at youth, I'd do a better job as a mother."

"Oh, now, don't stew over the past. You did fine. Charlene made her own choices."

The waitress took their order. Rene stared out the window.

Funny how a few weeks of one's life could either widen or warp the world. The last few had seemed like months.

"I see that look. You're worrying about the girls." Kaye said.

"It's hard not to. I know God is able to take care of them. But sometimes, at night, I'll be sound asleep, and suddenly I sit bolt upright in bed. It's like a panic attack."

"I've been waking abruptly, too, just like you. You know, I think that's the Holy Spirit reminding us to pray at that minute."

She'd been waking up, too?

Pinpoints of fear prickled along Rene's arms. *God, I have no choice but to choose faith.*

As the waitress appeared with their luscious slices of key lime pie and cold sodas, Kaye's last sentence registered.

"You're right. We need to pray without ceasing."

Kaye patted Rene's hand. "I'll pray now. For our food and for your girls."

As Kaye asked God's blessing and protection, the wave of fear passed. Rene echoed Kaye's amen then gazed across the street. A late model BMW pulled up to the gate outside a small office building on the corner.

Kaye slipped her straw into her drink. "What criminal mischief are you watching over there?"

Rene smiled. "Just a car pulling in at the corner office."

A dark-haired gentleman wearing a three-piece suit stepped out of the BMW. After unlocking the gate, he gave it a shove. The gate wobbled, and he returned to the car and drove through.

"Remember when I told you that someone at Charlene's office convinced her to get 'professional' help for Emily." Rene nodded toward the building as the man knocked on the side door. "She ended up right over there."

"Handsome goatee." Kaye slipped whipped cream into her mouth. "Who is he?"

"It wasn't him. They saw a woman."

The office door swung open, and a woman with long red hair emerged. Her short skirt, not much longer than her lab coat, revealed shapely, tanned legs. The man embraced her then draped her over the back of the car in a passionate kiss.

"Hoo-boy," said Rene, shielding her eyes. "Maybe they should shut that gate."

Emily waited by her desk as Maria dropped a stack of books on top. She scowled and crossed her arms. Too regimented.

Maria noticed her expression. "The books will heal you and get you through the program, dear."

These junky books were destroying her vacation. Maria, Bill, Mom, all of them were ruining things. If Bill hadn't come along, her plan would have worked. Might still work. She bit her lip, bottling up the angry words seething in her throat. Speaking up might make things worse. Maybe even drag things out.

Maria's hands rested on her hips, and her brows arched. "Get started, and your inner girl will get her joy back. You need some."

Inner girl? What psychobabble.

Emily had all the joy she needed. Given the right environment. She pressed her lips together. Maria would never have the satisfaction—

"I expect you to answer me, Emily. Don't clam up when I say something to you."

Who did Maria think she was? Mom?

Whine, play dumb, and Maria would back off and totally forget about the books. After all, she hadn't asked her to read last week. "I'll never get done with all these books. I'm a slow reader. And they look hard."

"Relax. You only have to read an hour a day. All I ask is that you do your very best." She slipped a small one out of the stack and handed it to Emily. "Why don't you start with *Joy of Life?*"

Gag. How about *Torture of Life?*

Maria stood straighter as if that settled it. "Now, I'll be back at five o'clock when your special time is over, and then we'll work together in the kitchen." She started to turn but hesitated. With a frozen smile, she lifted Emily's chin with her index finger.

Emily shuddered. She didn't want this woman touching her.

Maria's nose almost touched Emily's. Her breath reeked of onion, and a hard expression replaced the smile. "You'll be in your room when the maid comes at four. It's against protocol to come out. Don't talk to her. Understand?"

Those wide blue eyes penetrated Emily's, as if reaching into her brain. Holding her breath, Emily stared right back. Her skin quivered when the woman's coarse hair wafted against her arm.

All right, all right. Put on a positive face and Maria will leave. Emily nodded, mostly to knock the finger loose.

Maria left the room and shut the door. Her footsteps faded down the hall.

Emily dropped to the rug and wrapped her arms around herself. The book landed beside her with a *thunk*. She shuddered and scraped away the touch of Maria's finger, which still crawled on her chin.

As she fanned away the fumes of Maria's lingering breath, faint bumping and snuffling sounds came from under the door.

She crawled over and gripped the knob. She pressed her eye against the crack and eased the door open so Maria wouldn't hear.

A dog's wet nose hit her in the eye. Before she could scoot away, a black muzzle pushed through the opening. Dark eyes and silver-sprigged ears followed. Like a smiling racehorse charging out of the gate, he forced his chest inside. Emily lost her balance and snorted out a laugh as he burst in.

It was the dog from the first night.

"Hey, boy," she whispered as she shut the door. "I wondered where you went. You act like this is your room."

His plumed tail waved as he wiggled into her lap, licking and pushing against her hands with his nose.

Like she was his long-lost friend.

"You remember me? Where have you been hiding?" As Emily massaged the loose skin under his neck, he slowed, blinking and concentrating on his bliss.

"How did you get in here?"

He wiggled, forcing his nose into her face and dragging his tongue over whatever he could reach.

Bleah. She wiped her face on her arm.

Emily dodged his tongue with a snort and tried not to laugh too loud. She grabbed his soft ears and stroked them with her thumbs until he settled down.

"Look at all those black speckles." She pushed him off her lap, and he rolled over with a wag of his tail.

"Oh, I see. A big baby, huh?"

She took her hairbrush from the desk and passed it through

the silver hairs of his chest, lifting them upward, then letting them fall. He lay still and closed his eyes.

After a minute or so the door creaked open. Emily stared up into Maria's solemn face. She held a plate of cookies in her hands.

The dog flipped over, probably remembering what Maria had done to him before. "He isn't hurting anything. You won't make the dog leave, will you?"

Maria raised an eyebrow and set the cookies on the desk. "I see you've found a friend. I don't mind you playing with the dog. But you have to study."

She picked up the book Emily had dropped and handed it back to her. "This isn't doing you any good on the floor. How about if you sit here at the desk, and I come back in fifty minutes and check your notes? Write down all the important points."

Anything, as long as she could keep the dog. "Yes, ma'am."

The door clicked shut, and the dog blinked earnestly at her. His eyes moved to the plate.

"You beggar. Come here." She held out a cookie, and he devoured it in a couple of gulps. His nose probed her hand and whiffled over the rug. He found no crumbs and his eyes begged for more.

"All right." She gave him another cookie. "That's all you get, you silver beggar. That's a good name for you, Beggar."

Emily bit into a cookie and leaned against the bed. She opened the book. "Lie down, now." Her bare feet caressed the dog's warm side as she read the first page.

She hadn't read far when she slammed the book shut. Beggar jumped up. "No way. Nature is not God. People are not God. I do not believe this garbage."

Beggar whined, and Emily shook the book. "She wants notes? She'll get notes. I'll copy some sentences, but I am not reading this idiotic book. She might think I'm dumb. But I am not stupid."

Emily reached between the mattresses and brought out her journal. "First though," she said, pointing her pen at the dog and climbing into the chair. "I've got a few things to write for myself."

She clenched her jaw and scribbled her complaints into her journal. When she finished, she glanced at the clock. Oh, man. She set the journal on her lap.

Only eight minutes left to write something for Maria.

She searched through the book and copied the main ideas and subheadings on a piece of Maria's green paper. But like a handwriting activity, she gave the words no thought. Hopefully, the lies wouldn't pollute her mind.

She wrote furiously. Until the tap on her window.

Frowning, she reached across the desk and pulled back the curtain.

"Mom?" She glanced back at the door. "What are you doing out there?"

Mom waved and signed, "I love you."

"Hey," Emily mouthed, holding her book up to the window. She made a gagging sign.

Mom just wagged her finger as if Emily should keep studying. Well, forget sympathy. Of course, Mom couldn't tell anything by the cover.

Emily shook her head and dropped the book.

Before she could signal anything else, Mom blew her a kiss and disappeared.

Emily kicked at the desk leg and the curtains fell shut. If

Mom only knew the hogwash Maria was making her read, she'd probably leave right now. Emily had to tell her.

The bedroom door flew open, and Emily jumped. Her journal! She eased it under her loose cotton shirt. That was close.

"Um, hi, Miss Maria."

Maria approached the desk.

"I took a few notes." Emily hoped one paper was enough.

"Good. Let's see what you have there." Maria held the paper at arm's length to read. Her eyes must be going.

"You summarize well. Yes. All things exist as part of the divine nature." Maria perched on the edge of the bed. "This is good, honey, and I like this point—we must commit to care for the earth."

No big deal if one knew what to copy.

"These are good notes. You understand the book?"

Always play dumb. "Not so much. It's kind of hard."

"Well, it's time to learn some things in the kitchen. We can review the concepts while we fix dinner. That's what I'm here for, isn't it? To help you?"

Okay, that backfired. "Yes ma'am, thank you." Emily pressed the journal against her stomach. Could I play with the dog a minute first?"

"Sure. Wash your hands before you come, and we'll peel potatoes." The door shut and Emily waited for the footsteps to fade.

With her back to the door she pulled the journal from under her shirt, and cracked it open to her latest entry. "Dear Diary, The truth is, all things are *not* part of divine nature. God is divine and He *created* them. He created me too. He wants us to take care of the earth. But the earth is not Him. Dogs and cats and trees are not Him, but He created them."

She breathed in deep. "Hmph." *In the beginning God created the heavens and the earth.* That Bible verse was so basic, she'd known it all her life. How could anyone not get it?

She slapped the journal shut and drove it arm-deep between the mattresses before heading to the kitchen. Beggar clicked along behind her.

In the kitchen, Maria plopped a yellow glass bowl, heavy with potatoes, in Emily's lap. "You can peel these." She handed her a paring knife.

Emily drew the blade over the first potato.

"Be careful, it's sharp. Don't you know how to peel potatoes?"

A thick chunk of white came off with the peel.

"Not that way." Maria grabbed the knife. "Here, use the potato peeler." She jerked open the utensil drawer and tossed the peeler across the table. "Just keep your finger off the little metal piece in the middle. Point it away from you. Surely you're experienced with one of these."

Emily stroked the peeler twice across the potato. "What are we making?"

"German potato salad. I think you'll like it. It's served hot."

"You're not making your own recipes?"

"I modify them. You know how one recipe leads to another."

"What were you going to tell me about that book?"

Maria stared at her. "You just have to read and meditate on what the books are saying. Find that inner peace. Remember the title, *The Joy of Life*? Remember the notes you took? God is all around us. God is the trees. God is the fruit in this bowl."

She waved her arm at Emily. "God is you. God is me, we're all part of God. You are divine. Isn't that sweet? That should give you joy. Think about it." Facing the window, she arranged bacon on a cookie sheet with a fork.

With that logic, Maria was a potato. How could she be so confused? God *created* the trees and fruit and people. Creator, not the *created*.

Emily rubbed her bare feet over Beggar's side. Whatever. "Miss Maria, God *created* the heavens and the earth."

Maria froze and turned slowly, glaring at Emily. Bacon dangled from her fork. "No, honey, God *is* the heavens and the earth, and God is *you*, and God is *me* too. We're *all* God." The bacon hit the floor.

Well, Maria just dropped her god and she was going to eat god for supper.

Maria scowled. She reached for the meat and flung it in the trash, her blue eyes wide. "You should not be talking back."

Emily's gaze dropped to the bowl then up again. The tilt of Maria's head just now, it reminded her of someone. But who? With the light silhouetting Maria, her features were hard to discern. But when she had said those words about God—

Maria's big eyes drilled into her.

Emily peeled a potato as if Maria wasn't there. Just ignore her.

And anyway, what was that rotten smell? She plowed her hands through the bowl, but found no rotten potatoes. Eventually, Maria gave up staring and turned around.

Emily shook her head and dug the peeler into a potato eye. Poor confused woman.

Chapter 9

At dinner, Mom pulled out the chair for Emily with a grin. "Come sit down. How's it going, Emily?"

Emily squeezed between the wall and table then traded hugs with Mom. The lace tablecloth dragged along with her shirt.

Emily sat. "Hey, Mom," she mumbled, straightening the cloth. She leaned her cheek against Mom's shoulder.

Maria frowned at no one in particular as she placed the steaming plates on the table.

"I hear your stomach growling, Mom. Hope you like the potatoes I helped make. And the tomato and okra recipe." The green and red dish would be nice for Christmas. Emily would tell Grandma about it. At least by then they'd be long gone from this idiotic place.

She glanced up. Maria and John had dug into their food without praying. Their silverware clanked against their plates. John's gnawing sounded like the pig she had fed at her friend's farm. Maria shoveled potato salad into her mouth and left a smear of mustard beneath her lower lip. Emily held her breath to keep from laughing.

Maria set her elbow on the table, and waved her fork at Emily. "Your mom should be proud of your cooking. This is good." She pushed a piece of potato into her mouth with her pinkie.

"Thanks, Miss Maria."

"I've missed you so much, Emily," Mom said. "How did you do today? Maria tells me you are making tremendous progress in your therapy."

What therapy? Peeling potatoes and cutting up okra was nothing. This was just glorified chores. And Mom was way too enthusiastic.

Emily pushed her hair behind her ear. "I'm fine, Mom. How did you do in the shop today?"

"Some very needy people are going to be surprised with the clothes we're sending out. Gorgeous things. Fit for a queen."

"You're an awesome seamstress. Everybody knows it."

"Imagine what a change it'll make in their lives."

"How's that?"

"They'll have a new outfit to wear to job interviews. It improves their self-esteem."

"That's nice, Mom." But it wasn't the point of being here.

"I'm so happy we're part of Earth Mother Acres. Just the name of the place makes me feel love and warmth."

Please. Emily wanted to shake Mom's shoulders. What was wrong with her brain?

Within minutes, Maria gathered her plate and John's even though Emily and Mom hadn't finished their meal.

"You and John are so clever to come up with this charity work," Mom said.

"Think about this, Char." John leaned back with a toothpick wobbling from the corner of his mouth. He hiccuped and gestured toward their plates. "Our food is fresh and organic, not canned. Every garden plot uses the best organic soil and is tended with loving care. We do more than hand out food. We care about peoples' health."

Mom bobbed her head. "Anyone can hand out cans."

John nodded and crossed his legs.

"Emily's learning so much. I hope you know how grateful I am."

Emily squirmed and clamped her lips to avoid screaming the truth. Not that it'd do any good. Mom never listened to anything she had to say.

Maria patted the top of Emily's head. "She's definitely brave in the kitchen. A very fast learner. And it helps having a fan club like you."

"When I'm in the shop, I think about where we are in our lives. Each day I realize something new. Emily is getting over her bad experience, and we're moving on to happy thoughts. Like your booklets say, we're aggressively gaining positive outlooks instead of running from experiences. Doing for others is the best way to move ahead. What a great Christian experience."

Emily caught Maria glancing at John with a raised eyebrow, but Mom babbled on.

John picked up his tea. "How are your studies coming along, Char?"

"Reading about positive thinking and good deeds, that part is easy," Mom said. "For me the hardest part is self-discipline. And with all this delicious food cooking on the other side of the door at study time, I just about go crazy."

"How's the nature music we left in your room?" John said.

"A little different, I guess. Sort of lulls me to sleep."

Beside the table, Beggar whined as if he needed to go out.

John rose and Beggar followed his heavy work boots as they clomped down the hall. The front door creaked open then slammed.

"The music gets you in tune with Mother Earth," Maria said. "How about dessert?"

Mom laid her fork down. "I'm so stuffed."

"You have to try my famous tiramisu." Maria rose and

retrieved a dish from the refrigerator. She held it up. "Ta da. It's the best this side of the Suwannee." She turned her back to dish it up.

Seizing the opportunity, Emily leaned toward Mom.

"Maria told me *we* are God," she whispered.

"What?"

Emily repeated herself, but Mom just wrinkled her brow.

"No, Emily, you remember incorrectly." Maria turned toward the table.

Did she have supersonic hearing?

"The word was God's *representatives* on earth. Make an effort to be more attentive, please." Maria waved the dessert knife in Mom's direction. "Your mom knows I'd never say anything so ridiculous. Keep on studying your books, and your comprehension will improve."

"Emily did have a little trouble in school," Mom said. "Of course, I can't picture you saying such a thing, Maria. She just misunderstood you."

The whole world was turning against Emily.

She slumped as Mom hugged her shoulders. "Keep studying, sweetheart, and I'm sure it will all be clear in the end." Mom smiled as Maria placed the desserts in front of them. "Doesn't this look scrumptious, Emily?"

Emily pressed her fist against her cheek and gouged her fork into the food. She blinked back the acid in her eyes. "Looks great."

Chapter 10

Rene steered her green Accord off the highway east of Gaskille and coasted to a stop beside the Faithful Disciples sign.

Beyond the parking lot, rows of cut Bahia grass lay baking in the sunny field. A vacated mower rested under the lone sycamore. When Rene opened her window, the grassy fragrance rolled in on a mass of hot air. She squinted at the sign's purple lettering. "I don't see anything about service times, do you, Kaye?"

"Nope."

Four late-model cars lined the front of the corrugated building, which seemed more like a large warehouse than a church.

"There's a space." Rene pulled into a spot near the front door.

She squeezed the steering wheel. If only she could wrap Emily in a big hug right now.

And Charlene. That hard-headed daughter of hers. Always doing the exact opposite of everything Rene suggested.

A grandchild ought to live close by so her grandma could teach her to put up jelly and bake pies. Go shopping. Have fun.

Emily's whole summer would be over soon, eaten up by this silly trip.

The corner of Rene's mouth turned up as she pictured Emily's brown eyes and soft wavy hair. Such a good girl, polite, spunky, and she listened to older folks. More like her handsome daddy than her stubborn mom.

When he wasn't drinking.

She'd warned Charlene about that tendency. Of course the girl didn't listen. And now Rene wished she could slap a knot into Charlene and him.

"There it is." Kaye pointed to the foil sign on the glass door. "Sunday at 11:00. Why can't they put it on that other sign where everyone can see it?"

Rene put the car in reverse. "All right. That's all we needed. You going with me?"

Before Kaye could answer, a black BMW swung into the reserved space next to her, barely missing the Honda.

Rene stomped the brake, jerking them forward.

"Whoa."

The black door flew open and the driver leaped out. He strode swiftly into the building, unfazed by the close call.

Kaye cupped her fingers over her mouth. "Isn't that the handsome Mr. Goatee we saw across from Benny's Restaurant?"

Rene arched an eyebrow. "Sure looks like him."

The next morning Emily bit into a sugar cookie and studied her nails as she drew her fingertips across the sunny spot on her desk. Too bad she didn't have any nail polish. She'd paint them when she got home.

But not like Maria's witchy claws, all crawling with germs underneath. That's what Grandma said about long nails, anyway.

She traced the shadow on her desk, her morning sundial.

The door burst open, and she turned her head. Confirmed. Maria rarely knocked.

"It's an hour until lunch, honey." Maria strode to the desk and gathered the notes beneath Emily's elbow. "I'm looking forward to reading this, but you need to go stretch your legs."

Emily stood, half asleep from boredom, and stuffed the rest of the cookie in her mouth.

"Scoot."

"Yes, ma'am." She paused at the doorway, hating to ask for favors from Maria. But then, maybe she had misunderstood her last night. Grandma always said to give people the benefit of the doubt. "I've been thinking."

"That's good." Maria rolled the papers and stuffed them under one arm, "What about?"

"You know that old piano in the living room? Could I play it?"

Maria brushed loose crumbs onto the cookie plate. "I work in the office, you know."

"I won't play too loud." Emily followed her to the kitchen. "And I've had a few lessons."

"Not loud, okay?" Maria disappeared down the hall.

Entering the cool dark living room was like entering a separate world. The black piano stood neglected and tall against the dark pine walls. She touched its ancient crackled paint. How long since anyone had played it?

She raised the lid and folded it back with hardly a sound. A sweet pungent smell met her nose. Just like Grandma's piano whose keyboard's missing ivories helped Emily to find middle C.

That instrument had character, like Grandma. Old, but special. Its wood resonated with songs once played.

She touched middle C, and a loose string echoed inside. With one finger, Emily picked out "Yankee Doodle." The notes, metallic and strange, twanged like intruders in the house. So different from Grandma's. Despite the piano's poor tone, Emily sang quietly.

After awhile, the aroma of fresh coffee wafted in from the kitchen.

"Miss Maria," Emily called out. "How old is this piano?"

"I don't know." Maria paused. "My grandmother passed it to my mother, and she passed it on to me."

"Don't you play?"

"Never learned."

With one finger, Emily picked out "Aura Lee," a song she learned in the school chorus. The sad melody sounded perfect for this room.

Maria's voice came from the rear of the house. "Hey, good job with those songs. How long have you taken lessons?"

"A few months." Tony's mom taught the lessons at her house, and Grandma paid for them. That's how she and Tony first met away from school. Mom had no money for lessons in Citra. She could barely pay the rent. And no piano among the beat-up furniture of their rental house.

"Play more if you like, but I can't be talking, okay?"

"Okay."

Emily played a few more school tunes then switched to church songs. When the first line to "Jesus Loves Me" became clear, Maria emerged from the kitchen holding a black mug.

"Come to think of it, Emily, I think you've played long enough. Thanks for the recital, though."

Emily shut the lid and ran her hand down its length. She followed Maria into the kitchen.

"Do you realize I've been forgetting some of your vitamins?" She handed Emily a plate of yellow-frosted cookies. "Here's a snack since you shouldn't take vitamins on an empty stomach."

Emily frowned. "I just had cookies. And I took a red pill at breakfast."

"Never mind that. This is another one you should be taking for your eyes and mental acuity. I've been so busy the last few days I forgot about them."

Emily ate a cookie then swallowed the brown capsule with milk.

"We're cheating with those cookies between meals, so don't let them ruin your lunch." Maria leaned against the sink and sipped her coffee. "Your mom said you had a little trouble in school. This should fix you up. I'll take your mom some vitamins with her lunch."

"Can you take her some cookies, too? She loves icing. Grandma always makes this kind for us."

Maria shook the bottle. "Don't let me forget these vitamins anymore. Mentally challenged or not, we'll have you all fixed up before you leave."

Emily's mouth flew open. "I'm not mentally challenged."

Maria tilted her head and raised her brow. "I'm only repeating what your mom said.

"My mom didn't say that. She wouldn't."

Would she?

Charlene sat in the bedroom chair, one foot tucked beneath her. Muffled clattering of lunch dishes and muffled voices drifted through the wall. She smiled. How nice of Maria to include the culinary training along with Emily's therapy.

With her chin in her hand, she leaned toward the window. In the gardens, women in straw hats labored chest-deep in tomato bushes and okra. Others plucked squash from turgid, thigh-high plants.

Not even Kaye's gorgeous vegetables looked this good.

Suwannee soil must be so rich.

She glanced at the door. Surely Maria and John wouldn't mind her watching like this. After all, she wasn't communicating with anyone. Such an odd rule.

Visiting with others could help her pass the time in the shop.

Sewing labels and buttons kept her focused, but not busy enough to keep annoying thoughts out of her head. Like how Bill had completely fooled her. Poor Emily. *God, I'm so sorry.*

The girls at the real-estate office had drooled over Bill. Her handsome catch. Her handy man. She snorted. Yeah, he was handy all right.

Out in the garden, a woman parked her golf cart on a grassy runway. She filled her baskets with cucumbers and drove toward the far end of the complex. The cart disappeared past the mechanics garage.

Past Charlene's Civic. How kind of John to take care of it for her. What a good, capable man.

Whoops, there she was again, thinking about reliability. Admit it. She had to be the world's worst judge of character. Come to think of it, Mother had always complained about her choice of friends. Maybe if she had listened—

Enough. Think of something else. Like the car.

Good thing it broke down here instead of on the highway.

And hurray for dependable men like John.

Picking up her pen, she reread the title of her assignment, "How the Circumstance of No Car Draws Me Closer to My Sponsors and to God." This would be simple. Her stomach rumbled. She would rather eat first, though.

She hated eating lunch alone in the shop.

John and Maria must have good reasons for their rules, though.

An hour later, Charlene picked up her cookies and sat next to the shop window. On the other side of the dusty glass silent limbs waved in a noiseless breeze. Nothing could be more depressing. Not even the faintest bird sounds came through.

If she didn't get some fresh air she would smother.

She wrapped a napkin around the bottom of her tea glass and shoved the door open. A lively world of birds, squirrels and sunshine exploded around her. With a deep, cleansing breath, she headed for the shady chapel John had shown her the other day.

Moments later, she plopped onto the cool concrete bench in front of the fountain. What a perfect spot to finish off her lunch. She nibbled her cookie and watched a pair of fantail goldfish glide between the dappled light and ripples of the waterfall.

The patina-covered lips of the sun god smiled at nothing in particular. If John and Maria knew what the sculpture stood for, they probably wouldn't have it on the property. But nobody worshipped the sun god anymore.

She took another bite of cookie and surveyed the little nature room behind her. She hadn't noticed the five ash pits along its edges before. They must be for shish kabobs or weenie roasts. But why five pits? Each to his own, though. Strange, though, that nobody had mentioned cooking out, and it would be fun. But how would they work that in with all the solitude?

As she reached to knock a bug off her leg, the *snip-snip-snip* of hedge clippers sounded from outside the room of azaleas.

Uh oh. Clients.

"Hi, Char." A man's soft voice shot electricity through her veins.

She jumped, snapping the cookie, and turned.

"John." She caught her breath. "You startled me."

His eyes moved to the bench where crumbs now littered its surface. "Bring your lunch out?"

"I thought I was alone then some worker came up to prune the bushes out there, and you dropped in at the same time. I almost flew out of my skin." She couldn't seem to stop chattering.

"Sorry, I didn't mean to scare you." His low voice contrasted starkly with her childishly loud one.

"It's all right. I brought part of my lunch out. It was such a beautiful day. Do you mind?"

"I understand how peaceful it is. Celestial, isn't it?" He winked.

Bill used to do that same patronizing thing.

"But I guess we'd better stick to the protocol because other clients are out and about. Running into them, even accidentally, would destroy their solitude."

She scrambled to brush cookie crumbs off the bench. "I didn't mean to goof things up."

He extended his hands in exaggerated reassurance. "Don't worry about it. No harm done. Your lunch hour is almost over, anyway, isn't it?"

"Just about."

"I'll walk you back."

At the shop, Charlene stopped inside the door. "Thank you, and again, I'm so sorry. I just wasn't thinking."

He shut the door with a whisper. "You have a good day, now."

She set her untouched drink on the shelf behind the machine. But her hand lingered for a long moment, trembling in the stifling silence. She glanced at the noiseless trees, still waving beyond the window pane.

With a sigh she returned to the machine and flipped on the small bulb. She'd think about the suffocating surroundings later.

But right now her brain was crawling like a kicked-over ant bed.

Chapter 11

"You're sure Emily's all right, Maria?" Charlene gripped the dinner table. "Don't I need to look in on her?"

"She's okay, Charlene, don't worry. It's just a little diarrhea." Maria stuffed a piece of biscuit into her mouth. "I practically had to make her lie down. She's feeling better, but I insisted that she rest. Most of our children have stomach problems once they switch to organic food. The body's purging out the toxins."

"We eat healthy at home, though."

"Maybe it's the variety, then."

"Here, drop some butter on your new potatoes," John said. "I dug them up this morning. Taste like boiled peanuts." He coughed and cleared his throat. "Bet you use margarine at home. Butter's healthier."

Charlene glanced at the butter dish. "Really?"

"Which is better, Mother Nature-made, or man-made?"

"I'll try to remember that," she said, cutting a pat for her plate. Maybe Emily had amoebas from the river, or a mosquito-borne disease. "Did she have a fever?"

"Now, Charlene, trust me. Don't be so over-protective. It's not healthy for a child."

"I-I guess you're right. And I appreciate you taking such good care of her." Like Maria said, other kids experienced similar problems. No need to be rude about it, as if she didn't trust Maria.

The next morning, Emily sat cross-legged in the middle of her bed and tied the final knot in the back of her embroidery. Scissors, the craft bag, and colored threads lay scattered about the pink chenille bedspread. Even with her energy drained, her gut felt so much better today. Yesterday was horrible, hugging her knees against her chest, praying that each painful wave that cut through her insides would be the last.

And that stupid clock, *tick, tick, ticking* the whole miserable time. The longest day of her life.

She'd heard the grownups' conversation during dinner. That comment about Maria taking good care of her—*Pfft*. Maria had brought her one glass of water the entire day.

The doorknob turned, and Maria poked her head in. Speak of the devil.

She sashayed over to Emily's bed and sat down. "Did you finish your doily?"

Emily spread it over the bedcover and ran her hand across the textures. "What do you think?"

"Nice job."

"Can I keep it?"

"Of course, honey. It's all yours."

"Thanks." Emily folded the fabric and pressed it to her chest. *But please stop calling me honey.*

"Your mom told me what you like before you came. There's more needlework in the bag."

Nothing could be as special as the piece the other girl had started.

"But now it's time for writing," Maria said. "This is the point in your therapy where you write about what happened with your stepfather."

"That creep? I don't want to write about him."

"Writing about the experience is part of your healing. You need to face it head on so you can move forward."

A knot formed inside Emily's chest. She didn't want to relive that morning with Bill.

The dumb jerk. With his winks and nudges. Emily should have mentioned his behaviors to Mom. But Mom would have brushed them off as annoyances.

If only Grandma had been home when Bill came back for his lunch, none of this would have happened. She couldn't blame Grandma, though.

His leering face came to Emily's mind, and she shuddered. Thank God Mom came home when she did. And to think Bill had lived under the same roof with them for months.

Maria patted Emily's knee. "I'll be back in an hour. Just get it over with."

Nosy old hag. She just wanted to learn the gory details.

The door clicked shut and Emily pressed the rough embroidery against her face. She should have clawed Bill's eyes out.

Maria would never get the satisfaction of learning the details. At least not from her.

Emily's pulse throbbed from the inside of her knees up through her elbows, rocking her entire body like a boat anchored in the current.

Anchored in more ways than one.

Maria was not going to poke and prod into her business. All her Mother Earth talk and those lies about God were not going to change Emily's faith or reel in her anchor.

Only a few more weeks and this so-called therapy would be over. Emily lowered the embroidery. "And good riddance."

She unfolded her tingling ankles and hobbled to the restroom on half-numb legs.

With a flick of her wrist she slammed the toilet shut. *It's none of your business, Maria.*

She flushed. That was for her stepfather.

The tank filled and she flushed again. That was for his meaty hands and rotten breath.

The third time was for Maria.

She kicked the bowl for good measure.

Ow! She grimaced and grabbed her throbbing toe as she turned the water on full blast. She spat until her mouth ran dry, then loaded her hands with soap.

She washed three times. Just like the Father, Son, and Holy Spirit, a perfect number.

Emily squinted into the mirror. *It's a new day, baby.* If Maria wanted a story, then Emily would give her a story.

Back in her room, she picked up the pen and inked the first words onto the annoying green paper.

Last year my stepfather decided to add excitement to his life. He bought a small silver gun and a mask, and set out to rob all the banks in our town.

After forty-five minutes of writing, she grabbed her journal from beneath the mattress and read the last entry: *I know Jesus loves me, and I love Him. He is going to get me out of this place. He is Lord, and God is His Father. I love You, Jesus.*

She had barely replaced the journal when the door opened. Maria peered inside. "All done?"

Smiling, Emily held up the story. "Yes, ma'am. All done."

At lunch, Emily toyed with the food on her plate. Her stomach growled, but she refused to put grimy gator meat in her mouth. Some people loved it, considered it a delicacy. But gators were scaly reptiles, for goodness' sake. Gross.

When Maria looked away, she slipped another bite to Beggar.

At the sink, Maria arranged balls of bread dough on a cookie sheet. She glanced at Emily's nearly empty plate. "You must have liked the gator. How about some more?"

Her stomach lurched. "No, thank you. I'm saving room for that garlic bread."

"Well, when you're done, I have chocolate chip cookies for you to eat with your vitamins."

Cookies. Good. She could load up. Emily rolled the gel cap against the tablecloth. "Why are the vitamins brown?"

"What do you mean?"

"Sometimes they're red, and sometimes they're brown."

"Oh, that's nothing. I brought a new brand of lutein from the pharmacy. Lutein is for the eyes. It's another little something your body needs."

Emily dropped the last bite of gator meat into Beggar's mouth and rubbed his head. "Good dog," she whispered.

Chapter 12

Charlene glanced up as John plopped her lunch on the sewing table.

"There you go, Char. Smoked gator. A delicacy. River's full of gators, but we don't usually serve it."

He seemed mighty happy. Must not be upset with her anymore.

"My first husband used to bring gator home from Orange Lake. I haven't had it for a while." She bowed her head to give thanks.

"You got a lot done today," John said, interrupting her prayer. "Look at all these boxes. On a roll, huh?"

He must not have realized she'd been praying. *Thank you Lord for this food, and please bless it.* "Um hm."

John paused then crossed his arms. "The little chapel and the great outdoors are tempting, aren't they?"

Okay, maybe he was still annoyed. She set the cover of the dish aside and fanned the steaming meat.

John flipped over an empty five-gallon bucket and pulled it up next to her. Not good. Mother used to do the same thing before putting Charlene through one of her little wisdom talks. She raised her eyebrow ever so slightly.

"Just keep your focus until y'all are out of therapy and back home." John grinned and leaned so close that his gator-meat breath hit her in the face. "Pay attention to why you're here so you don't get distracted. It won't be long."

She hadn't meant to break the rules. If she apologized again, maybe he'd leave. "I'm really sorry about yesterday."

"Just keep a single mind, and things will go quicker for you. It's a small thing, walking in the garden, isn't it?" He locked his hands around his knee. "But a slight change in ambience and thought could send you down an emotional detour and 'short-out' the positive patterns we are trying to achieve with the protocol."

But what about a little fresh air?

"Everything you do factors into Emily's healing."

Charlene leaned away from his moving lips. Really, why all the fuss about stepping outside? She wasn't a child, after all. She took a deep breath. This was probably the point where someone else would quit. But she'd do whatever it took not to mess things up for Emily.

"I'll stick with the plan. You have my word, John. I couldn't be more grateful for what you're doing."

"Our success rate is high for a reason." He stood and scooted the bucket back in place with his foot.

"You can count on me."

He winked. "Enjoy that lunch, now."

His shoulders seemed to square as the door opened. Sunlight flashed across his disheveled ponytail before he disappeared from sight.

Charlene closed her eyes and exhaled hard, trying not to think about the stifling room around her.

Emily stumbled up the porch steps, doubling over as she headed down the hall. Not again. Nothing was worse than these ripping pains. Dumb old diarrhea. Beggar followed behind her.

Reaching the bathroom just in time, she closed her eyes,

holding her breath until the agony passed. Another spear hit and stars prickled behind her eyelids.

Minutes ticked by as numbness tingled her legs. She pulled the last of the toilet paper from the roll. Just this once, she wished Maria would barge in. With more toilet paper.

The back door slammed. Maria must be back from town. Cupboards banged. Grocery bags rattled. Hurray. Imagine being glad about that.

"Emily?"

"In here."

Footsteps approached. "Are you alright?"

"Can you bring me some more toilet paper?"

"Just a minute." Maria pushed a roll through the crack in the door. "What's going on? I gave you a new roll just this morning."

"I'm not wasting anything. I can't help it." Never mind that they were skimpy little rolls to start with. Grandma bought good solid rolls of paper. Less puff, more paper.

"Well, I'm running late, and we need to get back on schedule. Go to your room when you're done so we can discuss your little problem."

A few minutes later Maria stood above Emily as she sat on the edge of the bed. "Young lady..."

Emily wedged her heels under the bed and stared down at her legs. Wow. A stick figure. Even she could tell she'd lost weight.

"You need to look up at me when I talk."

She tried looking up, just to keep the peace. But she couldn't. This was killing her neck.

Maria drummed her fingertips on her arms. Their purple downward curve matched the arc of her ugly old lips.

Emily inched her knees away from the touch of Maria's skirt and rubbed her aching neck.

"The recurring diarrhea is your body telling on you."

"Ma'am?"

"When you have rebellion in your heart, your body tells on you. It tells me you're hiding things."

"I'm not hiding anything."

"Is that so?"

Whatever.

"That's all I'm going to say. You can't hide rebellion. It always peeks through. Open your mind and embrace the program. Embrace your lessons."

She'd never open her mind to that hogwash.

"You have a few minutes left to study." Maria pivoted and headed toward the door, her brown skirt brushing against Emily's leg.

Didn't the woman own any other clothes?

She needed to stay on Maria's good side just in case it would shorten the so-called therapy. Be the first to apologize, Grandma said. "Will you forgive me?"

Maria paused at the door without turning. Emily could imagine her confused face. "What?"

"Will you forgive me?"

"Umm, yes, honey. I suppose."

Beggar laid his chin on the rug as the woman's footsteps faded toward the kitchen. Emily lowered herself beside him and caressed his warm ears. She stared across the room at nothing in particular.

Now what would Grandma do?

The thumping on Charlene's bedroom door snapped her out of her nap.

She leaped off the bed, knocking her hair pick off the desk, and straightened the covers. Naps weren't in the schedule.

"It's open."

Maria nudged the door open with her elbow. She carried a china cup in one hand and a fat photo album in the other.

"Sorry. I waited for you, but I guess I drifted off."

Maria set the cup on the desk. "Here's some hot tea. The caffeine will help you write. This time of day we all need a boost."

Charlene slid into the desk chair. She should have been using her time more wisely. "I'm so embarrassed. This late afternoon sun just puts me to sleep. I couldn't help but lie down."

Maria edged the cup away from Charlene's elbow and sat on the bed. "Never mind, Charlene. I'm the one who made you wait. Our client at another cabin needed my help."

"It's fine, really. I had a busy day too. I filled six boxes."

"Forgot my tea, I'll be right back." Maria darted for the door.

Charlene sipped her tea and stared out the window toward the back lawn. The speckled shadows on the cracked sidewalk reminded her of her mother's gray porch and the iced tea she and Kaye shared. How peaceful it would be to sit with them on that porch right now. For the first time since they arrived at the retreat, she actually missed Mother. She needed to spend more one-on-one time with her when she got back. Actually sit and talk to her instead of just living in the same house.

Maria returned and took a seat. Having tea together made the session seem more like a personal visit than therapy.

"What's the assignment today?"

"I have to brag on you, Charlene."

"Why?"

"I have never seen such neat, precise work. The labels, the buttons. We haven't had to re-do anything."

"Thanks. Just doing my best."

"Few clients have your work ethic." Maria blew across her tea and took a long sip. "Thanks for tidying the shop, too. It hasn't looked this neat in years. You did a good job."

"Sure. The broom and mop were right there. You know what the Bible says, 'Whatever your hand finds to do, do it with all your might, as unto the—'"

Maria cleared her throat loudly.

"—Lord'."

"Let's talk about today's assignment." Maria gestured toward the photo album. "Take a look at that."

Charlene heaved it onto her lap. "State photos?"

"Open it. These photographs were taken in California and Colorado."

Maria sipped while Charlene turned pages. "I want you to pretend you've moved. Started fresh somewhere else with all the money you want."

"I would never, ever leave Florida."

"It's only pretend, part of the therapy. Your letters and essays go in your portfolio."

"Okay."

"In this exercise, you'll describe your new life in detail. Tell about your new home. What street is it on? Where does Emily go to school? Imagine your new church and your workplace. Choose any work environment you like."

Charlene flipped through photos of neighborhoods, landscapes, and interiors.

"The pictures will help you describe your bedroom, kitchen, and bath, your front yard, your backyard."

The next section contained people and pets.

"These are your new friends and neighbors. What are their names, and what do they do? Choose a pet. Give it a name. A personality."

"This sounds like fun."

"These are Colorado pictures. The ones in the back were taken in California. Decide where you would prefer to live."

"I just can't imagine leaving Florida. I love Gaskille. It's part of my blood."

"But if you had to choose, California or Colorado, which would it be?"

"Maybe Colorado. I've heard about the beautiful mountains there. At least in the summer. But I hate the snow." She shrugged. "I guess I could pretend, though."

"Good." Maria flipped to the beginning of the Colorado section. Now this may take a while. Write your letter, and paint a perfect picture of your new life."

"It's a letter, then?"

"Yes, and at the end you're going to invite your mother to come live with you in your new home. Your task is to sound so convincing she'll want to join you."

"Oh, my." Charlene chuckled as she skimmed through the book. "Mother? She's worse than I am. Generations of us have lived in Florida. Before the Civil War even."

"It's only an exercise." Maria tapped her cup with her fingernail. "Take your time and have fun with it."

Charlene laughed. "I feel like a kid again, dreaming about the future." Now if she could erase the alcoholic and the child-molester then add a Prince Charming, she'd be all set.

89

"Dream big." Maria rose to leave. "If you do well, you and Emily may be able to go home in about three more weeks."

Alone in her room, Charlene selected a handful of pictures. Consumed with the sense that she actually lived on that aspen-lined street in Colorado, she wrote page after page of her letter. If only she could Google and fill in some clever details about the flora and fauna. But she had plenty to write as Emily's new friends, Sarah and Janie, came alive in her mind. She even imagined a slumber party where the girls played Monopoly in their imaginary living room.

This was fun. No wonder Emily enjoyed writing so much.

After she signed the letter, she stretched her arms behind her back. Another knock. Finished just in time.

"Come in, Maria. You'll want to take a vacation in Colorado after you read this."

"I bet I will. Are you tired?"

"Exhausted. Creative writing knocks the stuffing out of me."

Maria laughed. "So it does, so it does."

"Emily and I should take a vacation out there sometime."

"Great idea. Why don't we make this even more real? Address this envelope to your mother." She dropped a cloud-covered envelope that matched Charlene's stationery on the bedspread and held out a yellow *Good Job* sticker. "Now don't laugh, that's a pretend stamp to put in the top corner."

Charlene applied the stamp and chuckled.

"Why don't you take some free time? You've earned it. Dinner will be ready in about fifteen minutes."

After Maria left with the envelope, Charlene lay on the bed and studied the bead board ceiling. The activity was a lot of fun.

But what was the point?

Chapter 13

Alone in the kitchen, Emily lined up the glasses beside the sink and reached for another ice tray. Icy splinters shot across the counter as she lifted the aluminum handle and dumped the cubes into the bin. Maria ought to have an icemaker. These aluminum contraptions dated back to the sixties and reminded her of Grandma, always asking her to fill them, a job Emily hated. Making Emily fill the trays was just a ploy so Grandma would have company in the kitchen.

Nobody had lived with Grandma since Granddaddy died. Emily couldn't even remember him, so except for her neighbor, Grandma must have been pretty lonely before they moved in.

Emily glanced at the wall clock. Almost time for dinner, and Maria was nowhere around.

She turned on the spigot, and it vibrated like a cricket, tickling her eardrums. Closing her eyes, she held the tray under the water, and imagined she was in Grandma's kitchen. She'd be so glad to be home, she'd fill the trays three times a day if Grandma wanted.

A shiver ran up her neck as the door to Maria's room clicked behind her. She whirled around but no one was there. A whiff of rotten sardines wafted across her nostrils then vanished.

Lucas leaned against the headboard and rubbed his black heels back and forth over Maria's chenille bedspread. Her cramped little office/bedroom offered no place else to sit. A little more shine wouldn't hurt his shoes, anyway. Grinning, he stifled a laugh as Maria tossed the open portfolio on the bed.

She hadn't seen him. Of course his stealth was superb.

After pressing the power button on the copier, she slid open a desk drawer. As the noisy machine warmed up, she scrabbled around for a book of stamps.

Her fingers peeled off the yellow "Good Job" sticker from Charlene's envelope and replaced it with a postage stamp. He'd taught her that trick. Good listener, this one.

She smoothed the stamp then held it out to admire.

That Charlene chick didn't have a clue.

Maria made copies of Charlene's letter and tucked them in the portfolio. The original with the Colorado photographs went inside an envelope that matched the stationery. This went into a large brown envelope. Way to go, Maria.

Once the brown envelope arrived at its destination, his Colorado girl would re-mail the letters inside. The perfect lie.

How he loved a lie.

Lucas blew a stream of cigar smoke toward the copier.

Well, Granny, now you'll think your daughter and grandchild have moved away. Gone, gone, gone. There's the postmark to prove it.

Lucas crept off the bed and stood behind Maria. She still hadn't heard him. He brushed his fingertips against her shoulder. She whirled as if an electric shock had jolted her. He chuckled and kissed her forehead.

"How did you get in here?"

"Never mind." His hand slid up her neck as he lifted her chin and found her soft lips with his fingers. Such a small neck. He could easily wrap his fingers around—but no, not yet. And probably not that way.

He squeezed her arm and smoothed the hair away from her temple. She closed her eyes and inhaled his scent. Now that he'd trained her, she seemed to enjoy his tobacco.

"When?" she whispered.

"You're doing great." His lips drifted to her ear. "Right on schedule."

"But when?"

"Patience. Just know that right now I'm very pleased with you."

"Can't you give me some kind of time frame? I've got to wrap my mind around it somehow."

"Not long, not long. Then it will be you and me, and this place, my precious queen."

She reached around his neck and smiled. "Of course I want this place, but it's the 'you and me' part I want to hear more about."

"Let me take care of John first, little beauty. The wheels of greatness turn slowly." Like the demise of the previous owners, his arrangements had to appear natural. Above suspicion.

Stepping back from her, Lucas slung the white coat over his arm then leaned in and caressed her temple one more time. "Just follow the plan carefully."

Her eyes searched his as she reached for his arm. "Stay a little longer."

Wordlessly, he planted a kiss on her upturned lips and walked out of the room.

Emily savored her final bite of seared rabbit and glanced around the dinner table. John, wearing his same old dirty glasses, sopped gravy with a chunk of bread. Across the table, Maria half-listened to Mom's chattering about some new place in Colorado.

If only Emily could get a little privacy she could give her note to Mom. Not a simple task with the old bat watching.

The rolled up paper tickled the bottom of Emily's foot where it had slipped below the arch. She bent over as if scratching and adjusted it. When Mom read it she would find out Maria was calling her mentally-challenged and they would clear out of here.

She had to figure a way to get Maria away from the table. Or get Mom's attention without being seen. Maybe that would work.

"Miss Maria, can I help with anything? Can I get tea or dessert?"

"How about some iced tea? I'm too tired to get up. John?"

"No, thanks, I'll go let the dog out." His chair scraped on the floor, and he ambled down the hall.

Emily fetched the tea then set it on the table. She stood behind Maria and wiggled her fingers to get Mom's attention. "I have a note for you," she mouthed.

Mom tipped her head and wrinkled her brow.

Maria turned around in her seat. "What is it, Emily? Is there something you want to say?"

Emily crossed her arms and glared at Mom.

"I think she just wants to get back home," Mom said. "That's all."

"I see." Maria lined up the silverware on her placemat. "Don't feel bad about that, honey. It's natural. You've been a little under the weather. That's bound to make you more homesick than usual."

Maria pushed back from the table and stood. "Wholesome foods take some getting used to. If your problem doesn't clear up, I'll have Dr. Mike come down. There've been some other bugs going around, too."

Oh, no. Dr. Mike was not going to look at her. She'd stay well, no matter what.

Emily pretended to scratch her foot again and slipped the note out of her shoe. She pressed it against the palm of her hand. "May I pick up the plates? I don't mind helping."

"Sure. Thanks, honey. Just put them in the sink. The cleaning lady will get them tomorrow."

That poor cleaning lady. She always had stacks of Maria's dishes to wash.

Emily lifted Mom's plate and dropped the note in her lap. Well, that was smooth. This time maybe Mom wouldn't give her away.

"Charlene, what did Emily drop in your lap?"

Emily froze. The woman must have eyes under the table. She didn't miss a trick.

Mom picked up the note and unrolled it. At first she said nothing then swallowed. "It says, 'She called me mentally challenged.' What is this about?"

Emily took a deep breath and stared at the dishes in her hand.

"Could you excuse us, Emily, sweetheart, so that I can discuss this with your mother?"

Emily put the dishes into the kitchen sink without a sound and walked out. What lies would Maria tell? If only she hadn't been so careless with the message. Around the corner, she leaned her back against the wall and listened.

Maria lowered her voice. "Again, Charlene, your precious

daughter has misunderstood me. You and I previously discussed her academic problems. I feel you know me well enough to realize that, as a professional therapist, I would never call a child mentally challenged to her face. Am I correct?"

"What could have been said to make her feel this way? She's been through a lot with her stepfather. I don't want her thinking she's part of the problem."

There. Emily punched the air in front of her. Take that, Maria. You tell her, Mom.

"I'll simply reiterate that, as a professional therapist, I would never call a child mentally challenged to her face or lead her to believe such a lie. You and I both know that teenagers can be highly interpretive, full of imagination when it comes to their sensitivities. As you surely know, they don't bond well with adults."

Yeah, right, you twisted liar.

Charlene said nothing for several seconds. "Emily and I haven't really had bonding problems in the past, though."

"She's having trouble bonding with me, Charlene. Perhaps she feels a little conflicted or thinks I am trying to replace you. It's common during therapy to experience this type of issue. The best thing for Emily is for you to show her how much you support the program and our methods."

"She's certainly not herself. You're probably right about the bonding."

How could Mom betray her like this? She slumped, her chest a hollowed out stone. Mom was totally on Maria's side.

"As I said, it's not totally uncommon. She's doing a great job in many areas, but we have to work through some of this willfulness. The trick is to remain detached and let her do this by herself."

Yeah, by herself. Emily scraped tears out of her eyes with clenched fists.

"That's the only way she'll gain the strength she needs. Do we agree?"

Emily imagined her mother's nod and gave a bitter snort. She was completely alone in this stupid prison.

The next morning, Emily sat under an oak tree on a wad of moss to keep the sand off her clean pink shorts. Good thing it was mostly sand under the tree. She flipped her ponytail behind her back. Maria had allowed her to trade art time for free time today. A nice surprise for once.

She dragged a piece of flint rock around the oak roots, around the sleeping Beggar, and under her knees to create a road. The boring yard offered little to do except make dioramas like this one.

The other girl, the one who'd been there before her, had left similar roads, giving her the idea. She had followed the faint tracks, almost obliterated by the rain, and discovered they wound in and out of the palmettos. She improved on them and added more of her own.

Her materials were primitive, but museums actually paid artists for things like this. She gathered a handful of sticks and made a fence. Then she scooted a lone brick, one she had found under the porch, beside her village road to form a bank. The grass around her was the ocean.

Rocks formed the outline of John and Maria's pitiful End of the Lane Church. What a place. Her old church, with a cross and pulpit up front, was far better than theirs. A place where people didn't eat and drink while the pastor preached.

What a rude idea, anyway, eating in church. She shouldn't have done it.

A row of sticks represented Maria, John, Mom, Dr. Mike, and the others. They stood in front of a cross made of twigs and palmetto fibers. She poked "Pastor William" into the ground in front of the congregation. His sermon would have been different from John's. Very different.

She wrapped her arms around her knees and gazed into the sand, the empty throb still in her heart after all this time. Sundays would never be the same back in Gaskille. After Pastor William died she'd never felt the same about attending church. Couldn't life just stay the same for once?

Emily's foot scraped sideways, accidentally erasing part of the road. She gazed at the destruction.

Bam. Change. Detour.

Just like her life.

She took a rock and created another road around the damage.

Her life wasn't entirely ruined, though. Tony had tried to befriend her. And there was Grandma. Since they had moved into her house, she could see her all the time instead of just Sundays and holidays. Two good detours in her life. Then there were the new music lessons.

She gazed at Pastor William's stick standing beside her bank. Grandma, a retired nurse, had asked Emily to help her with his care those last two weeks. As a widower, he had no one else. She and Grandma made a great team spiffing up his old home, expecting him to get well. But a big stroke had ended it all. Emily blinked hard and tossed a rock into the bushes. He shouldn't have died.

If he had known about Bill, he could have talked Mom

out of marrying him. They sure wouldn't be in this situation if he had.

Emily threw another rock against the tree. Hard. Beggar opened his eyes and sat up, watching her. "How could Mom fall for Bill, anyway? Or drag her to this place? Stupid!"

She gouged a hole in the sand with a stick, and Beggar blinked and turned his head as sandy crumbs flew up. That loser Pastor Mario. Trying to take Pastor William's place. She drew a circle in the dirt near Beggar's foot.

"Mario is a reptile. He'll never be my pastor," she murmured. "And I'm never going back to that church, even if I have to lock myself in a closet."

Beggar shifted as if listening.

"And you know what else? There's nothing the matter with me. I don't care if Mario's a pastor or not, he's a freak."

Beggar groaned and lay back down.

"Emily?"

She jumped, and Beggar let out a startled bark.

"Sorry, sweetheart." For once, Maria's apology sounded sincere. "I really didn't mean to startle you. It looks like you're having a good time out here."

Maria had never come outside before.

"You know, another girl used to play just like this."

Creating dioramas was art. Training for museum work. Not playing, for goodness' sake.

"She had long wavy hair, too."

"What was her name?"

"Susie."

Emily glanced at her roads. Susie's roads. Susie's embroidery. "Where did she go?"

"She graduated from the program." Maria held out her

hand, revealing a brown capsule. "Here, you forgot your vitamin. Were you in a hurry this morning?"

"I took a red one, remember?"

Maria held out a small bottle of water and a peanut butter cookie. "Actually, no. An extra vitamin wouldn't hurt a thing, though. Take this one and humor me."

Emily reached for the brown gel-cap. "I know I took one," she said, swallowing it with the water.

"That's okay." Maria took the bottle, and perched on a nearby log. She flipped her gauze skirt away from the weeds and revealed her maroon toenails. Creepy how her toenails curved over her toes. Maria should go back inside. Just go away. Back to her cave.

"Emily, we have to chat."

Not another talk. Emily took a slow breath.

"Sometimes young ladies say and do things for attention. They might even lie, which can ruin a person's life."

Not more finger-pointing. Maria had ruined the cabin for her, and now she was ruining the great outdoors. Just go away. Or Emily could change the subject. "Miss Maria, how did you know peanut butter cookies were my favorite?"

Maria's eyebrow arched. "About that lying. Your mom tells me everything." Her blue eyes bored into Emily's. "You accused me of calling you mentally challenged. Did you also accuse your stepfather of something he didn't do?

Emily narrowed her eyes. "No, ma'am."

"I suppose you sent your innocent stepfather to prison with your lies. Now you're punishing your mother by dragging out your treatment. She loves you very much and would do anything for you. Is this fair to her?"

"I'm not sure what you mean."

"Will you stop acting mentally challenged, Emily? I know the truth. That robbery story you made up? That was a lie."

So she knew about Bill's attack. Probably from Mom's paperwork.

"Attention-getting is all it is. Your stepfather didn't attack you. You're the one responsible for ruining your family." Maria raised both eyebrows. "I bet you think you're being cute, too."

Maria rose with hands on her hips and leaned over like a first grader about to stick out their tongue. "And yes, I'd call that mentally challenged. I'd also call you a liar." She turned and pranced back to the porch. The brown skirt snagged on a tall Spanish needle, exposing pasty white calves and cracked heels. She snatched at the cloth.

Emily closed her eyes. One minute the birds had been singing and the sunlight shone so beautifully through the leaves, and the next minute her ears were reverberating with Maria's accusations. The woman's rancor throbbed around her like silent thunder.

Emily turned her attention back to the diorama and touched the single black stick. She pushed it face down in front of the cross.

Bow, you witch. You're the liar.

Emily uncrossed her clammy arms, but another javelin thrust through her gut, sucking her breath away. She grimaced and pinched her cold dehydrated skin until it hurt. It might bruise, but the pinching distracted her from the pain in her abdomen.

Maria's voice slashed through the bathroom door. "Do

you need more paper?" Right about now, the woman would be drumming those talons against her arms.

Emily held her breath as another sword drove into her. When would this end?

"I hear that paper rolling and rolling in there." Maria paused. "Your body is telling on you." Another pause. "I know all about it. It happens every time."

Emily had no choice but to subject herself to the woman's mercy. "Please, Miss Maria, I just need one roll of paper."

"I'll get you some. But this wouldn't happen if you'd follow the program correctly. It might just speed things up for you if you had the right attitude."

A roll of paper appeared through the doorway as if the old witch had had it all along. She wanted Emily to beg. "Here, take it. And stop your lying."

Please, just get away from the door. Emily moistened her lips and tried to blink away the blotches of black ink growing across her field of vision.

She was going blind right here in the bathroom, with Mom so close and yet too far away to know what was happening.

She blinked until the spots receded, then stood and held onto the sink. Numbness prickled along her legs. She forced herself to march up and down and tried to restore the circulation.

The black curtain dropped over her head again, letting faint sparkles of light through as if the pinpricks had floated up from her legs.

Emily touched her eyes and fumbled for the doorframe. Within seconds the blackness dissipated allowing her to shuffle to the bed hugging her belly.

Maria had disappeared.

Emily shivered and eased under the bedspread. She willed her bed to warm quickly.

The clock's rhythmic tick interrupted the silence and assaulted her ears. *Stupid thing.*

After a fitful drowse, she woke to find the bedroom door hanging open. Beggar stood blinking into her face.

Through dry, stuck lips she managed a whisper. "Hey, Beggar." When he laid his muzzle on the bed, she gathered her knees up tighter and closed her eyes. She felt his breath on her chin but lacked the strength to stroke him.

He bumped his wet nose against her and moved away, his toenails clicking around the foot of the bed. Suddenly his weight landed on the mattress behind her. He nestled against her back as she drifted off again.

Emily knew Him. Even in the fogginess of her dream, she recognized that face. A hundred sunlights radiated from His hair. As He bent to extend the glittering key in His open hand, the shifting contours of His robe shimmered like diamonds, and the scent of roses perfumed the air. So many colors.

Her mouth refused to move, and she could only think the pleading words. "Jesus… Jesus… I need your help."

Low peals of thunder rumbled her body. His hand moved closer, and she sensed the key's warmth. She needed this key. But her arms, like heavy beams, refused to move, and the vision faded.

Maria's shrill voice cut through the atmosphere, calling Emily to dinner. Beggar leaped off the bed and stood by the door.

Bit by bit she roused. The plain walls of the bedroom materialized. Still groggy, she pushed away the covers and slid to her feet.

All through dinner the dream's energy swirled and hummed in Emily's head. She chewed the hot tomato-y pasta and green beans without tasting them.

Maria and John slipped her a sideways glance from time to time but remained silent. Mom hardly said a word, as if she didn't even know Emily had been sick.

After dinner, Emily climbed back into bed. Beggar sniffed the air a few times before curling up on the rug.

She snuggled into her pillow, closed her eyes, and inhaled.

Hadn't the smell of roses been part of the dream? She lifted her head and took a deep breath, her eyes blinking in concentration.

There it was again. Roses. Emily nestled back down.

Good night, Jesus.

Chapter 14

On Sunday morning, Rene stared through her windshield at the Faithful Disciples Church. Hot sun reflected off the building's green metal roof, but the pewter sky beyond threatened a storm. A stiff morning breeze whipped sand across the parking lot stirring the low limbs of the live oak overhead. "Maybe we shouldn't be here today."

"We're not backing out now, kiddo," Kaye said as she applied her lipstick. "Nice of them to give their visitors the shady spot, isn't it?"

In front of them, two families entered the church door.

Rene reached for her purse and threw her keys inside. "Somehow I feel sneaky."

"It was your idea, and we have every right to be here."

"I have a bad feeling."

"Same here. One more sign we're doing the right thing."

They entered, and Kaye led the way to a seat up front. On the stage, tuneless flute music drifted from a small keyboard behind potted palms. A tall blond usher escorted three women to the opposite row. Within ten minutes the auditorium was half-full.

Kaye leaned over and whispered, "I feel like the mother in a wedding up here."

"I've never heard bird songs in church, have you?"

"It sounds like an apiary."

Rene elbowed her. "I think it's *aviary*. Apiaries are for bees. Look." Onstage twelve men in black and purple vests filed in. They sat in a semicircle of folding chairs, their shoulders touching.

105

"Hmm," Rene said, "the twelve disciples."

"Don't be mean, now. They may be perfectly all right."

A plump usher strode to the podium. His full cheeks and bald head gleamed. "Good morning, ladies and gentlemen." He paused while the crowd settled. "I present to you—our pastor, Dr. Mario." With a flourish of his hand and a slight bow, he backed away. Mario burst from the side curtains like a TV game show host.

The congregation applauded and rose. Someone in the back whistled.

Rene tried to catch a glimpse of the whistler but couldn't. "You'd think this Dr. Mario was the president," she mumbled.

"Thank you. You may be seated." Pastor Mario's voice rolled out like melted butter. He opened his palms and quieted the applause then gave a nod as the usher slipped into his seat with the other eleven disciples. "It's so good to see you all today."

He stepped away from the podium and shaded his eyes. "And I recognize a few more faces coming in now. Welcome." After glancing left and right, his eyes rested on Rene and Kaye. "If you are a visitor, would you please raise your hand?"

Rene hesitated. Then she and Kaye lifted their hands together. No sense hiding. He'd already homed in on them. Four or five other hands went up.

"Thank you." He nodded as more applause filled the room.

"We would like to give you a visitor's information card to fill out," Pastor Mario said. "We'll get to know you better, and can send you a little more information about our church." He smiled and stroked his immaculate goatee. It glimmered under the stage lights.

"We are *so* happy to have you. After our service, I invite

everyone to join my wife and me for cappuccino and fellowship in the front lobby."

As he returned to the podium, his voice cooed. "Our theme today, beloved, is your success—something I'm confident you can attain in the near future."

He paused, looking thoughtfully across the audience as if considering his next idea carefully. "We all know that positive attitudes are vital, the key to reaching our pinnacle.

"So today, I am going to lay out seven important secrets that will spread their fingers across your backs and push you right up to the mountain peak.

"These seven secrets will supercharge your positive attitudes, creating a dynamo in you that cannot be stopped.

"In fact, my friends, these secrets will make you wonder just how you're going to contain all that success."

Rene eyed Kaye and faked a yawn.

"Who would like to hear those secrets?" He clasped his hands expectantly and nodded at the raised hands.

"So let us begin. The seven secrets for success." He opened a notebook on the lectern.

"Who has their notebook?"

Rene peeked around as the audience rustled. Almost everyone held up a notebook.

"If you forgot yours, there are pads of paper and pens behind the seats. Just help yourself, please."

"Smooth as oil, this guy."

Kaye leaned close, "Just pick up the pad and go along with it for now."

Two ushers carried a white board onto the stage. Pastor Mario turned to the board.

"Is this a sermon," Rene whispered, "or a classroom lesson?"

A message on positive attitudes sounded appealing. But not when it wasn't based on Scripture or the name of Jesus.

"Shh. Don't be obvious," Kaye said through her teeth, pretending to smile. "Give it time and write some notes."

After 30 minutes of smooth talking, Pastor Mario snapped his notebook shut and stepped away from his lectern like a male flamenco dancer. "Did that help you today?"

Rene and Kaye stayed in their seats as the rest of the congregation stood and clapped on cue. A happy melody filled the room.

"Will you have positive attitudes this week?" He pumped his hand like cheerleader.

Another crescendo of applause rose from the audience.

The tune meandered on as members put away their notes. The sermon had ended, but everyone sat down again. On the other side of the narrow window, the sky had darkened. Rain pebbled against the sheet metal roof. The congregation quieted as if anticipating more.

The music faded and the lights dimmed except for a spotlight on the preacher.

Suddenly, the rain let loose, drumming solidly. No chance of staying dry, even with a mad dash to the car. Rene stared through the glass. Church and nature seemed choreographed together.

When she turned her attention back to the stage, the platform had transformed into an orange inferno. Silken "flames" fluttered upward in an eerie dance behind colored footlights along the stage's curved edge. She traded glances with Kaye, who frowned and raised an eyebrow.

Pastor Mario stepped over the flames and stopped at the edge of the stage. Footlights cast ghostly shadows onto his face. "From out of the blazes," he said with a laugh.

Rene glanced at Kaye.

Pastor Mario spread his arms wide as if sprinkling water over the audience. "It's time for us to receive from the s-s-spirit." He hissed the last word. "Today I will ask the spirit to impart the secrets of a positive attitude to you. Who wants those secrets living within you?"

Pale hands flew up across the dark auditorium. Overhead, the rain's heavy pounding increased.

Rene pushed her back against the seat. "I can hardly stand this."

Kaye covered her lips with her hand. "That's *not* the Holy Spirit he's talking about. And this has nothing to do with Jesus."

"You ought to feel my pulse. I hope I don't have a heart attack in here."

The flute's tuneless wanderings were soon joined by the slow drub of a drum whose quiet bump-bump-bump mimicked the beat of a heart. As a queue of congregants formed along the far wall, the drum grew louder. Faster.

Pastor Mario laid his hands on each person. "Receive the spirit" he said to some. To others, he said "Woof," and pushed them backwards. A few fell flat on their backs.

"Kaye, this reminds me of faith healing," Rene said. But they're not praying in Jesus' name. This is wrong."

"Weirdest thing I've ever seen. Definitely not what the Bible says."

"These poor people. Look at them. I wonder what kind of strange spirit he's infecting them with."

In the lobby after the service, Rene glanced at the other

trapped congregants. Small groups clustered or milled about, dropping donut crumbs and sipping cappuccinos. The building creaked and groaned against the gusting winds and rushing torrents.

"I feel like a spy," Rene said through clenched teeth.

"Act natural," Kaye mumbled, holding a Styrofoam cup under the coffee dispenser. "Here, have one." She held the filled cup out to Rene.

"You're trembling."

"Let's keep our hands full. I don't want to shake anybody's hand."

Blue lightning tinged the room as thunder cracked. Everyone gasped, and the level of chatter rose higher. A small group moved away from the door.

"Want to make a run for it?"

"Yeah, and break our necks in their parking lot." Kaye reached for a cookie. "Might as well eat their free snacks."

Across the room, Pastor Mario shouldered his way through the crowd with a smiling blonde at his side.

Rene tapped Kaye's foot with the side of her shoe. "Look who's coming." The woman, probably in her mid-twenties and definitely much younger than Mario, latched onto him like a prom queen. She had the dress. All she needed was a printed sash.

"Good morning, ladies," he said, bending toward them. He hadn't seemed this tall from Benny's window, and his life-sized Barbie matched him shoulder to shoulder.

"Good morning," Kaye and Rene said in unison like school children. Rene glanced over his shoulder toward the darkened glass door. The weather hadn't improved in the last few seconds.

"I was hoping you'd linger a few minutes so we could meet you." He tipped his head toward the exit with a whitened smile. "But you didn't have much choice, did you?"

"Sure hope my vegetable garden isn't ruined," Kaye said.

"Sure hope not. Maybe it'll spring back," he said. "But we're glad you could be in here out of the rain with us. We appreciate all our visitors."

Rene smiled. "The facilities are gorgeous. You certainly keep them up well."

"Thank you. Our ushers told me you are Rene and Kaye? This is my lovely wife Linda."

"So very nice to meet you," she said, flashing teeth as white as her husband's.

Rene cleared her throat and smiled. "It's nice to meet you too. Thank you for your interesting teaching today." She suppressed the urge to look at Kaye.

His wife? Then who was the redhead?

Chapter 15

Emily followed Mom into the cool interior of the End of the Lane Church. Sunday services again. The old building's musty woodiness mingled with the smell of roasted coffee. Near the door, Donna straightened snacks, creamers, and sugar packets on a wooden table.

She handed Emily a handful of napkins with two crème-filled donuts. "You look like you could use a couple of these."

"Thanks. I love them."

Emily averted her eyes from the stained glass window when she walked past. No need to look at that ugly thing again. A few feet away, Mom ran her fingers over the back of a mahogany pew where a spear of sunlight sliced across its dark surface, exposing its hidden red grain.

Like blood.

Mom was probably saying *Praise, You, Lord, this is all so beautiful.* Yuck. Nothing here was beautiful.

Up front, John tuned his guitar with loud but uncertain chords. He hooked his boot-heel under the chair, strummed, and turned pegs until he got the sound right.

Emily headed toward the circle as he lit into "God Is So Good, God Is So Good," singing the chorus over and over while others joined in.

With a sigh, she glanced at Mom's face, but it was as happy as ever. Didn't she get it?

Eventually John's songs ended, and he pulled a large leather Bible edged in gold from beneath his chair. "This, brothers and sisters, is a special treat." Holding it open, he riffled the pages. "Just in, the New Times/New World Version of the Bible, the latest translation."

He displayed the title page. "Look here, it's autographed by the translators." Approving murmurs rose from the small gathering.

"Today I want to talk about our good deeds." He motioned toward a client in a pink dress and gave her a long proud look.

The client blinked self-consciously and concentrated on her clasped hands.

"Here we have Cindy, lovely little Cindy. A dear part of the kingdom. She's given so much love, so many sacrifices."

The straggly, brown-haired woman seemed too small, too ordinary to contribute any real sacrifice.

"She'll get her reward." John waited a beat. "You see, obedience is sacrifice, loving our neighbor as ourselves. And that's our Cindy, through and through."

What was he talking about?

"Good works have definitely earned Cindy her salvation," he said. "She's got that mansion coming, those riches, those gold streets. Yes, indeed, Cindy, thank you for your good works. You're an example to all of us. Let's show her our appreciation." He led the applause as sponsors stood with their clients and clapped.

Cindy glanced nervously at the faces around her then back to her hands in her lap.

What could she have contributed?

Once everyone settled into their seats, John held the Bible in the air again. "You see, we're obligated to study this book and the books you've been provided. It is a new world, and I challenge you to press forward with your good works and earn your salvation."

Forget that. Maria's stack of books hadn't included a Bible.

He pointed the end of the Bible around the circle. "Each one of you also knows that obedience to your sponsors brings you closer to God. The message is simple. Obedience, submission, and good works. They earn you a place in the kingdom. The good works you do at Earth Mother Acres are the ticket to pleasing God."

He did a final fist-pump with the Bible then tossed it on the floor and picked up the guitar. "Keep up the good work. Earn your way into the new kingdom."

Emily grimaced. He never opened the Bible. And he threw it on the floor. Dis. Re. Spect. Ful.

New chords vibrated from the guitar as John asked if anyone had any questions. But he failed to look up and find out. Instead he led them in another song.

Emily dropped a final bite of donut in her mouth. John was nuts and so were the others. They had clapped for Cindy without knowing why. But not her. She shook her head and kept her face turned away from Maria, hidden on the other side of Mom. A little vacation from the woman.

Mom raised her hand.

John finished the verse then nodded in her direction.

"Could you play 'Jesus is the Sweetest Name I Know'?"

Almost before Mom finished her question, Dr. Mike's Styrofoam cup flipped out of his hand, tossing coffee in a wide arc across the floor. He fumbled as if trying to catch the cup but things worsened when his arm knocked a snack table over. His actions were so dramatic, Emily could have sworn he did it on purpose. The table's edge smacked into the coffee puddle and splattered it further. Dr. Mike's donut hit the floor and rolled like a little white wheel, leaving a powdery trail before it fell on its side. Counselors scurried to drop napkins into the wetness and pick things up as if it were some kind of real emergency.

The whole time John stood quietly with his guitar in his hand. He shot a look at Maria who appeared to be stifling a smile.

Mike righted the thin metal legs of the table, and the room finally came back to order.

John turned to Mom who still waited on an answer. "We don't know that one. How about a verse or two of 'Beautiful Earth'?"

For a split second, Mom's gaze dipped to the floor.

She nodded.

Good. So maybe she was starting to get a clue about things.

In Gaskille, the after-church crowd packed into Benny's as usual. Rene sat opposite Kaye with the same view of the psychiatrist's office as before. The office and the wooden gate remained closed.

"What about that church service?" Kaye asked as their waitress slid salads in front of them.

Rene poured Thousand Island dressing over her onions. "If that's who sent the girls to a retreat, we've got some big-time praying to do."

Kaye speared a cucumber. "What would you call that place? I know it isn't Christian, but just what do you call it?"

"I read a Christian blog the other day. The writer said that the Bible encourages us to test the spirits to see if they are Christian. The first test, did the church exalt Jesus? Failed."

Kaye's nose wrinkled.

"Okay, and two, do they proclaim the Word of God?"

Kaye shook her head.

Rene's gaze settled on the building across the street. "Well, well, guess who just drove up."

Kaye twisted around as the black BMW pulled to a stop, and its goateed driver jumped out to open the gate. "No blonde wife in the passenger seat?"

"Can't the guy wait until after lunch?" Rene stabbed a tomato. "Oh, yeah, number three. Are persons repenting of sin, and being baptized in water and the Holy Spirit? Did you hear that today?"

Across the street, the car pulled through the wooden fence and out of sight.

After a few seconds Rene nodded. "Glad to see he shut the gate this time."

Today was Monday, with 1 ½ weeks down, and 3 or so to go. Emily jammed sticks in the sand beside the sleeping Beggar. Like shish kabobs, green stems of unripe beautyberries drooped overhead. Together with the palmetto fronds, they formed a dense backdrop for the primitive diorama next to her knee.

Beggar twitched as a gnat landed on his eye. He rolled over, crushing a road she had just built. Nice rockslide.

Emily's stomach growled. Maria had refused to switch the schedule around today, but lunch would be soon.

A black and rust butterfly lit on a small pile of rocks. Emily's rock houses had all collapsed, and she gave up on them. Instead, she worked on improving her skills of weaving little mats from sticks and palmetto fibers, something she'd learned from her friends in their orange grove fort in Citra.

She should call that BG, before Grandma's house.

Except for Tony, she hadn't met any kids in Gaskille who were like her friends at North Marion Middle.

Emily let out a deep breath and picked up a woven square. Mom would never move back to their old home.

The butterfly flitted to the top of a beautyberry and opened its wings. A monarch or a viceroy? A teacher had explained the difference once.

Whoops. BG again.

The butterfly, startled, lifted away, darting up and down through the foliage. Its drunken path led to the main road down by the river. That's where she'd like to go, just for a change. To liven things up.

If she asked permission, Maria would probably tell her to stay in the yard.

Emily shot a glance toward the house. The tree stood between her and the porch. Maria wouldn't be coming out until she rang the bell.

It was now or never.

She crawled through the opening of the palmettos. As she pressed through the fronds, they slapped together behind her. There was no way Maria could see her in here before she reached the road. All she had to do was watch for snakes.

The noise of a car in the driveway brought her to a stop. Maria never had visitors. A car door slammed and then the screen door. From the porch, Maria's voice mingled with a man's, but Emily couldn't place him. She lifted her head at the same time Maria clanged the bell for her to come in. Shoot. Maria was early. She ducked again.

Creeping out of the palmettos, she hid behind the oak.

She yanked the knotted rope then let it go so Maria would think she'd been on it.

Good trick, Emily.

Maria didn't have a clue. Next time she would have to start exploring sooner.

She studied the ground as she approached the porch. Maria held the screen door open for her. "Wipe your feet, please."

Boots blocked the doorway. Her eyes traveled up to a black medical bag and the large freckled hand that held it. Dr. Mike. She jerked her head around to Maria who made no attempt to conceal a smirk.

The witch. She'd lose that smile if Emily got hold of her.

"Since you've been having some problems, Dr. Mike is going to take a look at you." She motioned toward the living room. "Why don't you see her in there, doctor?"

Emily pursed her lips as the woman sashayed away. With rubbery knees, she followed Dr. Mike's enormous Wranglers down the hall. The floor creaked under his boots.

In the living room, dusty amber light seeped through the brittle window shades. Small bright tears in their papery surface revealed the barest hint of the brilliance outside. Dr. Mike paused by the sofa and flicked on the table lamp. Its puny light added little to the darkness.

If only she could get back outside. Back to her one secret place of freedom.

Dr. Mike motioned toward the overstuffed sofa. "Why don't you sit right here?"

His booming bass voice rattled her insides.

Emily scooted higher on the sofa's arched surface, trying not to slide off or touch his bag. Whatever padding was inside the sofa crunched like hundred-year-old moss.

She glanced sideways at the giant cowboy's face.

He chuckled. "You don't need to be afraid of me. I don't bite."

Seen up close, his squinty blue eyes and red ponytail made him appear less sinister. But he would never examine her. Nobody else would, either. She clasped her fingers around her knees, wedged her heels beneath the edge of the sofa, and focused on a forgotten dust bunny that lay under the rocker. It must have lain there a long time, undisturbed, a silent eavesdropper to all conversations.

Dr. Mike grabbed a ladderback chair from the corner and flipped it around backwards. It groaned under his weight.

Just keep that chair right there, Mister.

Her eyes lit on the bag again. Shiny torture instruments gleamed in its recesses just like at her doctor's office. She hated them all. He picked up the Popsicle stick and held it like a large flat pencil.

"Can you open your mouth?" An earthy smell, as if he'd been in the sun, drifted off him.

Emily clamped her lips together and stared at the curling moustache hairs which formed two Cs beneath Dr. Mike's nostrils. A few blond bristles mixed with the reds.

Like Grandma's hairdresser told her, redheads sometimes turned blond then white. This old toot was aging.

He smiled. "Could you please open your mouth so I can see in?" The man was nice enough, but no, she wasn't doing this. She sat like a stump.

"Well, okay, then, I'll look in your ear." He traded the stick for a light. "Just hold still for a second." He looked into her right ear as she tilted her head down and studied his snakeskin cowboy boots. Brown with a distinct diamond pattern down the front. Hmm, real snake's scales, maybe a rattlesnake. The scales seemed like they would chip off if they were bumped. Dirt clung to the boots' soles.

Dr. Mike sat back. "Uh huh," he said. "I see."

He pulled out a little notepad and jotted something down. "Emily, do you know what I see?"

"Earwax?" She pursed her lips together and met his gaze.

"I see where you need to be open and not hide anything from Miss Maria. Just cooperate with her, and you will get well. What you have is a resistance syndrome."

That sounded ridiculous. So he was playing Maria's little accusation game. Play dumb, though. "Oh."

"Take your vitamins and cooperate. That's all. It's as simple as that."

"Yes, sir."

"No arguing back. No telling lies." He patted her head and stood. "Do you think you can do that?" He pulled the chair back into the corner then grabbed the bag with one hand and adjusted his large silver buckle with the other. "It's not too complicated, and between you and me, it will make your stay so much shorter. Wouldn't you like that? A shorter stay?"

That would suit her just fine, but she kept her mouth shut.

He hollered down the hall. "Miss Maria, I'll get back with you in about an hour. I have some other appointments." The door creaked open and the porch boards complained as he stepped out.

Before the door could slam Beggar burst in. His toenails clicked as he raced down the hall and leaped into Emily's lap, licking her face and trembling from head to haunches.

"Ow." She shifted his weight and swiped the slobber off

her face "Your toenails are sharp." As Beggar settled, Emily's gaze returned to the ladderback chair.

What in the world had just happened?

Chapter 16

Charlene picked the tiny stitches out of the jacket's label with her seam ripper. Even with the lamp bent close, she found herself squinting in the poor light of the workshop.

A movement behind her shoulder. She jumped. The ripper flipped out of her hand. Dr. Mike stood near her elbow.

"Oh. You scared me. I didn't hear you come in."

Maria stepped from behind him and placed a lunch tray on the sewing table. "Sorry to scare you. How's it going?"

Charlene retrieved her tool from the floor. "It's going fine. I-I guess I was just concentrating."

Dr. Mike traded smiles with Maria. "I'm only here for a quick visit," he said.

Charlene held up the jacket by the collar. "This crooked label was driving me crazy. I can't stand to make a mistake."

"That kind of thing happens." Maria turned to Dr. Mike. "Charlene's one of our best clients. God must really be proud of her."

"Your daughter reflects those same careful tendencies, Charlene."

"Thank you, Doctor. I've tried to raise her right despite the circumstances that have tried to destroy her."

"We understand."

"Dr. Mike visited Emily at the house a while ago," Maria said. "He gave her a little checkup—"

Charlene shifted around in her seat. "A checkup?" They didn't need to be giving Emily any exams, especially after her experience with—

"Yes, her ears, her throat, just to calm your fears. Around this river we can't be too careful, you know. Her recent stress could weaken her immune system."

"But nobody told me she needed an exam." Whatever the type exam, they still had no business looking at her child without consent. "What's the matter? Is she sick?"

He waved his hand. "Oh, no, no, no. She's not sick. Her body's adjusting to natural foods, though. And that's just fine."

Charlene took a breath. Maybe she was too quick on the draw. These were professionals. They knew what they were doing. After all, look at the reputation of the place.

"I appreciate it, Doctor. But if there's a next time, I want to be there."

"If you insist, of course."

"I'm glad she's okay. Maria already mentioned the diarrhea."

"She's lost a little weight. But it's not serious."

"She's not a big eater to start with."

"I only stopped by to get you up to speed. I'll keep a close eye on her."

"The medical service is covered by the retreat fees. There's no charge," Maria added. "We're lucky to have Dr. Mike. He's so well thought of at the hospital."

Of course, it was nice of him to make a house call. Most doctors didn't do that anymore. Maybe she shouldn't blow this out of proportion like a raving ingrate. "I'm so—" she reached for his hand, "I'm so grateful, and you're so sweet and kind. Thanks for caring about my Emily."

"You're welcome. Any worries, you mention them to Maria here. I'll be nearby. Take care now, and keep up the fine work."

They turned and walked away in quiet conversation, Dr.

Mike's broad torso contrasting distinctly with Maria's narrow one.

Of course they meant well. What lovely people. But if the doctor needed to check Emily again, he should let Charlene know. Ahead of time.

John swung the post office box open and reached for the handful of mail leaning against the inside wall. Snapping a green rubber band around the bundle he dropped it into the battered shoebox under his arm. Maria could go through the letters.

As he stepped outside, the cell phone he'd left on the van's front seat rang. His pace quickened, and he swung the vehicle's door open with a loud metal squeak, snatching up the phone on the fourth ring.

"Hello, Maria." He barely disguised his annoyance. She'd probably ask him to look through the mail for something. It never failed, and he hated looking through mail.

"Did we get anything from Gaskille, Florida?"

"Hold on. I have to set everything down to see." Inside the van he propped the phone where the stuffing had been plucked from a hole in the passenger seat. He dug through the contents of the shoebox and squinted through dust-speckled glasses at return addresses. "Well—" He picked up the phone and cradled it between his chin and shoulder. "Yeah, here's one from Gaskille, from the courthouse."

"Open it and see if it's the child support check."

"How about you doing that? I'll be home in just a few minutes." The stack of mail landed in the box as he started the motor and threw the van into reverse.

"It'll only take—"

"Maria, I can't drive and talk. It's not safe." Anything to keep from having to plunder the mail. He wasn't exactly lazy, but she did this to him every time.

"John, please—"

"I'll get back with you after I drop these packages off at shipping." He punched the end-call button and threw the phone in the box with the mail. If she wanted to know so much, she should pick up the mail herself.

At Main Street, he turned left then checked his rearview mirror. A white mass blocked his view. Cigar smoke hit his nose, and he twisted his head, barely missing Lucas' grinning face over his shoulder. The wheel jerked in his hands.

An oncoming car blasted its horn. John veered to the right, dodging a head-on collision. Over-correcting, he snatched the wheel the other way. Straightened. Pulled into a driveway and slammed on the brakes.

With his nerves on fire, he turned. His eyeball scraped across Lucas' white sleeve. He grabbed his eye. "Ahh! That hurt, man. Get your arm off the headrest."

Lucas laughed and placed his foot on the console. "Don't be such a girl." He reached for John's shoebox and climbed into the front seat, dropping it on the floor. His black-marble eyes glinted, and the smile widened under his moustache.

John slammed his hand against the steering wheel. "Don't *do* that. Man, I nearly hit that guy." With his heart returning to normal, he scowled out the front window, breathing in and out through his teeth. "You scared the fool out of me. Why do you always do that?"

Lucas chuckled, obviously pleased with John's reaction.

A heavy woman wearing a cotton housecoat stepped off

her porch and waddled toward the van. John frowned but waved her a never mind as he backed up. "I'm going to be messed up for the rest of the day."

"You'll be fine," Lucas said. "Just stopped by to say hi."

"Hi, then." No smile yet, though he ought to be more respectful to the boss. This was Lucas. And you didn't mess with Lucas. "Everything's going fine here, as far as I can tell you."

"Oh, it is, indeed." Lucas pulled out another cigar. "You want one?"

"No, I'm good."

"Pull up to that warehouse on 45th Street. I'll get out there."

"Can't stay longer?" John asked, though Lucas never did. Gag! It had only taken a couple of minutes for him to stink up the van.

"I'll check on the farm later. You're doing a good job, John." He blew a smoke ring toward the ceiling, held the cigar over the dash, and grinned again. "Still interested in my little lakefront cabin up in West Virginia?"

John stared at him for a brief second then focused on the road. "It's all I ever wanted. You know that." In fact it was reason *numero uno* of their work here. After the elderly Smiths died, Lucas bought the Earth Mother Acres property. John and Maria only had to finish this last season at the place before moving north.

"Nice timing, wasn't it," Lucas said, "the way the Smiths died?"

Convenient, all right. Only days after Lucas made his offer. No way was John going to ask him for the details.

Forget all that, though. Once he and Maria carried out Lucas' plan, the cabin in the mountains would be theirs. Such a simple trade. Work for land.

"I didn't hear your answer."

"Good timing, yes. Very good."

"Atta boy, John. Soon you'll be fishing in that lake with the sun against your back. Not a care in the world." Lucas blew more smoke. "Set for life."

Forty-fifth Street was just ahead.

"Whoa, pull over."

Lucas opened the door and slipped out.

John undid his seatbelt and locked the door behind the man. If Lucas followed his usual pattern, he'd be gone a few months. Good riddance. In the meantime, John would keep the van locked. Just in case.

The office door eased shut, and Maria dropped its latch into the eye. Her fingernail bumped against the dull paint and left a purple line even after she rubbed it with her finger.

Never mind. The house needed a paint job anyway. She pressed the lock down once again, just in case. Couldn't have Emily or the maid intruding on the business.

Lining up the mail in *ABC* order along the bedspread, she pulled a check from each envelope. Anything to make this job easier. Copying all the different signatures would take days.

At the desk, she squinted at the first check. Who knew why squinting helped, but one day she'd actually go take an eye exam.

Pay to the order of Jill Gary. She reached in the desk for the Gary file and placed the cheat sheet on top of the machine. With the light on, she placed a paper over the signature. A simple signature, but it would take practice to make it look natural.

This time she heard Lucas come in, but she didn't look up from her tracing. Three more letters, and she had this one down. Even with that, her shoulders quivered with expectancy—and then the touch came, warm and soft, massaging her neck. He dropped to one knee touching her cheek with his own. His hair brushed her ear, and she breathed in the sweet cigar scent as his fingers drifted along her writing arm and covered her hand. He held it lightly, guiding her to the end of the name. With his feather touch, he made the signature easy. Perfect.

"Keep writing," he breathed in her ear.

She shivered.

"You were born for forgery," he whispered. "A natural."

Drawing his hand over her shoulder, he lifted her hair and brushed his lips across the back of her neck. Then he stood, letting the hair fall back into place. When she turned, he had disappeared. He never stayed long enough.

She touched her neck where the sensation of his breath still lingered.

Only then did she notice the latch, still hooked from the inside.

Chapter 17

Emily bounded down the front porch steps and headed for the end of the rutted driveway; before the witch could see her and change her plans. Forget exploring the front yard. She needed to wedge a little more distance between herself and the woman—and this prison. At least while she could.

Near the end of the driveway, Emily slowed. Out of nowhere, Beggar appeared, prancing proudly at her side. She patted his shoulder. "Good little poochie."

They reached the decrepit sign Emily had seen that first night. Gray lichens still clung to its rotten legs.

"See that, Beggar? Nobody ever pays attention to this poor messed-up sign." She knelt and scratched at one of the larger lichens, blowing the crumbs across a blue spiderwort bloom which had already closed in the heat.

Like the shriveled flower, Emily was going to curl up and die if she didn't get out of this place.

She patted Beggar's head and stood. "Come on. Let's go see what's down the road."

Jays squawked in the oaks and cypresses, and a mystery bird sang, "Go on home. Go on home" and "Em-uh-ly, Em-uh-ly." Thousands of cicadas filled the air with their buzzing.

City people thought it was quiet in the country, but Southern woods were as noisy as all get-out. Up ahead, two squirrels leaped from the trunk of a sabal palm and spiraled up the loop of a thick vine. Beggar lunged after them then loped back to Emily after they disappeared into the crown of an oak.

Above her, sunbeams passed here and there through the

translucent green canopy, hitting the ground in dusty rays, and reminding her of the woods near Orange Lake. She twirled through the beams and stirred up the lazy dust motes. Beggar danced on his back legs. Then, dizzy from spinning, Emily dropped to the sand.

Her hands rubbed across its smooth surface, still undisturbed from the last rain. Obviously, no cars had passed by. Emily disengaged a long stick from the weeds and pulled off its moss. She climbed to her feet and sauntered down the road, dragging it behind her as it cut a snaky trail in the sand.

Beggar trotted beside her, sniffing the edge of the dense palmetto undergrowth, the same bushes that had scraped the sides of their car that first night. Along with the dark wax myrtles that rose here and there, the dense woods provided a perfect cover from Maria's nosiness.

Up ahead a black and orange butterfly lingered over the road then disappeared behind her.

Something rattled in the bushes. Maybe a bird. Maybe a gopher turtle. It might even be a rattlesnake, but surely Beggar would have barked at a snake. Instead, he darted confidently through the bushes. Emily chased after him, maneuvering through the limbs and vines and barely missing a healthy patch of poison ivy.

"Beggar, come back. Beggar!"

On the other side of the underbrush, the river glittered like diamonds in the sun. Beggar stood on the damp sand lapping thirstily at the water as it rippled around the cypress knees. He trotted proudly to her with a dog-grin. Water drops trailed from his muzzle.

"Wow, Beggar, look at the cool place you found." Emily squatted beside the river and dipped her fingers in the water.

She ran her hand over the scaly surface of a cypress knee. A few feet away, the smooth remains of a gargantuan tree pointed straight out into the river. Its trunk slanted downward like a round gray dock and disappeared into the water some thirty feet out. A trio of water turtles dove off its far end with a splash. Remnants of its former limbs rose from the log's surface like jagged masts with Spanish moss for sails.

Beggar jogged back and forth by the upturned roots as if expecting her to join him.

"You want me to climb out on this?"

He wagged and danced on his back feet.

"Well, okay, I'll try." It had to be ten feet high. But she could do it. Her buddies from Citra would have been right behind her waiting a turn. So why should she be afraid?

She crossed between the cypress knees and gripped a root. She climbed it like a monkey up a ladder.

At the tops she eased out on the log and straddled it like a horse. She inched along its slanting trunk. "The water looks like coffee down there, Beggar. I bet it's deep."

He perked up his ears and cocked his head to one side as if he understood.

"You silly, I never thought I'd be doing this today," she said as she climbed over a broken stob.

Twenty feet from the bank she paused and gazed into the trees where a hidden orchestra of insects, animals, and birds filled her ears with their sounds. She peeked back at Beggar. "Thanks for showing me this. It's great." As long as she didn't fall. She spread her fingers over the log's hot grain feeling the sun against her back. The current below her tree swept away to the west. But her gaze remained on the river's black ripples.

Black. Like her heart.

She wouldn't be stuck in this place if she hadn't played hooky that day. Hadn't stayed home so she could run away to Dad in Citra. Mom still didn't know about that plan.

If only Bill hadn't come home that morning.

If only she'd left the house before he arrived.

And the weird thing was, she'd been so caught up in her ruined plans that Bill's creepiness just hadn't sunk in.

Now she shuddered. Bill was a jerk. A sick one. Good thing he was in jail.

And Mom really was trying to help Emily. In her own way.

A tear rolled down beside her nose, and dripped on the log below. "God, just get me back to good old Gaskille, and I promise, I'll spend less time pouting and more time with Grandma."

What about Tony? She didn't want to think about him. But his face wouldn't leave her mind. If he were around, he'd be like all her other friends from Citra. Laughing right along with them.

And he was trying so hard to be nice.

It didn't mean he had to replace her Citra friends. He could be a friend, too. "All right, God. I'll be a better friend to him."

The sound of his voice came back to her. "Call me as soon as you get back," he'd said.

"I'm sorry I ignored him, God. Forgive me?"

Another tear dropped to the log. Emily stared as a stick floated under the log.

What if she'd actually gotten back to Citra?

Of course, her friends would always be there.

But Dad... She pictured him spread-eagle on the broken orange couch. The scene then morphed into another more fearful one she'd never allowed herself to catch hold of.

This time she did.

In it, bean cans and dirty dishes filled the sink. Mouse droppings littered the Formica table. Cigarette butts and beer bottles littered the floor, and dried splats of puke lay crusted around the toilet.

And in this picture the house was vacated.

The curtains Mom had once starched and ironed were now stained and fluttered out of open windows. The ugly vista was all too clear, branded behind her eyelids, and yelling at her to stop her nonsense. Going back to Citra wouldn't change him.

She sniffed back the burning in her sinuses. It wasn't fair. A kid her age couldn't straighten out a grown man, couldn't stop him from wandering out on the highway or tangling with the neighbor's pit bull.

Emily couldn't keep him from falling in the lake with alligators and moccasins, the stuff of her nightmares. She shuddered, recalling the story her friends told her about a hundred moccasins dangling from a stranger's dead body.

Emily couldn't hold things together for her dad. Not a kid like her. Not by herself. And Mom had failed, too.

The truth was, Dad would have come for Emily if he'd quit drinking. Because he did love her. He loved Mom. Emily knew he did.

She pressed her palms against the log and sat up. She slapped its trunk with both hands. Why couldn't Dad straighten up and take care of his family?

Beneath her feet in the water, a water lettuce bobbed and twirled, caught in the fork of a broken jag. Just like her and Mom, trapped in this awful place.

Behind her, Beggar whined.

"Shh. It's okay, boy."

It wasn't, though. And she couldn't expect to live in Citra without Mom.

But now with Bill gone, maybe Mom and Dad could get back together. That is, if Dad quit drinking.

All this time since they'd left Citra, Emily should have been praying, not trying to run away.

She dug her thumbnail into the wood. "I'm sorry, God. And just for right now, would you help us get out of here? Please?"

As the sun burned against her back, Emily wiped her face and turned around on the log to work her way back to the shore. Somewhere behind her, a big fish splashed. The water lettuce she had noticed a minute ago had broken free and now bobbed downstream at a steady pace. She stared after it.

"Thank you, God. I know you're listening. I know You are."

With renewed energy, Emily eased forward and approached the pointy limb she had passed on the way out.

At its base, a flash of green caught her eye. The same bright green as her stationery up at the house. A paper? Out here? Someone had jammed it into the base of the broken limb.

She inched closer and used her pincher fingers to maneuver it loose. A small pencil rolled out and dropped into the water. She watched it float away then unfolded the wet paper, smoothing it over the log. Barely faded, it hadn't been here long.

Wow. A drawing of a dog. Of Beggar.

A good one, too, with the same ears-up look, same spots, everything. Judging by the bumpy lines, it was probably drawn on this very log.

Emily stared at Beggar. "It's Susie's, isn't it?" He woofed and lowered his elbows onto the wet sand.

134

She refolded the picture and stuffed it inside her shoe. "I'm saving this picture, Beggar. *Our* little treasure."

She clung to the fat trunk. Up ahead in the shallows, water plants rose and fell in the amber ripples. Minnows skittered beneath their shadows, inches above the sandy bottom. To the left, the tin roof of the house peeked above the foliage, yet not as far away as she'd earlier imagined.

But too close for comfort.

She involuntarily shivered then pressed her hand against the gnarled hardness of the log. Her and Beggar's secret place. Time was ticking, though. She scooted toward the water's edge and leaped off the roots, landing on her hands and feet in the sand.

After brushing off her fingers, Emily poked her finger into her shoe and adjusted the paper. Maybe she could get Susie's address from Maria and mail the drawing to her.

The bell's clang resonated in the still air.

"Perfect timing, Beggar."

They raced toward the house, but by the time they arrived at the porch, Maria had gone back inside.

Emily entered the kitchen with Beggar close behind her.

"You satisfied?" Maria spread dark purple jelly on a slice of bread slathered with peanut butter. "Find what you were looking for?"

Had she seen her in the woods? Or did she think Emily had been in the yard? Emily shrugged then nodded.

Maria laid the top on the sandwich. "Anything interesting?"

"Yeah. Bright sunlight. Squirrels jumping all over the place. Birds, sand, plants, trees. All kinds of stuff."

"Lunch is almost ready. Why don't you go wash up?" A purple glob fell from the knife, and Maria jerked her foot back. It hit the floor and Beggar whiffled it up. "I don't even need a maid with you around, dog. Maybe we'll just keep you."

Beggar's eyes pleaded for more. "No, you go back under the table."

Emily's stomach grumbled, and she quickly washed and dried her hands. As she sat at the table, Maria placed a plate and a glass of tea in front of her.

"My grandmother always fills the glass to the top with ice like this," Emily said. "Then she hands me a long teaspoon and the sugar bowl. The glass is so full I can't even stir it."

"That's funny. But this is real southern tea. Already sweet.""

Grandma's was southern, too. Emily wished she could be back there right now. Helping Grandma take care of Pastor William. Too bad he was gone, now. They'd need to find a new church right away. One better than Maria's, for sure.

"You know what Pastor John preached about on Sunday?"

"Yes?" Maria's sandwich paused in mid-air and her wide blue eyes peered from under her tent of hair.

"He said we work our way to heaven with good works, right?"

"Right." Maria's mouth twitched, and she seemed to be holding her breath.

Emily paused. Maybe she'd better not say it.

Maria put the sandwich back on her plate and moved her chair back. Just a little.

"In church—at King's Tabernacle—we memorized a verse." Emily drilled her eyes into the tablecloth and tried not to mess up the words. "If thou shalt confess with thy mouth the Lord Jesus, and shalt believe in thine heart that God hath raised Him from the dead, thou shalt be saved. For with the heart man believeth unto righteousness: and with the mouth confession is made unto salvation."

Thank goodness for memory-verse assignments.

"We learned salvation isn't by works, and you can't earn it." She looked up at Maria. "That's what the Bible says."

Maria groaned, grabbed her stomach, and leaned forward. Her voice came out deep. "No..."

"Are you okay?" The legs of Emily's chair scraped against the wooden floor as she scooted from the table and touched Maria's hand. "What's wrong?"

Maria's blue eyes faded to a foggy gray. They turned to Emily as she jerked away from her hand. "Don't touuuch meeee." She growled the words, her voice as low as a man's. Her face contorted. Her eyes, those of an ugly, pained stranger, focused on Emily's mouth.

The odor of dead fish floated across Emily's nostrils, and she backed away from the table, her nose buried in the crook of her arm. "What is that gross smell?" Her voice came out muffled.

"*I* am your mother and father while you are here," Maria snarled. A bubble of phlegm seemed to clog her throat. "*You* submit to us. *You* will not rebel."

Emily took another step backward. "What are you talking about?"

Maria hunched over, rose, and disappeared into her office. The door slammed.

Emily followed but stopped outside the closed door. Her legs trembled, but she tucked her hair behind her ear and flattened it against the door. Only a light shuffling could be heard on the other side. Then the bedsprings squeaked. Maria must have sat on the bed.

Motionless, Emily stayed glued to the door, but the room was silent.

Emily tiptoed back to the table and sat down. She picked up her tea glass. Her hands shook so bad she set it back down. Maybe she should find Mom and tell her what happened.

Before she could get out of her chair, Maria's door eased open. Forget that plan, the witch was back.

"I'm sorry, Emily. I got a little sick just now. It must have been a reaction to something I ate. I didn't mean to scare you, honey." Maria retrieved the vitamins from the kitchen counter. "Here, dear. I don't want you to get sick, too. Take your vitamins, and don't worry about me. You stay well."

As Maria held out the brown gel cap, a lingering whiff of rotten flesh drifted across Emily's nose.

Chapter 18

At supper Emily swallowed the last bite of her mashed potatoes and laid her fork down. Across the table, John flipped his chair around and straddled it. His toothpick bobbed up and down between his lips as he studied the table.

Maria gave him a look then glanced at Emily. "Honey, will you run in the other room and play some songs? I bet your mom misses your music."

What a fake, always acting syrupy around Mom. Emily squeezed from between the wall and table. She wanted time with Mom, but arguing with Maria never did any good.

"Here," said Maria, lifting Emily's flowered coffee cup and saucer. "Take your drink with you."

As Emily entered the living room, the decaf coffee sloshed into the saucer. She put the rim to her lips and drained it before setting it on the piano. Coffee cups were so much more feminine than mugs. When she got back home she'd hide all of Grandma's mugs and get out the china cups and saucers.

If that day would just hurry up and come.

Maybe if Emily put on a positive face, Maria would cut off some of their time. With such a strange woman, though, nothing was certain.

Since Maria's episode in the kitchen at lunchtime, the woman had acted perfectly normal. She seemed to be okay for the moment. But that stuff about her being sick—whatever happened sure didn't sound like a sickness to Emily.

Pastor William had mentioned something once. *Demons.* Emily struck a low note on the piano. The vibrations filled the room and faded as John's voice filtered down the hall from the other room. "I've got to brag on you, Charlene." He cleared his throat. "My extensive experience with writers tells me you and Emily are very gifted. Your last essay? A work of art. I could picture everything you wrote about that new Colorado home."

Colorado home? Emily frowned and hit high C on the keyboard. The note clinked. Mom couldn't be thinking of moving again.

"With all the detail," John said, "you even made me want to go there. You worked your pen like an artist's brush. Of all the exercises that our clients have ever written, yours was the best description of your imaginary new home."

Oh, imaginary. Emily hit a few random notes.

"You mentioned Emily's writing," Mom said.

"I love Emily's writing. I wouldn't have thought a fifteen-year-old could write like that. She's following in your footsteps. Incredible."

He sure was laying it on thick. Emily had done nothing in her writing but jot down main ideas.

"I always thought she had talent," Mom said, "but it makes me feel good to hear it from professionals."

Professionals? Pfft!

Maria jumped in. "I almost forgot. My gooey caramel cake is going to melt in your mouth. If you don't burn your tongue first."

"I owe so much to you both," Mom said. "And to Earth Mother Acres. My heart's at peace knowing Emily is getting the help she needs. The writing and imagining have helped me too. They've allowed me to think things over in my own life."

Mom was getting as crazy as John and Maria.

John mumbled something Emily couldn't hear but then his voice rose again. "Sounds good to me. Since it came up, Charlene, let's make that tonight's topic. Write about how you owe everything to Earth Mother Acres."

Emily gasped. They didn't owe a thing to this place.

"One more thing," Maria said, picking up a pill bottle. "John and I are worried about your eyes. I saw you all hunched over that label yesterday when I came into the shop with Dr. Mike. He reminded me you could be taking bilberry for your eyes along with the lutein you're taking."

"You're always so thoughtful. Thank you."

"Start with two. We'll get those eyes fixed right up."

"Thank you, Maria. Thank you so much."

"I'll get you some water. The coffee's too hot to wash down the pills."

Emily ran her finger down the keyboard then played "Jesus Loves Me."

Maria called out. "That's good, Emily. Come on back now and have your dessert."

Emily reluctantly stopped playing and headed for the kitchen. Her only real dessert would be to get in the car and drive away with Mom.

Charlene stumbled out of the bathroom and clung to the dull wood of the doorframe. She curled icy fingers against her neck and squinted, waiting for the black speckles to dissipate from in front of her eyes. Her shaking legs made it hard to stand for very long. As the reeling room settled, her eyes drifted to the toppled lamp. Caught up in the same sickness as Emily, she'd accidentally knocked it to the floor on her first run to the bathroom.

She ought to be at the shop, but waves of vertigo sent her careening sideways like a drunk. Landing on all fours beside the bed, she clutched the bedspread and pulled herself to the mattress. The room finally righted itself. Panting, she crawled beneath the covers as best she could, and curled into a shivering heap.

Please, God, no more trips to the bathroom.

As her breathing settled, a warmth returned to her body, but not to her feet.

The metallic clatter of the trashcan lid and the slam of the back door filtered in through the window, intensifying the throb in her head. The lingering aroma of fried bacon nauseated her.

Charlene woke to find Maria pressing a hot washcloth against her forehead. An unpleasant whiff of lavender hit her nose.

"Thanks," she whispered. "I'm so cold."

"You've been through a lot this morning. I brought you some Pepto Bismol." Maria shook the pink liquid and poured some in a tablespoon. "Here, open up."

Charlene swallowed the medicine and slumped back on her pillow. "Could you turn the clock around?" she whispered. It spun around when the lamp fell.

"It's just noon. You've been resting quite a while, and that's good."

"I'm so sorry. I would have gone to work—"

"It's all right. You'll be back to normal before you know it. This is just a passing phase of diarrhea. It's an adjustment."

Charlene's eyes closed again. "Thank you for understanding."

"Don't think twice about it." Maria adjusted the washcloth. "Pastor Mario called and we discussed your progress. I told him you were making great headway. You won't need to reimburse the fees unless you suddenly quit on us."

Charlene lay still.

"I know that won't happen. You were lucky to meet this pastor, the way he helped you and all."

"Yes. I know."

"He thought you might offer us your testimonial for other potential clients. It could point them in the right direction."

Charlene licked her dry lips. "Happy to."

"He appreciated that you had the courthouse re-route your child support money here. Of course, it doesn't begin to compare to the $30,000 that he's donated. But it's a small way to "give back for all we're doing for you.""

Charlene tried to answer, but her lips didn't cooperate. She didn't mind helping, though all the paperwork hardly seemed worth the effort for a couple of checks. They'd be gone soon.

"We've got the basic paperwork filled out, and you can sign it in the morning. John and I agreed to hand $20.00 back to you. We just won't mention it to Pastor Mario, and you'll have a little something for your trip home."

"I'll do my part."

"That's it. We're pleased with your progress."

Maria stood, "Could you endorse this child support check so I can take it to the bank before it closes?"

"Hand me a pen."

"You're such a good client, honey," Maria said after the check was signed.

She patted the cloth on Charlene's head. "You rest, now. I'll bring you some chicken soup in a little bit."

Lucas leaned his elbow against the Colorado mountain wall a few feet behind the mailbox. He enjoyed dropping in on his people. No matter how far apart they were.

Beyond this little niche of his, the rocky lane doubled back in a nice hairpin turn. He knew the place well, having shoved several cars off it before. He leaned around the wall and searched for that dip in the gravel. Yep, right about *there*.

He peered across the expanse between the mountains and inhaled the cool air. At these altitudes, a thousand feet higher across the valley, mornings in the Rockies could be pleasant in June, even cold.

He drew in the cigar smoke, blowing it back out as the sound of a vehicle approached. A shiny red Jaguar pulled to a gravelly stop as it threw bright reflections over the box's weathered tin.

The window lowered, and a finely manicured hand reached out to the box.

He laughed inwardly at how close she was to him without her knowing.

The box opened with a creak, sending a skinny-legged spider scurrying to the red flag on its other side. The woman pulled out two brown envelopes, a few bills, and some ads. With a toss of her long wavy hair, she rummaged through the car's console. This chick was nothing like her ugly sister back at the Acres.

A chuckle burbled from his guts as he observed the silver dragon letter-opener in her hand, a present he'd given her. Via someone else, of course. Something to symbolize his essence. Anything to self-promote.

The woman could not hear him, of course. He blew a little cloud through her window. This time she looked around. Frowned. Aha. She probably smelled it, then.

Reveling in his stealth, he slapped his thigh with a loud guffaw then settled down to pay attention.

Sometimes finely-tuned people, like this woman, *could* detect him. Others seemed a little dense. Neither trait could be discerned by looking at someone.

When she turned back, he noticed the stars and moons around her neck and fingers. More of his stuff. Oh, baby. A giddy thrill rippled through him. Probably still had the fairy set with the large stolen emerald back at her house. This girl was good.

The woman's blade sliced through the first brown flap.

He grinned. Such a rich sound. Go, baby, go.

This package came from the woman's ugly sister Maria. Back in Florida. Inside were the checks and letters from Charlene. He laughed. She'd written all about moving to Colorado, and the old lady in Gaskille would buy it hook, line, and sinker.

Rene. She was trouble, that one. Always praying, praying, praying. And her neighbor, too. Strong forces against him. Just about ruining his plans. A few more humans like that would clip his wings. This letter should stop them, but if not, he could swat her flight right out of the air. Like a fly. All he had to do was get her on a plane to Colorado.

He shook his head. Sometimes Rene and her friend even jumped a step ahead of him. He wished he knew how.

He glanced at the manicured woman as she removed the stamped letters and placed them back in the mailbox. Good girl, keep right on going.

She pulled out the handful of checks and smiled. They'd be in the bank tomorrow along with some from his other enterprise in California.

She shoved more letters in the box and glanced over her shoulder behind the car, scanning the surroundings.

The nervousness on her face revealed she sensed his presence. He leaned close to her face as her fear grew. Her warm breath touched him.

His hand waved. *Look I'm right in front of you, honey.* He blew in her face, and she blinked. Cackling and slapping his thigh, he stood.

She quickly raised the flag and closed the window. Really spooked, this one.

The tires kicked up gravel as the car moved away, allowing the reflection of the box to glide slowly across its mirror-like windows. The spider, still straddling the curling letters of Colorado's Faithful Disciples, remained motionless. Lucas crushed it between his thumb and middle finger then wiped the remains on his starched white pants.

With the ironing board set up in the kitchen, Emily flattened the torn pocket and pressed the steam button. The iron hissed as a small cloud rose. Maria had told her Mom was sick. Her own intestines burned from last night's dysentery.

She pressed another torn seam and hit the steam again. Though she'd improved, her head still buzzed. Using one hand, she pulled up her shorts. Her waistline was skinnier than ever, but if she said anything to Maria, the old witch would call Dr. Mike again.

Good old Maria.

Emily reminded herself to remain civil. It could make the stay shorter, after all. "What should I do with the torn uniforms, Miss Maria?"

"Torn ones?" Maria stood at the sink peeling carrots. She waved her hand as if it were no problem. "Just iron them like the others, and put them on the end of the rack."

"My mom could fix them up real easy."

"That's the plan."

Emily flattened the tear and pressed the sides together. "The garden workers must be hard on their clothes."

"Don't worry about it. We just fix them, and they wear them again."

"What do people wear home when they finish the program?" She pressed the steam button again.

Maria frowned at the iron then filled a measuring cup with faucet water. "Here, keep that thing filled."

Emily took the cup and poured the water into the iron. "Well?"

"Well what?"

"What do clients wear when they leave?"

"Whatever they came in. Their own clothes."

"Could I iron my regular clothes when I'm done?"

"You in a hurry?"

"I didn't mean that. I just want to look nice. They're all wrinkly."

"Sure. Go ahead."

Emily dove into her room and grabbed her outfit from the closet. She glanced at the top shelf and stopped. The metal box had been moved to the left side.

Goosebumps covered her arms.

Maybe Mom had come in.

Emily returned to the kitchen to find Maria on her knees, rummaging under the sink. From Emily's vantage point, Maria's long hair formed a graceful line with the skirt. The woman was almost pretty the way her hair draped close to the floor.

Emily tossed her outfit on the ironing board. "What are you looking for under there?"

"Oh, special pans. I know they're here somewhere—aha!" Maria stood holding a pair of round cake pans like some kind of trophy. She pointed to the laundry basket. "How many more dresses in there?"

"Just two." Emily quickly finished ironing her shorts and arranged one of the dresses on the board.

"You're mighty quick. Good job."

Wow, something positive. "Thank you." Maria *could* be nice. Sometimes. "Miss Maria, what are you making with those carrots?"

"A surprise."

"Is it carrot cake?"

Maria pulled a grater from the cupboard. "Not telling."

Emily shot more steam onto the dress and flipped it over. She waited a beat then ventured. "Do you ever have dreams?"

"Yes, why?"

"I had this dream. About Jesus. I saw Him, and He was all shiny white, with sort of a diamond-y outfit. And—beautiful."

Maria leaned over the bowl. "You can go." Her voice sounded low like a man's again.

"Ma'am?"

"You can go. Go."

"You mean free time? I'm not done —"

"Off. Turn it off. Go." Just like the other day.

"You want me to put the rack away?"

"Get out." It came out like a lion's growl.

"O-Okay." Emily unplugged the iron. "Thank you, Miss Maria."

She grabbed her outfit from the rack and hurried to her room. She hung the clothes up and slid the hangers to the side.

Her eyes dropped to the floor where the clothes still lay from that first night. She'd almost forgotten about them. Stain and all, the clothes must have been Susie's. But what had the girl worn home?

Emily bent to look at them again. She pressed the thin shirt to her nose. The cedar smell of the closet filled her nose.

She'd wash that stain out.

For Susie.

On her way outside, Emily passed Maria, still grating carrots and stretching her neck as if loosening it up.

Nothing seemed to be wrong with her now.

Rene clutched the letter and marched through the tomato patch.

"Morning," said Kaye, rolling a speckled tomato into a plastic bowl. "I'm trying to kill these baby stink bugs. They're sucking on my tomatoes and leaving yellow spots all over them."

Rene thrust the letter at her.

Concern darkened Kaye's eyes. She brushed sand from her gloves. "What's going on?"

"Just—take a look at this."

As she read, a frown grew over Kaye's face. "What on earth? A few weeks at that place, and now Charlene's decided to move to Colorado?" She shook the pages. "This doesn't make sense."

"This too." Rene held up the photo of the mountainside suburb Charlene had mailed with the letter.

"I don't understand. What's *wrong* with her?"

Rene pointed to the postmark, and Kaye shook her head. "Colorado," she sighed. "I'm sorry, Rene."

"I'm not. I'm just plain mad." Rene had prayed for her daughter far too many years to let this trick of the devil happen. She crossed her arms. "There's no way I can just sit back and accept this. I don't believe for a minute it's God's will for her to take off to Colorado. She needs to be home, and Emily does too. You and I need to pray."

"Absolutely. Right here and now." Kaye pulled off her gloves and set them on the ground with the letter. She grabbed Rene's hands and closed her eyes.

Rene shut her eyes, too, and took a deep breath. Praying together was more powerful than one praying alone. Thank God for a friend who understood that.

"Lord," Kaye prayed, "we lift this situation up for You to intervene. You are all-powerful and can do anything. We don't believe for a minute that moving to Colorado is Your will for Charlene. We know it's a trick of the enemy to get her away from her family and onto a path of destruction. Please put a stop to these plans, and bring Charlene and Emily home to Gaskille. We ask this in Jesus' name."

Rene squeezed Kaye's hands. "Amen. And thank you. Let's just keep praying that way."

"We'll get her back home."

Rene picked up the letter and smiled. "Yes, we will. With God's help."

Chapter 19

"Silly dog, I hope you didn't kill any minnows out there." Emily brushed the sand off Beggar's feet with the corner of the bedroom rug. Seriously, though, minnows were too quick to get stepped on.

"Next time we go out, we should catch a jarful." She'd caught tons of them down at Orange Lake back home. Emily gave his ears an affectionate squeeze then paused with a frown. "No. Never mind. Can't do that. Maria would figure out we've been to the river and find our log."

Her lips brushed across the top of Beggar's head, and she hugged him, pressing her cheek against the warm fur of his neck. "I'd absolutely die if I couldn't go out on that log. And I'd be dead if you weren't there with me, Beggar." She clung to him until he twisted away and dragged his tongue across her face. "*Pth*. Quit that!" Emily wiped the slobber on her shoulder.

He tried again and she rolled him over. "Aww. They should let me take you home with me. That wicked old witch doesn't love you like I do."

The sound of a mower outside drew her attention. With her hand on the dog, she crawled on her knees and gazed out the window. Being cooped up in here with all that good daylight outside just wasn't fair.

The ugly workshop blocked her view of the mower, but beyond that, gardeners in green dresses moved about, doing whatever it was they did out there.

Mom would be coming from the workshop soon and tapping on her window.

Emily glanced at the desk. Maria's book stared back at her. She needed to show Mom the propaganda Maria was making her read. Mom would be so angry, she'd have them packed and on the road in thirty minutes.

Yesterday's chapter focused on monkeys evolving into people. In her journal, Emily had drawn a large exclamation point and written beneath it: So why, if monkeys evolved, do we still have monkeys in the world?

From behind her came a knock at the door, interrupting her thoughts.

"Emily?" Maria's head appeared. "I need you to take the linens off your bed and throw them in the hall so the maid can wash them."

Emily raised her eyebrows and nodded. That was close. Maria might have taken those off herself and discovered her journal under the mattress.

"I'm going to step out. When I get back, I'll go over your notes, okay?"

Not really, but anything to keep the peace until she could talk to Mom. Emily smiled and gave her a thumbs up.

After the door shut, Emily moved quickly, stuffing the journal, Beggar's picture, and the embroidery deep between the mattresses. She ripped off the linens and threw them in the hall.

Beggar lowered his head when Emily came back in.

At the desk, Emily opened Maria's book and picked up her pen to take Maria's idiotic notes. This was only penmanship. Just penmanship. She could handle that much.

Once she filled a green sheet of paper with notes, Emily sank to the floor beside Beggar and patted his head. "Roll over, now."

Beggar pushed his muzzle in her face and licked.

"Cut that out." She hid her face with her arm. "Let's peek under the door and watch the maid's feet." Beggar wagged his tail but stayed put as she crawled to the door.

A cool breeze flowed under the crack and brushed Emily's cheek. Nothing to see under there but shadows. Forget it.

Beggar whined and wagged a little harder.

"You have to go?"

When he danced on his back legs, she opened the door. He charged out like a greyhound at a racetrack.

The maid's voice floated down the hall as she greeted Beggar. Her footsteps padded through the living room and the front door banged.

Emily closed her door. Alone again.

She threw herself onto the bare mattress, tennis shoes and all. One toe poked out of her right shoe, and she pulled it in like a turtle's head. The clock over the door ticked, marking the rhythm of her loneliness. If she didn't need to keep track of the time, she'd jerk out its battery. She clamped her lips together and threw her pillow across her stomach. No. She would not, repeat, not feel sorry for herself. But it seemed like home would never happen. Tears seeped out of the corners of her eyes. She wiped them away.

She wrapped her arms around her pillow and closed her eyes.

The bang of a door electrified her from sleep. Her shoes hit the floor, and she lunged for the chair with a thumping heart. She pictured Maria's finger in her face, scolding her for not studying.

The knock came. "Emily, bring out your notes. We need to start dinner."

She took a deep breath to settle her nerves. "On the way."

At least she had one page of notes. Emily glanced down. Maria still hadn't noticed she was only copying the main ideas. Apparently, she didn't care whether Emily learned anything. She was just a slave-driver.

Emily grabbed the paper and headed to the kitchen. Maria scraped at some carrots over the sink. Again. With that familiar brown skirt draped over her wide back end.

A day or so ago, for just one minute, Emily had seen something pretty in Maria. But not now. Maybe it was the way she moved her arms as she peeled the carrots. Even the backs of her arms looked mean.

Emily shook her head. Enough of that stinking thinking. She pressed her lips together. Maria did have problems. But Emily was tired of her own disgusting thoughts.

Maria smiled over her shoulder. "Just put that on the table, honey. Did you have a good study session? You look a little sleepy."

Emily nodded.

The woman held out a peeler. Steam rose from the pot beside her. "Would you like to do potatoes? Just peel them and cut them up real small. Here's a cutting board."

"Sure."

As Emily peeled the potatoes, Maria hummed a tuneless song.

Emily sighed. She should be ashamed of herself. Her thoughts weren't fair to Maria, and she ought to be practicing forgiveness. *Sorry, Lord.* From now on she would try harder to be kind.

"Only three potatoes?"

Maria sliced into a green bell pepper. "It's just John, you, and me tonight. Your mom still isn't feeling well."

"Mom never gets sick. This is two whole days. What's wrong with her?"

"Don't worry, hon. It's just a bug."

"You mean the D word?"

"She'll be fine."

Emily's mind wandered to last Christmas when Mom had nursed her through the flu, bringing her medicine and crackers. She made her drink Gatorade, something they usually couldn't afford. Hydration, Mom called it. Day after day, Emily's temperature had soared.

Emily thought she was dying, but Mom was with her the entire time. Come to think of it, how had Mom gotten the two weeks off from work to stay home with her?

After Emily recovered, they moved to Gaskille.

Emily's potato peeler trembled as the realization hit.

Mom had been fired.

She wrapped her forearms against the hard rim of the bowl, but her hands still shook. An anchor pulled at her heart.

She'd created this deep dark hole.

The move from Citra had been her own fault.

"You done, honey?"

She didn't move.

"Emily, the potatoes need to go in the pot." Maria held up the lid. "Be careful not to splash."

And all this time she'd been mad at Mom.

"Emily, are you listening to me?"

Still in a stupor, Emily raised the bowl over the steaming vessel and dropped in the potatoes. Water splashed onto the floor.

"I'll wipe it up," Emily said. Cleaning was the least she could do to straighten out the world she'd been so busy ruining.

"Yes you will. The maid just mopped that floor an hour ago. Here are some paper towels."

Emily had to figure things out, but not in the middle of the kitchen in front of Maria. *Other thoughts, Emily. Other thoughts.*

She dropped the paper towels onto the mess and rubbed it with her shoe.

Maria had mentioned the maid. "What's her name?"

"Who?"

"The maid."

"Why?"

"I just wondered. She's here every day."

"Don't worry about her, Emily. Cindy's just another client to you. There's no contact with other clients. Even thinking about them is a form of contact."

Emily snorted. As soon as she got home she'd talk to every Cindy and Susan and Brenda she could meet. She'd talk to everyone. Every day. Maria couldn't control that.

"Since all you can do in here is make a mess, why don't you find something else to do?"

Anything to make the clock move faster. "Piano?"

"Keep it low."

In the living room's cool darkness, Emily folded back the old piano lid and inhaled the familiar sweetness of the wood. A quiet peace drifted over her, comforting her like a well-worn afghan. Her fingertips rested on the keys, and she closed her eyes. A yearning welled up inside her chest.

Jesus, I'm going to make a song for you.

Her fingers pressed one note then another, playing not a

song she knew but a new one. Long notes filled the room.

At least she had Him as a friend. Maria couldn't take that away.

Within minutes, Maria's voice interrupted. "That's nice, but you know, I am getting a big headache. Why don't you go outside?"

Emily breathed deep and smiled inside.

Thanks for being there, Jesus. I know you can see what I have to put up with.

So would You please get us out of here?

Chapter 20

Charlene's plastic bucket clattered against the shop wall as she flipped it over and lowered herself onto it. Its sound ricocheted across the silent gardens. Barely halfway between the house and the garden plot she gave out. She had to rest. Not surprising after two days of sickness, though. Or was it three?

With her hands in her lap, she leaned against the building. She stretched her legs in the direction of the shadows, and enjoyed the coolness of the concrete blocks against her back.

Half an hour ago Maria had waltzed into her room and had awakened her from a dead sleep with that sing-song voice of hers. "Charlene, dear, I need you to pick some tomatoes for dinner." Never mind how sick Charlene had been or how cozy the warm sheets were.

She should have begged off. But Maria had rattled off her directions and left, slamming the door behind her. Final. That was that. No ifs, ands, or buts.

Charlene took her time getting up, but in a few minutes Maria and John would return from town ready to eat the burgers they were picking up. Burgers, of all things.

Picking vegetables was not part of Charlene's job description. But Maria had forgotten to ask John to bring the tomatoes up for dinner. Oh, well. Whatever they needed.

Charlene studied the sky. Bad weather moving in. She lifted a strand of hair off her face, noticing how her fingers still shook. She wrapped her hands around her knee and took a deep breath as she scanned the surreal landscape. The wild

Florida thunderstorms that bore down in the late afternoons were magnificent and full of power but not something to be feared, as some thought. God's protection extended even there.

Around the perimeter of the acres gray moss hung limp and straight in front of the darkening woods. *Father, it's so gorgeous.* Charlene leaned forward. *Thank You for surrounding me with Your protection. You're so strong. I love You.*

The response was more an embrace than a voice.

I'm always here.

Along the back of the property, a dozen Florida palms stood like tall sentries above a cluster of voluptuous oaks. Their topmost fronds pointed straight up in the muggy air. Their shaggy bottoms, normally brown, glowed bright gold in the waning sunlight.

Two sunlit egrets, followed by a third, glided fluorescent and white across the purple sky.

Her eyes savored the turgid foliage, somehow affected by the river's special nutrients. *Thank you, Father.*

In the stillness not one bird sang. Even her breath was amplified. "Thank You for this beauty. Thank You for this chance for Emily to heal, but I do miss home, and I know Emily does. Please take us home soon."

Time to get moving and pick tomatoes. Charlene stood and kicked the bucket to loosen the sand. Its noise sliced through the rarified air like a dull gunshot.

She grabbed its handle and headed for the foot-high picket fence Maria had told her about. Strange how none of the other garden plots had the white fencing. What use was it, anyway, being so short?

The soft earth inside its border of white slats was freshly

tilled and raked as if for a new planting. Just like the other plots, its corners were marked with small marigold plants. Beside it pendulous clusters of red tomatoes hung on six foot plants crowded so close together she couldn't walk between the bushes.

Forced to kneel inside the picket fence, her knees sank into the soft hot sand as she raised the lowest branches to hunt for the ripest tomatoes. The peppery fragrance of the foliage tickled her nose.

The warm fruit twisted off easily, and she placed them in the bucket. Maria got one thing right. The tomatoes were huge. Bigger than anything she'd seen at Pop's Organics. Six tomatoes filled a good third of the container.

Finished in no time, she braced against the bucket. She brushed off her legs as the humid air began to stir, softly at first, then lifting energetically as cool air rushed in to take its place. The wind picked up her skirt, and she batted it back down.

The moss, no longer still, whipped sideways under the trees.

Cold, fat bullets of rain pelted her skin and sank into her cotton dress, taking her breath away. They spattered her tomatoes and streaked down the dusty bucket. She ducked her head and hurried toward the porch.

White-blue lightening pierced the sky ahead of her. Thunder exploded on its heels, and shook the earth. Whoa, that had been close. Energized, she struggled toward the screen door. It slammed behind her as the world lit up again. A cannon-blast shook the air. She gripped the bucket, gasping as the scent of lightning filled the air.

Emily closed her eyes, waiting for Maria to finish her spiel on the other side of the bathroom door.

"Between you and your mother, Emily, I've put toilet paper in these bathrooms three times since yesterday. Here. And use some spray." She tossed a roll through the door, and slammed it. The paper hit the floor and rolled to the rug.

Emily brought the roll closer with her toes.

"If you weren't so headstrong," Maria hissed, opening the door a crack, "you wouldn't be in this fix." Her fingers clung to its edge. "Nothing's going to improve until you start cooperating with our therapy. That's Mother Nature's way." Maria's foot remained between the door and frame.

If Mom could only hear this. Maria always lowered her voice and kept her nasty little comments a secret when Mom was nearby.

"But I am cooperating, Miss Maria."

"You certainly aren't. This illness happens every time you start thinking and repeating your headstrong thoughts. I can tell by the way you play on the piano. I can tell by your study notes. I know things you don't think I know."

"But I'm not being headstrong, really. I like you, Miss Maria," she lied.

"This isn't about who you like, young lady. This is about your thoughts and beliefs. I can see you're not in harmony with the program. You have a resistance to everything we are doing. Mother Nature is trying to show you some things."

Mother Nature? Oh, come on. "I'm sorry, Miss Maria, I am trying to cooperate." Another pain hit, and Emily gasped.

"Mother Nature knows more than you. It's probably related to those fake dreams you were having." She tapped a fingernail on the door. "Every false thought earns you an attack of diarrhea. All I know is it's happening time after time after time."

"I'm sorry, Miss Maria." Emily turned the roll of paper around, searching for a loose end. "I promise to do better. I really do."

"Unfortunately, your promises aren't getting results. You'd better adjust your thinking, missy. Do you realize you made your mother sick the other day?"

Emily glared at the rolled and squeezed it flat. She clawed at its end and worked it loose. "I rarely see her. How could I make her sick?"

"You two are interconnected, and your actions affect her. There she is, all happy, working her fingers to the bone out in that musty old shop, day after day, and you're in here making her sick. Making her sick. She suffered two whole days because of your pernicious thinking."

"I'm sorry. I promise I'll think straight now."

"I cannot keep babying you." The hand disappeared and the door snapped shut. "I want to see a new girl. Get your thinking straight." Maria's voice faded as she walked away, "People die from these diseases."

Emily thrust a feeble kick in the door's direction.

Jesus, please help me. And Mom, too. Help us get out of this place. And Jesus, please make us well again.

After dinner Maria set a birthday cake on the table. "Ta da." Five candles blazed on top of its nut-covered icing.

"Whose birthday?" Charlene said.

John pointed a thumb at Maria.

"I know you'll love my birthday carrot cake. Cream cheese

icing and pecans instead of walnuts." Maria smiled, remembering how Lucas had stopped in today to help her with those pecans. She shivered, still feeling his warm hand on hers as she placed the pecans on top. With John in town, she'd given the maid the afternoon off and shooed Emily outside. Oh, it was a real birthday afternoon, alright. She straightened her skirt and smoothed her hair.

Charlene nudged Emily. "We need to sing happy birthday, then."

Maria grinned at the awful singing and bowed. "Thank you very much."

John stepped into the living room and came back with roses. "Orange, her favorite color." He kissed her cheek and set a package beside her plate. "And here's a little software you've been needing for those recipes."

"You should have told us," Charlene said as she stacked dishes. "Happy birthday."

"Nah, don't worry about it. It's another year, but I like my birthday cake." She handed John the cake server. "You cut the cake. And thank you, honey, the roses are beautiful."

He grinned at the floor and scratched the back of his neck.

"Blow out the candles, Miss Maria," Emily urged.

"Oh, yes, they're melting away." She blew, and wax spattered over the icing. "Sorry, everyone."

"Did you make your wish?" Emily said.

"I make my wish every day," Maria said, imagining Lucas' touch on her arms. One day soon.

"I only see five candles," Emily said. "How old are you, Miss Maria?"

Charlene touched her daughter's arm. "You don't ask adults how old they are."

"Mother Nature's been good to her, Emily," John said. "She's put in fifty-five years." He gave Maria's arm a squeeze. "She doesn't look it, or mind telling it."

Maria sat down. "That's right, I don't mind. When we were five, my twin brother and I survived a bad car accident. We were lucky." Of course everyone else had died.

"We're so glad you made it," Charlene said.

Emily pointed to Maria's unopened mail. "Why don't you read your birthday cards?"

Charlene looked across the table, "If we'd known today was your birthday, Emily and I could have prepared something. A card, a letter, a poem. We had no idea."

"Thank you, Char, that's not necessary," John said, slicing into the cake, "Y'all have too much to do without worrying about this sort of thing. Just enjoy the day." He dropped a slice of cake on the plate.

Maria read through the cards and smiled when she reached the third one. She waved it at Emily. "It's from my twin brother," she said, slitting open the envelope. She studied the card and the photo then allowed John a peek. For her own reasons, though, she wouldn't be passing it around.

He handed her a plate. "Uh-huh."

She stacked the cards and laid them beside her fork. "Thank you all for your good wishes, and, John, thank you, sweetheart." She blew him a kiss and pulled a couple of candles from her cake. "Here, Emily, you can have these," she said, dropping them on a napkin. "Young people enjoy licking the icing off."

"Thanks." Emily popped one in her mouth then glanced at John. "I was thinking about what you said at church. Why do you always say Mother Earth? The Bible says God is our Father."

164

Maria stood quickly and gathered her cards and gift. She knew what was coming. The girl didn't get it, but the mother might. With her head down she hurried to her office.

Shoving the door closed behind her, she lurched for the trash can and tossed the birthday cards onto a stack of recipes. She couldn't help but vomit. The girl kept bringing up God and Jesus. She wiped her mouth and spit as she held onto the can.

A few minutes later she returned to the kitchen and flopped back into her seat. "Sorry, I needed to put my birthday cards away." She stuffed a forkful of cake into her mouth, as Emily stared at her.

Maria returned the gaze until Emily blinked and glanced away.

Chapter 21

After dinner Maria returned to the bedroom and closed the door. She dropped to the floor beside her desk. As she leaned back against the drawers, her elbow hit a stack of folders piled nearby and sent them sliding across the carpet.

She'd pick them up later. John wouldn't be around much longer to complain about the crowded mess. He'd be elsewhere. By himself, surprise, surprise. Then she'd get that big fancy office Lucas promised her.

Her immediate task was to find that accordion folder with last year's recipes. Where'd she stash it?

She lifted the bedspread and looked underneath. Nothing. She pushed the hair out of her eyes and located it between the boxes under the desk. Dust flew everywhere as she dragged it out. With a sneeze, she unwound the string and rubbed her nose across the back of her hand. Here were her recipes.

Next month she'd apply for a copyright, publish the book herself, and sell it on Amazon and at the farmer's markets. She'd be rich and famous.

Now to get the manuscript formatted. John meant well with his little recipe-typing software gift, but Maria had no patience for learning it right now.

Emily could type and Maria should have handed this over to her weeks ago.

Maria riffled through the disorganized papers. Surely a fifteen-year-old had enough sense to put them in order.

The latest batch of recipes had been sitting on the corner of the desk for months. Reaching behind her head, she located the stack and dropped them into the back of the accordion folder.

She got to her feet and headed to Emily's room.

Half asleep at her desk, Emily doodled little squares on the green paper.

"I'm glad you enjoyed my cake."

Emily's pen jerked at the unexpected sound of Maria's voice. The woman never came into her room this late. She turned the paper over and twisted in her chair to face Maria.

"The cake was really good. I'd like to get the recipe for Grandma."

"Sure." Maria shifted the accordion folder in her arms. "Speaking of recipes, could you do a little job for me tonight?"

"I guess so."

"Remember we talked about typing recipes? John's gift reminded me."

This could be interesting. "Do you want them on your computer?"

"Sorted first. Could you do that for me tonight?"

"Show me what you want."

Maria emptied the folder onto the desk. A cookbook slid out, and she turned to its table of contents and pointed out the categories. "Break them into groups like these: meats, vegetables, desserts, and so on. That's all there is to it."

"Sounds easy enough."

"Stay up as late as you want tonight."

Well, she was awful jolly tonight. After she left Emily shut the door behind her and moved the jumbled pile to the rug.

Maybe she would read a few, get some ideas. She situated herself on the floor and picked up half of the stack.

What in the...? Sandwiched between the pages were three familiar envelopes. Maria's birthday cards.

A warning drummed in her ears. *Curiosity killed the cat. Curiosity killed the cat. Take them to Maria.*

She glanced at the door to make sure it was shut. Whatever. Maria would never know.

The first envelopes were from Colorado and California.

But the other one. Gaskille? An upside down photo slid out. *Mario*, it said on the back. Familiar name. She flipped it over. The front showed a dark-haired man and a blonde.

Her mouth fell open. *He's* the twin? Pastor *Mario?*

She studied the moustache, the eyes, the tilt of the head, the posture. It all made sense now. *That's* who Maria reminded her of.

Rene squinted at the numbers on the clock. One a.m.

She snuggled into the pillow Emily had made for her last birthday. It helped with her back pains. Once again she prayed for her girls, and then drifted into a semi-slumber.

Suddenly, a puff of air hit her face. Her head jerked back. She touched her face, the sensation still fresh.

It couldn't be a dream.

Her eyes bore through the darkness.

The curtains hung limp on the partly open windows.

A flicker. The clock registered 1:16.

A tiny *plip* filtered down the hall. Just the spigot in the bathroom.

Blue moonlight lay across the corner chair.

Nothing stirred
"Lord? Is that you?"
Nothing.
"Why are you waking me up? Should I be praying about something?"

She dropped to her knees on the rug and stretched her hands over the warm bed covers. "Lord, if Charlene and Emily are in some kind of danger, please send your angels. Deliver them from all forces of evil right now. Break this trap off of them."

A sense of danger thrummed inside her. "Lord, send your protective angels to them. "Anger surged up from her core. Anger at the devil.

She rose to her feet and pointed to the invisible enemy. Her words came out bold and clear. "Satan, I tell you, you're done with Emily and Charlene. I bind you in the name of Jesus. I cover them with the protective Blood of Jesus. You have no rights to them. I command you by the power of the Cross and in the name of Jesus." She punched the air. "Get your hands off of them. You're done, devil. Let go of them. In the name of Jesus. You must bow."

A quick gust of air sucked the bedroom curtains toward the windows then left them limp.

She stood for a moment in the silence as peace returned then crawled between the sheets again.

"Thank you for waking me up, Lord. Send your holy angels around us all."

Chapter 22

Charlene stared through the east window of the shop. Yards away, flash floods gushed across the checkered acres, filling the deep places, and transforming the driveway into a wide river. The rain sounded like Niagara Falls over the shop's tin roof, deafening her as gusty blasts battered the windows. She turned to the north window where the grapefruit tree bowed, its black silhouette twisting and swatting against the wall.

The sewing machine light flickered. She glanced at the clock. Five minutes till quitting time. Forget going out in this weather. Surely John and Maria didn't expect her to swim to the house.

She counted the boxes by the door. Nineteen taped and ready to go. Twenty in one day would be a personal record. She hurried back to her machine to finish the last box before John arrived to pick them up.

She snatched up the scissors and clipped a thread. It fell next to her foot.

Just ten minutes. That's all she needed.

The stormy diversion was nice, keeping other things from clawing at her mind, things trying to overtake her. Things plucking a raw nerve.

Like the incident at the fountain with John.

No wonder Emily wanted to go home. Being cooped up could get old, especially for a fifteen-year-old. She must be so lonely away from her friends.

Charlene slapped the presser foot into position and

stepped on the pedal. As the label fed through the machine, she silently apologized to her daughter. I'm so sorry, Emily. Sorry for bringing you here. Sorry for everything bad that has ever happened to you.

Her needle stabbed along the edge of the shiny gold letters, *Estrella.* Star. She chuffed. Emily considered her the exact opposite.

The shop door flew open, banging hard against the outer wall. She turned, expecting to see John.

A woman dropped her umbrella on the floor then grabbed the door and heaved it shut with a dull thump. Oblivious to Charlene, she wiped her face on her sleeve before folding the umbrella. Water pooled around her drenched feet.

Charlene stood. "Hello."

The woman spun and stared.

"Sorry, I didn't mean to scare you."

The woman's arms clamped across her chest as she glanced around the room. "I, I'm not used to anyone being here, that's all." She dipped her head and gazed at the floor. "I-I came to get my cleaning supplies."

"Here." Charlene pulled a torn uniform from her mending pile. "I don't have a towel, but you can dry yourself with this.

"Thank you." The woman took the clothing and blotted her face.

Charlene glanced at the peeling Earth Mother Acres pin on the woman's pink bodice. *Cindy. The one John praised at the meeting.*

"I'm always gone by five, but with the rain—"

Cindy rubbed the worn cloth over her arms and legs and scanned the room behind Charlene again, as if looking for someone. "We aren't supposed to talk to other clients, you know."

"I know. But look at that rain. I'm surprised you came out in it." Charlene offered her hand. "I'm Charlene. My daughter Emily and I are staying at the house."

Cindy's brow wrinkled. "At the house?" Her eyes welled with tears. "My dau—"

"Yes?"

"It's just…"

"Your daughter's going to be fine." Charlene gave an encouraging smile. "These people are doing a good job. They really know what they are doing."

Cindy squeezed her eyes shut and raised her face to the ceiling. Tears drained from the corners of her eyes in silent agony.

Charlene placed her arm around Cindy's shoulder. "It's okay."

Cindy pressed the uniform against her eyes and wailed. "Oh, God. Oh, God. I don't know what I could have done different."

"What is it?" Charlene breathed a silent prayer for wisdom. "Whatever happened I'm sure it's not your fault. I'm sure it's not."

Cindy blew her nose. "No, it's nobody's fault. They did what they could. They had a doctor, too. It just came on her."

A hot sensation raced up Charlene's neck. "What happened?"

Cindy silently shook her head and swiped her cheeks with the damp cloth. "I'm really sorry. I didn't mean to do that. You're the first person I've seen." She covered her mouth, but a moan escaped her lips. "Oh, God, help me."

"It's going to be all right, Cindy."

"At least she went in her sleep. Doctor Mike said it's a

youth thing, like meningitis." Cindy struggled for air. "I'm so glad he was there. Otherwise, Susie would have been all alone." Her face twisted, and she latched onto Charlene. "She was barely fifteen."

"My Emily's fifteen, too." Tears trickled down Charlene's cheeks.

"She stayed at the house, studying in the bedroom while I worked. I always tapped 'I love you' on the door, and she would tap back." Cindy groaned and wiped her nose. "We weren't allowed to talk until supper. Nobody knew about our tapping. We only did it when we wouldn't get caught."

Cindy's words sucked Charlene's breath away and hung like an electrified presence between them.

"The dog would follow me in the house. He always sat by Susie's door until I let him in her room. She loved him."

"Emily calls him Beggar."

"He's a beggar, all right. And so skinny. You'd think they'd treat him for worms. He was her best friend here."

"How did she do with the therapy?"

"She hated it. I tried telling her that it would be over soon." Cindy melted to the floor as if her legs could no longer support her. Outside, the raindrops slowed. "I didn't like being away from her, but these psychologists know what they're doing, and they've been so nice to us. Susie was doing okay, aside from occasional rebellious attitudes."

Cindy pulled a wet handful of hair around the side of her neck. "I wish we'd never come."

"Why didn't you leave?"

"I'm a single mom. I couldn't pay them back."

"You borrowed the money?"

"No, the church put it up. If you quit, you pay it back. "

A bolt of electricity shot through Charlene's limbs. "Are you from Gaskille?"

"Where?"

"Gaskille, Florida."

"No, California. Why? "

"As she searched Cindy's eyes, a strong pulse throbbed in Charlene's neck. "What is the name of the church?"

"Faithful something. Faithful Disciples."

Cindy's voice faded into the musty stillness, her lips still moving as silent thunder rumbled between Charlene's ears. It pressed the air from her lungs, until finally she could stand it no longer. With a sharp breath, she sucked in new air. The noise over the roof increased now, pelting like machine-gun bullets.

A deafening buzz filled her brain.

Cindy pulled a handkerchief out of her front pocket. The blood-like stains drew Charlene's attention. "Are you bleeding?"

"Stupid me," she said, glancing at the handkerchief. "I found a red pen in the trash and found out the hard way why they threw it out. Old habit of being thrifty." She sniffed and rose to her feet brushing moisture from her knees. "I'd better get my supplies. Sorry about all this crying."

Charlene raised her voice over the drumming rain. "Maybe the ink will wash out. And don't worry about the crying. I don't blame you. I would feel the same way. Nothing wrong with being thrifty, either."

Cindy gripped the key hung around her neck. She pulled its pink ribbon over her head and stepped to the storeroom.

"My supplies are in here." She unlocked the door, left the key dangling, and reached for a cleaning caddy inside. "I sure hate to go back out in that rain."

"It should let up in a minute."

Cindy carried the caddy to one of the windows and gestured toward the gardens. "Susie's right out there, you know."

Charlene wrinkled her brow. "What do you mean?"

"They fixed her a nice little grave."

"She's buried here?"

"In that white picket fence."

Buried in the garden?

A hurricane roared through Charlene's brain as she pictured the cheap slats leaning haphazardly in the gray soil.

She'd trampled the very clods above that lifeless child. A ragged gasp forced its way from her mouth as her stomach lurched. It was all she could do to not cry out.

Seeming not to notice, Cindy opened the door. "I'm sorry. I guess I'll be all right. I'm making my contribution and doing the right things. With God's help. This is a good place despite all my bad luck."

Charlene shook the horrible images from her head and concentrated on Cindy's words. "What do you mean?"

"Just all the people they help."

"No, I mean about your contribution."

"The child support."

Charlene pictured Cindy signing the form just like she had, the one Maria would have sent to her hometown. "When will you be going home?"

"A couple of weeks. Maybe a month to make up for the doctor expenses." She reached into the stained pocket again and wiped her eyes with the handkerchief.

"I'll pray for you, Cindy."

"Thanks, Charlene."

"I better get going."

Charlene reached for her arm. "I meant it. I'm praying for you."

Cindy nodded, grabbed her umbrella, and hurried out the door.

Stepping to the side, Charlene wiped moisture from the window and peered out into the mist. Cindy's words ricocheted in her head until it ached.

Susie had died here.

Was Emily in danger, too?

Rain poured over John's yellow slicker. His shovel sucked and slurped in the mud of the growing hole by the front yard sign. He tossed another glop down the hill. It landed like melted chocolate in the ruts. Once again he wiped his sweaty brow.

He hadn't meant for this job to turn into a dad gum project. All he'd needed was a big hole in the driveway. What he hadn't thought about were all the stupid roots he'd have to deal with.

He gazed into the pit and chuckled. Good enough. Mother Nature would be proud of it.

He swiped another rivulet from his face with the back of his gritty sleeve. *Hmph*. Little good that did.

One last kick at a stubborn clump of mud and his foot slid out from under him. His back end hit the mud like a brick. Should have left the stupid thing alone. He scrambled to his feet. Good thing nobody was around right now.

Throwing open the door of the van, he rinsed the shovel in the rain and slid it through the opening with a loud metallic scrape. Then he climbed in. Time to get to the shop.

As he slammed the door and inserted the key, a movement on the porch caught his eye.

Lucas all high and dry, sat in the rocking chair with his foot on a post, smoking a cigar. And watching him. With a smirk on his lips, Lucas blew a smoke ring in John's direction. He'd seen him slip.

Shaking his head, John returned a minimal wave and revved the engine. He lifted his foot, letting the engine idle as he wiped his face with a greasy red rag. He threw it on the passenger seat.

His mountain cabin should be a reality soon. Then he'd be away from Lucas and his stinking surprise appearances. Forever.

John put the van in gear. Time to go collect the garment boxes from the shop.

Cindy's words drummed between Charlene's ears, but she forced herself to push them aside. The puddle of water right beside the door needed to be mopped up before John came in. He might fall.

She snatched a petrified mop from the back corner of the room and gave the puddles a cursory swab.

When she finished that job, she stretched tape over her last box and stacked it with the others.

The door clicked, and Charlene pivoted. A dark silhouette stood against the brightening sky. Postured in a raincoat, the figure reminded her of a cowboy ready to draw. Behind him, the van's door hung wide open.

"John. Hi."

"What are you still doing here, Charlene?"

"I was just cleaning up. Besides, it was raining too hard to walk to the house."

His eyes roamed around the room, stopping at the boxes by the door. He checked his watch with a sigh then pulled off his wet raincoat. "Reckon this weather's about done for the day," he said, and flung it toward the open van door. It missed the passenger seat and landed on the floorboard.

She stepped toward the door. "It came down in sheets. Cats and dogs. I couldn't even get out the door." Her chattering made her sound guilty, but she couldn't stop herself.

"I know. I was out there in it. Drove through puddles up to the hubcaps." He grabbed an armload of boxes. "Couldn't see diddly in front of the headlights. But then these Florida thunderstorms can stop on a dime. Not much time lost."

Tension eased from Charlene's shoulders. *Thank you, Lord.* If John had seen Cindy leave the workshop, he would have said something by now.

"It's a good thing you brought the van instead of the golf cart. The boxes would be soaked."

He nodded agreement as he stacked the boxes in the van. "Can I help?"

"I've got it, thanks," he said, with his back to her. "But I do want to tell you something."

He leaned against the truck and wiped a shirt sleeve over his face. His gaze focused somewhere beyond her head. "First, we have a pretty bad washout in the road down around the house. Might be a sinkhole. That's a problem."

"I would say it is."

"It's the only way in and out of the Acres between here and the river. Of course, nobody can drive through the palmettos or cypress knees."

A wave of claustrophobia washed over her. They were trapped in this place?

He chuckled. "The good news is your car is fixed."

At least they had wheels, but at what cost? "That's great, John. I'll have to pay the mechanic with my credit card."

He cleared his throat. "You know, Mother Nature has a way of dealing with us, our attitudes and character."

What did that have to do with paying for repairs?

"Maria informed me of Emily's attitude problem. This could stop her progress."

"I'm sure she's just homesick. She's a good girl, really."

"Resistant."

"What can I do to help?"

"Do you want to go home?"

"I want to do everything we're supposed to." Her voice cracked. "I know God has... um... has led us here." Except that wasn't true. She wished she'd never heard of this place.

A half-smile twisted his lips. "We've got to pray for her to settle in and be comfortable. For this to be a pleasant experience for Emily."

"Sure. Of course."

John stacked the rest of the boxes and slung the van door shut. He stepped through the doorway and crossed his arms, looking down at her.

A million crickets buzzed inside her head. The way he kept watching her mouth was unnerving.

"When things aren't right, and they aren't working out, we've got to look at the cause, right?"

"Y-yes, of course." An odor settled in the room, thick, like a dead animal.

His eyes remained fixed.

She stepped back.

He lowered his voice a notch and came closer. "Not seeing Emily, you probably feel you have no control over that, either, right?"

Another step back. "No control, no. W-we never talk."

"Your attitude exudes powers over her. Influence."

The fetid smell grew heavier, and Charlene's stomach lurched.

She needed help. Inside her mouth she formed the name. *Jesus.*

John's arms flew out. He stumbled backwards for several steps as if someone had pushed him. He pulled himself together again and stood weaving back and forth, trying to catch his breath. "What did you just do?"

She shook her head. Nothing.

"You must have."

Her prayer.

His eyes riveted on her mouth again. "I *saw* Cindy."

Charlene swallowed hard. "Cindy didn't know I was in here. With the storm, she couldn't leave."

"You remember the agreement? The rules of the retreat?"

"I-I can't control the weather."

He headed toward the supply room door and flipped over two orange buckets. "Sit down here and let's talk."

Outside, the skies continued to brighten. A breeze stirred, scattering drops over the roof with a dull rhythm.

Charlene's heart pounded as she lowered herself to the bucket. "I am really sorry Cindy and I bumped into each other like that."

"And yet it was a breach of intent." He made a *tsk*-ing noise. "I hope God won't punish you. An agreement is an agreement."

What kind of guilt trip was he trying to put on her?

"I'm beginning to see a pattern. The washed out road. Your sickness. Your daughter's sickness."

Prickles ran along her neck again, and her chest tightened. Those coincidences didn't have a thing to do with her.

"Attitudes always come before the rules are broken. The bottom line of healing is following protocol. I'm concerned for you and your daughter. Really worried for you."

How could he say that? Her intentions were honest. Blaming her didn't make sense.

His eyes bored into the wall behind her. Why did he avoid looking into her eyes?

Jesus, I know I have done the best I could, Charlene silently prayed, *and I have tried to guard my attitudes, I have done everything for you. Just get us away from these crazy people.*

"You have to repent."

That rotten stench seemed to suck the oxygen out of the air, and she coughed. Just get this over with. Whatever it took to keep the peace with this man and find a way out of this mess they were in.

"Okay, I repent."

"Well, go ahead," he said.

With the odor in her nose, she could only whisper. "I'm so sorry—for breaking the rules—and I ask you—to please forgive me." Her chest constricted as if a python had wrapped itself around her and forced every bit of air out of her lungs. She glanced at John, barely able to squeeze out the last three words. "In Jesus' name."

John's chin flew back, and his feet flew up as he fell off the bucket. His back smacked the floor. Air rushed back into Charlene's lungs as she jumped out of his way.

The pythonic grip had let go and the horrid smell with it. John groaned and clutched his arms to his chest.

"Are you okay?" Charlene reached toward him.

He rolled away. "Don't touch me. I-I'll get up." His back to her, he rose unsteadily to his knees.

"Are you hurt?"

"Yes." His voice was low. "You don't have to pray. You don't have to pray that way, in that *name*."

"You mean in Jesus' name?"

John doubled over with a growl. His voice was hoarse and faint. "Just pray to the Great Spirit. You're safer that way."

"I always pray in Jesus'—"

He jerked forward again. "The Great Spirit is all encompassing," he croaked.

"But that's not what the Bible—"

He groaned even louder than before. This guy was so mixed up. Some preacher.

"Did you bump your head?"

"No," he grunted. "You go up to the house. That's enough for the day."

"Let me help you up first." She reached for his hand.

John snatched it away. "I said no." He spread his palms on the floor. "Get away from me."

With her brain on fire, Charlene backed away then headed out the door. If she could just erase this awful day. Wake up from this nightmare.

"Jesus." She moved robotically, numbly, along the wet driveway, her heart slamming with each step.

"Jesus, Jesus, Jesus," she prayed all the way to the back porch. "You've got to help us."

Chapter 23

Emily stood over the bathroom sink and ran her fingers over her scalp. If she could just clear out Maria's nagging voice: "Sick again. This is just too much. Another wasted morning in the bathroom. Rearrange your thinking, young lady. Get right with God before you run out of chances."

Maria had practically thrown the two rolls of toilet paper at her. Come to think of it, why didn't she just keep the bathroom stocked?

And what did she mean by run out of chances?

Emily returned to her room and curled up under the bedspread. Thunder rumbled outside under a darkening sky. Beggar leaped on the bed and flopped against her back with a whine.

"It's okay, boy," she mumbled, closing her eyes and hugging her pillow. "It's just noise." Beggar's agitated breathing slowed until he finally settled into a light and peaceful snore. Not long after, lulled by the gentle sounds, Emily drifted off, too.

In her dream, Emily knelt in a dark, musty cave. Her face and hands pressed against the cold bars of a rusty gate. Jesus reached through from the other side and laid warm fingers against her forehead. His hand glistened and sparkled. Then He was gone.

Emily shook the gate, but it wouldn't budge. If she could just get to the other side, to the light and warmth.

Now she was seated in the bottom of a rowboat. The waves tossed her vessel high onto the black crests then dropped it low into the troughs. Up and down, up and down. A vicious nausea grew inside her as invisible hands pinned her arms to the bottom of the boat. She struggled left and right, but she couldn't break free to grab the sides of the boat.

If she could just grab the sides.

"Get outside, dog. How did you get in here?" Maria's grating voice shattered the nightmare.

The bedroom. Thank goodness. Relief filled her lungs. For once she was glad to hear Maria's voice.

Beggar whined once, and his weight lifted from the bed. His toenails clicked against the floor as he slipped and slid down the hall. The back door banged.

Maria shook Emily's arm, and the nausea bloomed. Emily tightened her closed eyes.

"It's time to get up. Are you awake?"

"Mmm." She didn't dare move.

Maria jostled her again, shaking her foot. "Wake up, honey."

Emily drew in her feet.

"You've been sleeping all day. Aren't you feeling better yet? It's time to help in the kitchen."

"Give me a few minutes," she mumbled. A minute later, the rustling of Maria's presence faded away.

Good.

Emily lay still. If she could float back to sleep, maybe Jesus would touch her again.

At the dinner table, Emily rested her chin in her hand. Neither the food nor the sweet tea had cleared the cobwebs in her head. She spooned a glob of icing into her mouth.

John, wolfing his cake, only glanced up once. Mom picked at hers and stared into her plate. Nobody had much to say tonight.

Maria looked under the table and wrinkled her nose. "I thought I smelled a wet dog."

Beggar, who had sneaked back inside with John, lay wedged between Emily's feet. "If you're going to have that dog in here, you'll have to bathe him," Maria said.

A bath would be something new to do. "I could bathe him during free time tomorrow."

Maria pointed the fork toward Emily and spoke with her mouth full. "That's fine. Use the shampoo from the bathroom."

Dinner ended, and everyone stood up. Mom gave Emily a squeeze and whispered, "I love you," before planting a kiss on her forehead.

Mom seemed awfully quiet tonight. If only Emily could talk with her without John and Maria hanging around.

"Charlene, don't forget this." John handed Mom a fat book before she trudged off to her room. Poor Mom.

"Miss Maria, could I be excused? I'm just tired tonight."

Instead of answering, Maria waved her away with the back of her hand.

Emily changed clothes and climbed straight into bed. Even her bones were tired. She stared at the beadboard ceiling. Beggar jumped up beside her, and she wrinkled her nose. "You do stink, really bad. Especially up close." She patted his head. "Who cares, though? I'm just glad Maria didn't send you outside again."

She curled her legs up and tried closing her eyes. But there was the clock again. Ticking, ticking, ticking. Concentrating on the rhythmic noise only made it worse. If she could just doze off. She touched Beggar's fur behind her. His breathing had slowed like before. Amazing how dogs could fall asleep anywhere, anytime.

She lay awake staring at the dark ceiling.

Lucas filled his chest with smoke and lowered the cigar to the concrete bench. He crossed his legs and released a lazy cloud of smoke from his nose. It drifted around him as the aggravating swarms of crickets and frogs cranked out their deafening chirps and bellows down by the river.

The noise overpowered the popping of his five fires.

He hated that.

Nevertheless, here, inside his limbed cavern, he was in charge, and the chanting of his worshipful minions grew louder, eventually drowning out the night creatures. Ebony shadows wavered over the hedges, mimicking the twists and turns of their robe-clad bodies.

He rose partway and gave a sharp kick to the writhing sack in the middle of the group. The bag drew up like a giant surprised pupa, and he chuckled.

He aimed a smirk up through the gnarled limbs of the oak and twisted the cigar's stub against the concrete bench. He thumped it away. "You see, I win again."

The heavens offered no response, but that was no surprise. Night clouds drifted and paused over the full moon and blocked its pale glow. His gazed dropped below the tips of Spanish moss that hung like gray foxtails through the accumulating smoke.

On his left, one figure, her brown skirt almost hidden by a robe, vied for his approval as she made her circuit. She glanced his way, sprinkling powder into the fires so that rivers of green sparks writhed and twisted above the flames.

He tittered. Idiots, always trying to gain his favor. He had no favorites.

Five others passed behind him. He twisted around as they bowed and cowed, dropping glimmering tokens through the hairy roots of the hyacinths then backing away from the fountain's stupid sunny face.

Who cared what his servile followers were into, as long as it wasn't *Him*. He glanced up to the sky, unable to stop himself from looking in His direction.

Lucas' lips clamped together in determination. Nope, he wouldn't even give a *thought* to that Name.

Yeah, yeah, yeah, enough. This swaying and swerving had lasted long enough. The orange embers had cooled to gray ash, and now it was time. He snapped his fingers and the six figures formed two shadowy lines on either side of the revived, squirming bundle. They lifted. The loud ape-like call of an owl resonated sharply through the trees. Lucas snorted and led the way. Now and then he turned to watch as they plodded toward the woods on the far side of the shop.

Sleepers inside the house would never hear a thing. He sniggered with a shiver. Delightful. One more trophy for him, in honor of his sole purpose to kill, steal, and destroy.

Behind the shop, he unlocked the door to his special room.

Emily woke with a start at Beggar's low growl. Her eyes fixed on his sphinx-like posture, blue in the moonlight. He whined and rumbled again, his own eyes riveted on the outer wall as if he could see clear through to the shop.

"What is it, Beggar?" she whispered, reaching for him. But

at the bristling on his neck, she jerked her hand away. "What's wrong?"

Rigid, he ignored her.

Emily flipped onto the floor and crawled to the window, glad she had forgotten to put the shades down. The moon lit up the gardens and cast deep shadows across the property and inside the bedroom. The scene would have been beautiful had Beggar not been growling. She stayed in the shadows and eased the voile curtains open.

"I hear it, too," she whispered.

She stared hard, but nothing moved in the gardens. In the woods to the right, a square of light bathed the tree trunks and underbrush behind the building. "There's a window back there."

A muffled thump broke the stillness then all fell quiet. Shadows fluttered back and forth then downward. The brightness expanded as if a door had opened back there.

"Shh." Glancing at Beggar, she put her finger to her lips. The clock on the wall read one thirty. Who would be up at this time of night? It couldn't be Mom. She propped open the curtain and stretched her arms across the desk.

Beggar whined and leaped off the bed. He pressed against Emily, his front paws on the desk. Quivering against her arm, he growled. She patted his head. "It's okay, Beggar, it's okay."

His eyes searched hers. She rubbed his back, shivering as her fingers stroked the spiking hairs. "It's just somebody messing around in the shop."

His nose turned toward the window, and Emily leaned closer.

Two dark figures, one holding each end of a long narrow object, emerged in the patch of light.

Their faces tipped briefly to the side. "It looks like those two counselors from church." She hugged the dog's chest. "Shh. Let's see who's got the other end." A large man emerged and flicked off the light. "That's Dr. Mike."

Now only the black shadow of the building lay over the woods.

"Let's go back to bed, Beggar. The light's out. Everybody's gone."

She rubbed his head, and he gave her a dog-grin, as if to say, *Okay, I'm with you.* He leaped over the wad of bedclothes as Emily slid between her still-warm sheets.

Wide awake, she studied the way Beggar's fine chest hairs glimmered like silver. "This is really neat," she whispered, smoothing his coat. "We should leave the shades open all the time."

A muffled *whumph* came from outside.

Beggar jerked upright, growling and shaking. He leaped over Emily and hit the floor again. With his front paws on the desk, he growled even louder.

"Shh, get down." She rolled onto all fours beside him, and wrapped her arm around his chest. Just in time to keep him from barking. She peered over the edge of the desk.

It was a man.

"Stay down. He'll see you." She pulled his paws back to the floor. The man walked to the garden with a long handled tool, then disappeared around the shop's corner. "That looks like John. What's he doing out there?"

"Rats. I wish we could see." Emily stared, wide-eyed. If she could just see some movement.

She studied the shadows again. Beggar pointed his ears forward. Barely breathing, he growled softly.

An elbow and hip edged in and out of view behind the shop.

"This is too weird, Beggar. Someone's digging... or raking."

Except for those few seconds, the garden remained still. With her arms trembling against the desk, she remained at the window a long time.

What secrets were they hiding?

Chapter 24

Through the upstairs window of her bedroom, Rene gazed at the moonlit grass below. Nothing stirred the quiet stillness except a pair of scrawny cats sniffing around her trash cans. A large white one leaped onto the lid. The other prowled near the bottom, its mottled fur clearly lit by the full moon.

A few minutes ago, when she'd crept through the house, the silent rooms had revealed no prowler.

So what was this awful dread gnawing at her insides?

Rene pulled the curtains back further and peered through the pecan trees. A light from Kaye's house shone through the branches.

Rene reached for the phone.

Within minutes she found herself stepping through Kaye's tomato patch. Behind her, an unearthly yowl pierced the humid air. Only a cat. But Rene picked up her step anyway. A second cat answered the first, its threatening resonance coming from the hydrangeas near Kaye's back door. Right in her path.

Undeterred by her presence, its voice melded with the other cat's as they warbled up and down their throaty feline scales. Rene tightened her grip on her Bible and pillow as she backed against the screen door.

Kaye flicked on the back porch light. "Come on in."

Rene shuddered past her. "Glad to. Almost got caught in a brawl out there!"

"Let me fix that." Kaye grabbed two pie tins from the top

of the washing machine and stepped outside, beating the pans. "Get out of here. Scat!"

Kaye returned and latched the door behind her. "There's something in the air tonight. I can feel it."

"We've been taunting the enemy with those prayers, you know."

"It has to do with the girls. You can bet on it."

"All the more reason not to quit."

Late the next morning at the Acres, Emily bounded up the steps of the front porch. "Oh, I'm sorry, Miss Maria, I forgot to give Beggar his bath."

"Oh, you're fine, honey. You can wash him later."

She was in a mighty good mood.

"The reason I called you in early is there's something special for you to do. Come with me."

In the dim light of the darkened hallway, Maria's white ankles flashed like albino fish from the bathys-something, the deep part of the ocean.

"No studying?"

"Correct," said Maria, walking past the living room. "Something different."

Emily bent over, patted Beggar's skinny ribs, and mouthed the words. "No stupid books."

When they reached the back porch, Maria picked up a galvanized bucket beside the washing machine and grabbed the red mop handle. "Do you remember the maid? Cindy? Well, today you get to share Cindy's housework."

Maria handed Emily the list of chores. "I'll be back in a little bit."

Emily studied the small paper in her hand.

"Stay out of the kitchen cupboards." Maria said, heading out the back door. "Everything you'll need is next to the washing machine on the back porch and on the shelf above it."

Finally, something new to do. But why was Emily having to do Cindy's work? This wasn't therapy.

As the van drove away, Emily climbed on top of the washer. She located a bottle of floor wax but found nothing to clean the floor with. She backed away and drummed her fingers against her arm. "Grandma always uses dish soap." Beggar followed as she wandered into the kitchen.

Under the sink, she located the detergent bottle. "Ta da! Just don't tell Maria, okay, boy?"

She plunked the bucket into the sink, turned on the water, and squeezed the bottle. The emerald green soap mounded into bubbles.

After mopping the floor, she wiped her hands on her shorts and checked the list. "Now the trash."

A jam-packed brown paper bag lined the can. "We'd better take the whole thing out." She dragged the can to the back door and thumped it down the steps to the large galvanized cans at the bottom.

But when she lifted the lid of the galvanized can she froze. A dozen empty worm-pill cartons lay on top of its contents.

"Wow, Beggar." She shoved her kitchen bag on top and shut the lid. "Poor Mr. Wormy. All this time I thought Maria didn't care about you."

Beggar wagged.

"Come on, let's go wrap things up."

Inside the house, she placed a new bag in the can and grabbed the detergent bottle. As she replaced the bottle in the cupboard, it knocked two small boxes onto the floor. More worm pills.

Come here, Beggar," Emily said, hugging his neck. "Look at all this. Here, let's take one right now."

She crossed her legs and pried open a box. The bubble pack slid out, and she rubbed Beggar's chin. "You'll be like me, now. See? Mine are brown, too."

He blinked and panted as she flipped over the bubble pack and pushed her fingernail through the foil. The pill popped out, and rolled onto her palm. "Here you go, Mr. Wormy." She glanced at the letters and paused. "M/2? Your medicine says M/2?" She leaped to her feet. "Hold on a minute."

Emily grabbed the vitamin bottle from the counter, the one Maria opened each morning for her. She clawed at the flimsy lid then dumped a pile of brown and red pills into her palm. Two or three tumbled onto the counter and she caught a brown one. Her hands shook so badly she could hardly turn it over.

She stared at the letters.

M/2.

"No way. No way." Maria was feeding her worm pills? *Trying* to make her sick? Why? Why?

No wonder she had diarrhea.

At supper, Emily hugged the discovery to herself, barely speaking. She scurried to her room at the earliest opportunity.

The next morning at breakfast, events drifted along like always. The smell of the coffee, the dishes clattering, John and Maria ignoring her and making small talk.

Outside, the sun slanted in such a beautiful way through the back porch.

Birds twittered.

But Emily's throat tightened.

The hot breath of fear blew against her eardrums.

She *had* to act normal, like this was any other day. Or Maria would know she knew.

The fried eggs tasted like rubber bands. Chew anyway. Another bite. Chew, swallow, bite. Chew, swallow, bite.

Gigi, her friend's poodle, had gotten diarrhea from his worm pill. They did do that.

Emily scooted the last piece of scrambled egg back and forth on her plate and stared at the shiny brown pill beside her glass. M/2. Same worm pill.

She glanced at John hunkered over his coffee.

Did he know what Maria was doing?

Her teeth bit mechanically into her dry toast. Right now she had to survive the witch's tricks.

And Mom. Mom had been sick too. She had to warn her. But how could they get away?

Emily and Mom were alone. Stuck in the middle of nowhere with a car that didn't work.

Maria drained her coffee cup. "Take your vitamin, honey."

Emily nudged the pill under her plate but pretended to take it with a mouthful of milk. A satisfied smile curved Maria's mouth.

Emily grinned inside. *Fooled her.*

She maneuvered the pill onto her lap and finished her milk. *Very smooth, ha ha.* "Thank you for breakfast, Miss Maria. Can I help you with anything this morning?" Maybe she could drop the pill down the drain.

195

"No, Honey, just follow your regular schedule. Arts and crafts, then writing therapy. We'll save the dishes for the maid." She held up one finger. "Oh, I forgot. Do the dishes later, how's that?"

Emily grabbed the pill from her lap. Too bad the maid's absence couldn't get her excused from studying and reading. She needed some time to think right now. With the pill wedged between two fingers, she stood.

"What do you want me to write about today?"

"Write about why you deserve to be going home in a few days."

"Really? I'm about done?"

Maria turned her back so Emily couldn't see her face. "Yes, honey. I believe your time here will be over in a few days."

Sweat prickled on Emily's neck.

She had to act fast.

Chapter 25

Charlene ignored the toast crumbs littering the counter-top and the fried-egg dishes in the sink. She poured herself a cup of coffee and sniffed the brew. Scorched. Maria had left the pot plugged in again. Well, maybe it would clear out some cobwebs anyway.

She stepped outside with the cup in her hand, and glanced toward the empty driveway as the back door slammed behind her. The van was gone.

Thank goodness. Charlene needed solitude to settle this sword-fight in her head. She eased onto the bottom step and leaned against the rail post.

Cindy's words played and replayed in her head, just like they had all night, stalking her like a yellow-eyed panther. There was no escaping them. She crossed her arms and pressed the warm mug against her skin.

The woman's child was dead.

A few feet away, a pair of cardinals darted in and out of John's azalea bushes, singing a two-note song then flitting away. Charlene rose to her feet and stared blankly at the end of the short sidewalk. Pink oxalis flowers and a lone spider web glittered with dew. Flowers, beauty. What a contrast to Cindy's frightening story.

She closed her eyes. The surrounding woods droned with the ever-present cicadas.

If she could only back up a few days, not meet Cindy, not stay in the shop during the rain. But that wouldn't change the facts.

She needed to do something. But what? Hot coals burned her gut.

The voice in her head grew stronger. *There's been a huge mistake. It's huge. It's huge. It's huge.* She wanted to vomit.

She could still hear the secretary's words at her office in Gaskille. *Charlene, don't be an idiot. Emily's trauma deserves therapy. Therapy, therapy, therapy.*

But Bill did not hurt Emily. He only *tried.*

Her mother's words rushed in. *We'll take care of her at home with us. She's learned the truth that bad people exist. Emily's wiser now and needs our prayers, our love, and support. Maybe get her some pastoral counseling. We'll love on her, talk with her, take her to church, and she'll meet good people, nice boys, nice people. She'll be okay.*

Sitting right there in her old blue Honda, Charlene had gone against her mother's advice. No one would tell her what to do with *her* child. She was a forty-year old adult, for goodness' sake. And what would an old-school seventy-year-old know about therapists? Today was a new day in America, and since eighteen, like the law allowed, if Rene said white, Charlene would say black.

She'd shown her, huh? Right.

Charlene leaned her head back and closed her eyes. Idiot, idiot, idiot.

Fix the mistake. Hurry. Get out. Get out. Now.

She lifted the cup and sipped the acrid liquid. What about the thirty thousand dollars?

Get out.

She had no money.

Forget about it. Get out.

It would take years to pay back.

Just do it. Hurry.

She kicked at a clump of wet grass at the bottom of the post and closed her eyes. The world spun, but she stood anyway. Time to go to the shop.

As Charlene neared the building, a golf cart zipped by and rolled to a stop beside the garden's picket area.

Charlene squared her shoulders. Why should she avoid the other clients? She strolled to a dewy arbor of morning glories and brushed a line of black ants off the bench and sat down. Wherever John was, he couldn't see her.

She stared at the gardeners as the black crows of Cindy's story flapped through her mind.

There were too many similarities to be lies.

Out in the garden, the golf cart driver jumped to the ground and threw out her tools. They clattered to the ground beside a half-dug plot. How could the women work in this heat? By noon that green dress would be dripping with sweat. The straw hat offered little help.

Lord, please help that woman. And please help Cindy. There, see. She just needed to pray for Cindy. And her bad luck.

The golf cart gardener stabbed her shovel around the edges of the plot, loosening the divots. She moved quickly and neatly around the grassy sides, positioning the blade, stomping it, and pushing it down like a lever. The roots lifted easily from the underlying soil, and she jerked them loose with a gloved hand, shaking out the dirt. The center of the plot had already been dug.

Lucky Charlene. They'd chosen her to work indoors.

If only she hadn't met Cindy, she wouldn't be so confused. Things would be fine, just like before she and Cindy talked.

But *were* they fine?

She rose, tossed the remains of her nasty coffee, then headed for the shop. "Father, I am so confused. Please help me understand what's going on, and help me sort it out."

When she opened the shop door, the stuffiness of the concrete walls hit her in the face. What an empty void. She needed air.

She reached for the window crank but recoiled when her fingers brushed the matted spider webs. Crumbled June bugs and dead flies filled the windowsill's crevices. She brushed them out with the sewing machine's whisk broom and opened the window as far as it would go then opened all the others. The air remained tainted, though, by the filth that still clung to the screens.

Charlene sat at her machine and stared over the top of it. If she could just get rid of the painful gnawing in her gut.

She began her work robotically, pushing her foot against the pedal. An hour passed. Only one box was filled. She closed her eyes.

Make a move.

Stuffing the folded garments in a box, she dragged tape over the lid, and dropped it by the door. Bathroom break. She stepped through the door and headed up the driveway, drinking in the fresh air.

The golf-cart woman had disappeared.

The child's white picket fence had been moved to a new plot.

After her restroom break Charlene trudged back to the shop. The sun, now straight overhead, baked her skin.

That's it, she would open the shop doors and let the suffocating air out of the building. She picked up her pace.

The shops doors, a foot off the ground, folded easily against the outside wall, but they swung shut again. She needed a prop, like a bleach bottle, or large detergent container from Cindy's storeroom.

Inside, Cindy's pink ribbon still danged where she'd left it. Charlene wrestled the lock open again.

The store room's musty air filled her nostrils. Yellow light seeped through two grungy windows high on the left. On the right, at the top of a sturdy rack of shelves caked with dust, soap powder, and rust, sat one large unopened box of detergent. Twenty years old, judging by its logo.

Charlene climbed the racks and coaxed the box to the front of the ledge with her fingertips. Crud rained across her face. With her eyes closed she blew it away. She swiped her arm across her mouth, Phthew! She gave it one more tug. It tipped. She dodged.It hit the floor. Split open. White grains oozed like sand around her feet.

Only when she brushed off her hands did she notice the door to the left of the shelves.

She shoved the box aside with one foot, stepped around the shelves, and rattled the knob. Locked. Best case scenario would be a restroom so she wouldn't need to walk to the house anymore.

Except, after hearing Cindy's story, she ought to be grabbing Emily and getting out of here.

She thrust Cindy's key in the lock, and the door opened a few inches. Pitch black. Extending a finger, she gave the door a push. The gap widened. She felt around the doorframe for the switch. Nothing.

Then, like a tidal wave, the stench rolled in. She clutched her nose and backed up. Thick and rotten, like sardines, it filled the room. Her heel hit the fallen box, and she sprawled backwards, her shoulder slamming against the floor. She clutched the throbbing joint and clambered to her knees with a gasp, covering her nose again.

Something dead, probably. She kicked at the door, and it opened wider.

With eyes peeled, she waited for her pupils to dilate and reveal the contents of the black hole.

At first, only speckles of light seeped in through the painted windows. Soon, though, a full scene materialized. A tall angular mass loomed on the right. Fabric draped over hornlike projections on top of a throne. A long narrow table lay on its side in front of it.

Her eyes narrowed in disbelief. A chill crawled up her spine as she focused on the circular rug and its large pentagram.

Burnt jars and broken glass gleamed over the surface of the star. And everywhere, dark splatters. Lots of them.

Blood, maybe.

A buzzing, like high voltage, resonated in Charlene's brain, growing louder and louder. She opened her mouth, but nothing came out. She swallowed, but her throat constricted as if paralyzed.

As she pulled the door shut, she tried not to inhale the awful stink.

Her limbs moved like stiff wooden appendages. If she hadn't seen this, this.... She turned. A sword of pain stabbed through her injured shoulder. But pain was the least of her worries. No matter what, she had to get Emily out.

Now.

She looped the string around the knob and paused. That wasn't how Cindy left it. She unwound the ribbon and let it hang down.

Pinpricks of fear tingled in her arms as she backed away from the door.

Chapter 26

At her desk, Emily took another look at her pitiful drawing of Beggar then scribbled circles all over it. She'd have to work harder to draw as well as Susie.

She folded Susie's drawing and stuffed it under the mattress for safekeeping then flopped back into the chair. Waiting for time to pass was such torture.

Her assignment, finished a long time ago, lay on the desk as she pondered the life-or-death task ahead. Once Maria sent her outside, she'd race to the log and write her heart out to Mom. Tell her about the brown pills and the lies—convince her that they'd both be dead if they stayed at the Acres.

And hope Mom believed her.

She couldn't risk writing all that in the house. Not without being discovered.

The secret journal, hidden in her waistband, poked against her side. She stood and circled the room a few times, practicing a natural look before sitting back down. If she didn't press her forearm against the journal, it would slip through her shorts. Skeletal figure courtesy of the witch, of course. So she enlisted the help of her underwear.

The door opened, and Emily jumped. She resisted the urge to stand and drew more circles on her picture.

"It's free time." Maria clapped her hands and swept the essay off the corner of the desk.

Emily twisted around in her chair. "Since I'll be going home soon, could I walk down the road and look for butterflies again? I promise not to go too far."

"Well, I guess. Just be sure you're close enough to hear the lunch bell."

"Sure."

Maria brushed her hand over Emily's forehead. "By the way, how do you feel?"

Emily leaned away. "I've had some stomach pains this morning, and some diarrhea, but I'm okay now."

No, I haven't taken your brown pill today, you witch. And keep your ugly hands off me.

Once outside, Emily pushed through the palmetto thicket. She stepped only on the dead vegetation to ensure she left no tracks on the frond-littered sand. A straight line was the quickest way to the log. Chances were slim that Maria or John would come looking for her down there, but she couldn't risk leaving tracks. Beggar trotted behind, dodging the slapping fronds.

In a sandy clearing scattered with palmetto berries, she knelt down with one hand on the dog's shoulder. "We have to pray. Be still."

He looked into her eyes and sat down as if he understood.

"Father, You know what I'm trying to do. Please give me the right words to say, and—just do whatever you need to do to help us. In Jesus name, Amen."

She stood quickly and pressed the journal against her waist. "Let's go, Beggar. It's now or never."

Her heart slammed fast and hard as she raced to the log and climbed its roots. Keeping an eye on the cover of cypress and myrtles, she crawled forward on the bleached wood. Though the cabin's rooftop remained visible, the foliage blocked Maria's view. She tightened her elbow against the book. All she needed was the privacy to write.

A crow cawed noisily from a nearby cypress as if laughing at her.

She shook her head and inched forward. "I might be slow, but I'm working on it, you ugly bird."

Her eyes focused on the black water as it swept under the log and disappeared downstream around a bend in the mossy woods. A wave of dizziness washed over her. Maybe she ought to keep her mind on the log.

Another crow cawed in the distance. Or was it an owl? She shivered. "Just please, don't let Mom brush this off."

Beggar whined from his place between the scaly fingers of the cypress knees.

She lifted her arm and peered back at him. "Shh. Be quiet."

He lowered his head onto his paws with a groan.

A breeze stirred, and the elephant ears rustled on the bank. Emily froze and scanned her eyes across the undergrowth but nothing seemed amiss. In front of her, the far end of the log tilted like a pale ramp, dipping beneath the inky ripples. It touched things she didn't want to think about.

A stub of a limb rose in front of her. Grabbing hold, she leaned into it, and prepared to crawl over.

But the wood snapped under her hand. She dove, chest-first against the log. The limb's loud crack ricocheted across the river like gunfire. Off balance, she slid toward the water, clawing for a hand-hold, and helpless against the snag's wicked rake across her bare ribs.

Beggar leaped up growling, as Emily, kicked and panted, and pulled herself on top of the log with a gasp. She closed her eyes and clutched the precious book to her side.

Careful not to drop it, she thrust the journal between her teeth and turned around to face the shore. When she pulled it from her mouth again, tooth prints and drool marked the soft plastic. She wiped it on her shirt and hugged it to her chest, her lifeline. Maria's rules were so stupid, especially the one about no extra writing materials.

Behind her, Beggar barked.

"Shh. Beggar. What if the witch hears you?"

He plopped down with a grunt.

Lifting her shirt, Emily examined the stinging scrape across her ribs. Dark pearls of blood seeped from the fiery rawness.

If Maria saw this, she'd ask questions. Snatching an empty page from her journal, Emily pressed it against her side. Blood quickly saturated the cheap paper. It should clot and stick to her skin, keeping the stain off her shirt.

Another scrape burned on her shoulder, but it hadn't bled. She swiped her thumb across it. If she held her shoulders right, Maria wouldn't see it inside the armhole.

Her fingers trembled as she worked the pencil from its elastic loop. She sucked in a ragged breath and stared at the blank page. How should she start? Dear Mom, Maria and John are trying to kill me and possibly you, too?

The sun bore straight down, scorching her thighs as she pressed the pencil to the paper. Heat shimmered from the log like liquid glass, and the sunny spots burned like a stove. As she wrote, perspiration rolled down her neck and the middle of her back. She scooped the sweat from behind her knees with her fingertips and wiped it on her shorts.

Wrapping up her message, she discovered she'd actually beaten the bell. *Thank you, Lord.*

Now she had to get her note to Mom. Maybe she could slide it under the bedroom window.

The sound of the bell interrupted the quiet. Four loud peals instead of one. What was Maria's hurry?

She stuffed the book between her teeth, crawled toward the roots, and leaped onto the wet sand. At the edge of the road, she picked a few scroungy dandelions. Just for appearances. After all, she'd told Maria she was looking for flowers and butterflies.

She paused, secured the book under her clothes and trotted up the lane with Beggar. His nose zigzagged along the sandy ruts ahead of her. Along the way he disappeared into the palmetto bushes between the road and the house. Emily plowed through the woods, but slowed as she emerged near the porch.

Maria stood by the bell with her arms crossed. "What took you so long? Lunch is ready."

Emily climbed the creaky steps and handed her the flowers. "These are for you."

"I hope you brought a good appetite for my new peanut butter recipe." Maria followed Emily into the house and hooked the door latch behind them.

Lucas slipped to the corner of the porch as Maria's bell rang.

Today was the kid's big day. He shivered with delight. Kill, steal, and destroy. It wouldn't be long now.

The back of his white jacket brushed against the weathered planks of the wall just out of their sight. He peered over his shoulder through the cobwebs that fluttered beneath the rocker. Perfect view. The girl climbed the steps and handed Maria the dandelions.

Stupid kid.

He almost snorted out loud when Maria tossed the flowers off the porch and wiped her hands on her skirt. His kind of style. Way to impress, old girl.

Once he heard the screen door latch, Lucas stepped around the house and passed through the shadows with his fist to the sky.

"Stop me now!"

Chapter 27

Emily stepped through the hallway in front of Maria, aware of the woman's hot gaze on her back.

At the kitchen sink, Emily lathered her hands and washed away the dandelion sap. The journal slipped beneath her waistband, but she pressed it a little tighter against the sink.

She took her time drying her hands, glad for the clatter of Maria's lunch plates and silverware that filled the uncomfortable void in the room. Her fingers touched the paper where it stuck to the dried blood. Still there. She peeked at the abrasion on her shoulder. It was still raw and pink, but not bleeding.

The book in her shorts seemed fairly secure, and she took a deep breath. Only its pages could save them now. If Mom could believe its words. Now to get them under the window where Mom could find them.

Emily gazed into the black hole of the sink drain. She could have fallen in the river. Or dropped the journal. She shuddered and eased toward the table.

Maria stirred Emily's chocolate milk with a long spoon. Emily could have done that for herself.

Whatever Emily did, though, she'd better act natural and cheerful. "Thank you, Miss Maria."

But she wasn't normally cheerful, at least not around Maria. What was natural?

This was hard.

Emily smoothed her napkin on her lap and smiled down at the peanut butter sandwich Maria had cut into quarters. "Just the way I like it. Thanks."

"You're very welcome, honey."

Emily glanced up at the woman then averted her eyes.

Maria wasn't behaving naturally, either. Yesterday she'd plopped Emily's sandwich on her plate as one big hocking hunk. Today she'd even garnished it with a dill pickle spear.

Go figure.

Maybe Emily had misjudged her. Maybe Maria was just a middle-age nutcase. Maybe the pills were an ignorant mistake. A coincidence.

Emily rubbed her finger over the coarse bread. "Sunflower seed bread. I love it."

Maria tossed her a half-smile. "I know how much you like peanut butter, so I tried a new recipe today. You can be my little taste-tester."

Right. Now she was all chummy. Emily pulled the bread apart. "Where's the jelly?"

Maria pressed a finger to her cheek as if thinking hard. "We're out. Just drink your chocolate milk, and I'll pick some more up at the store next time. Sorry."

"But we had a whole jar of plum jelly this morning." Emily bit off a dry corner. "I saw it in the refrigerator at breakfast."

"It broke." She might as well have said, *Who cares?*, the way it sounded.

The peanut butter was thicker and saltier than usual. Emily really needed something to moisten it. She finally managed to swallow. "How about honey?"

Maria frowned and stood. "I can look, but take a sip of your chocolate milk. That'll help." She opened and shut a pair of cupboards with barely a glance.

Grabbing the pencil hanging on the refrigerator, she scribbled on the grocery list and took her seat again. "Happy now? Don't you know that flexibility is a mark of higher intelligence? Let's just make do today."

Maria put on a fake smile. "So, did you have a nice time outside? What did you see?"

As if the woman was really interested.

"Yes, ma'am." Emily took a sip of her chocolate. "I'll miss the butterflies when I go home."

Maria's smile seemed stuck on her face. But the flat, intense way her expressionless eyes drilled into her told Emily the truth. This was real. Maria was really trying to poison her with those pills.

Emily took another sip and set the flimsy plastic cup near the edge of the table.

Maria, her eyes following Emily's actions, neglected her own sandwich. She leaned her chin on her hand.

Chocolate had swirled in Emily's cup and now settled quickly to the bottom in grainy black particles. "Is this a new kind of chocolate?" she said. "I think it needs more sugar."

Emily reached across the table for the sugar bowl, and Maria shot out a hand. "Careful, don't spill—"

Too late.

Emily's elbow bumped the cup and propelled it off the table. It hit the floor, and a geyser of milk flew straight up. It landed, dripping and draining over the table, the wall, and the chair.

And Beggar's face.

He backed away from the spreading puddle.

"Can't you be more careful?" Maria's voice shrieked. "I can't believe you did this."

"It's not that big of a deal."

Maria waved her arms over the table. "You messed up

212

the entire kitchen—just go. Go to your room. This is not happening. *Go!*" she bellowed, jerking the table and chairs away from the wall as loose strands of hair fell around her face. She pointed at the dog. "Get him out of here."

"It's my mess. I'll clean it up."

Maria threw napkins on top of the puddle. "Go to your room and don't come out until tomorrow morning."

Emily clapped for Beggar as he dragged his bologna-like tongue through the milky lake. He ignored her, lapping up the treat as fast as he could. "Come on, Beggar," she pleaded.

Maria, her face contorted and red, kicked at the dog as she pointed them to the bedroom. He yelped, leaping away, and slunk into the bedroom behind Emily.

Charlene gripped the sides of the sewing table and squeezed. *Slow down.* She took two deep breaths. The trouble at Earth Mother Acres was more than just ignorance, more than foolishly believing in some Great Spirit, more than just ignoring God the Father and Jesus His Son. This place was evil at a new level. *Black and occultic.*

She stared at the threads poking out of the silver throat plate, aware only of the rise and fall of her chest and the wild racing inside her veins. She finally closed her eyes, inhaling the familiar hot smell of the machine's oily motor. She lifted the presser foot.

John or Maria might be back soon.

Like an automaton, she fed label after label under the presser foot, stitching them into the necklines of the jackets. She had no consciousness of time or quantity.

Jesus, I have to hide what I know. What can I do? We need to leave here. Help us. Help us. Keep us safe.

What about that stupid remark she'd made to John that first night?

I didn't even have to pray about it, it just felt so right.

Now it slapped her in the face like a big hairy hand.

Oh, God, I am so sorry, forgive me, forgive me.

Emily left Maria to tackle the chocolate milk mess in the kitchen and raced into the bedroom. She maneuvered the journal out of her pants as Beggar leaped on the bed. With trembling fingers, she ripped out the pages. She moved the desk quietly and jerked up the window. Her hands trembled as she unlatched the screen and gave it a shove.

It refused to budge.

No! Not after all this effort.

This was no time to mess around. She kicked her heel against the frame. The corner separated but something on the outside held it shut. She kicked again. Nothing.

It didn't matter. This little setback wasn't stopping her.

She folded the papers in half, shoved them under the corner of the screen, and lowered the window. They were far enough through the frame for Mom to see, but not far enough to draw anyone else's attention.

Dizzy from the effort, she lay down beside Beggar and closed her eyes. There was nothing else to do until tomorrow.

Charlene reached for the nearly-full box and dropped in the last folded jacket. After this, no more sewing.

Thank God for mindless work. For time to think and plan. Some poor women would benefit from the new clothes, and that was all fine and good, but she needed to think of herself right now.

Timing was everything.

She pondered her next step as she rolled the tape dispenser across the box.

Lord, I'm sorry. I wanted to do my best for You, but I failed. Please help us get away. I beg You.

She glanced through the window at the back of the house. Late afternoon shadows stretched across the yard. In a little over an hour she'd pass by Emily's window, round her up, and get her off the property.

Nobody would miss Charlene during study time. On the other hand, Emily's absence would be noticed. She had to risk it. To spend one more night in this place would be pure stupidity.

That meant they needed to get as far away as possible before Maria called Emily to the kitchen.

"Emily," she whispered, "I hope you'll trust me after I was such an idiot."

As she pulled off another length of tape, the shop door swung open. She jumped and the tape jerked from the roller.

Maria waved a hanger with a pink dress on it. "Hi, Charlene. I've brought you some mending. Can you squeeze this in today?"

The lilt in Maria's voice caught Charlene's attention. She stared, nodded her head, then turned away to fit the tape back in the dispenser while Maria hung the dress on a nail near the door.

"One of our best clients is going home today, and the

good news is you and Emily will be doing the same thing very soon."

Charlene gritted her teeth and forced a grin as she carried the last box to the door. She'd like to throw it at the woman.

"That's great news, Maria. We've accomplished a lot during our stay." As she pitched the box toward the others, it fell on the floor. She grabbed it up, hoping her nervousness didn't show in her laugh. "Never was good at basketball."

Maria ignored the comment. "This isn't a big job, just a torn pocket and so on. It's been cleaned and ironed. Just tend to it when you're done there." Maria returned to the door. "By the way," she said, "John will be here a little early today. After he picks up the boxes, keep your schedule as usual."

After Maria left, Charlene expelled a long jerky breath. Good thing she knew to wait for John.

But as she glanced toward the pink dress her jaw dropped.

The dress on the hanger appeared to have been in a cat-fight. Its bodice was torn halfway off and its pocket hung open like a flap. Across the front of it, as clear as day, was a bright red ink spot.

Cindy's red ink spot.

Maria entered Emily's room and shook her arm. "Emily. Emily."

No response.

Dishes needed washing, and floors were still sticky from the chocolate milk. Might as well get the girl out of bed. Maria had been a little hasty sending the kid to her room for the rest of the day.

Other methods existed to "graduate" her out of the program.

Right now, though, Maria needed help. She pulled up the shades and cupped her hand under Emily's nose.

Was the girl even breathing? She placed her ear near Emily's nose. Hard to tell. The girl couldn't have swallowed *that* much of the drink. Maria must have come pretty close to getting the job done after all. Her fingers flexed against Emily's pale neck. As she checked for a pulse she admired the purple paint on her own long nails.

Oh, yes, there it was, a pulse. Still alive, but not much use right now.

Maria stepped out of the room and pulled the door shut. She locked it from the outside.

The girl could mop in the morning, then.

She smiled at the promise of toying with Emily some more. Like a cat with a mouse.

No spilled drinks, next time, though. She'd finish the job. For Lucas.

Chapter 28

Charlene cradled the dress as she carried it to the machine. Repairing the garment was the least she could do for Cindy. Once she pinned the bodice back to the skirt, the stitching took only minutes. She hung the dress on its nail as John's van squeaked to a stop outside. "Thank you, Lord, for letting him come early," she whispered.

She swung the shop door open as the van slid into position for loading from the side. The motor idled while he strode around the vehicle.

She tried to sound casual. "Hi, John."

The van door opened with a *whumph* as he snorted back whatever was in his throat. He gagged as it caught in his throat and bent low, coughing.

Should she pat him on the back or what? "Are you okay?"

He hacked until his face turned red. His breath came in long gasps and tears filled the corners of his eyes. His hands grappled for the doorframe, and he lurched into the building. He swiped his mouth across one sleeve and rummaging through his keys. "I'm okay. Just a little stuff in the lungs. Must be from all the rain, huh?"

He disappeared into the supply room where his frenzied coughing started up again. Maybe she should help with the boxes. Get things moving.

As she tossed the first few into the van she recognized the ones already inside as the same shape and size as her boxes from yesterday. She dragged one close and examined it. Same weight, too. Someone had stuck a gold label on it addressed to *Nacy's Fashions, Fifth Avenue, New York, New York.*

Charities didn't require a Fifth Avenue label.

John's congested breathing grew loud behind her, and the hair prickled on her neck. She backed out of the van and turned around to find him rubbing his glasses on his shirttail.

"I hope you don't mind me tossing these in for you. I knew you weren't feeling well." She tried to distract his focus by sounding sympathetic. "Are you going to be all right?"

"That's all for now. Thank you." He rubbed his nose across the back of a wrist. "Has Maria told you anything about being dismissed soon?"

"Yes sir, that's really good news." That familiar stench filled her nose again. She forced a smile and willed him to leave.

"Maria took the liberty of giving your credit card to the mechanic. He's at his other place in town. That okay?"

"Uh, sure." As long as he didn't go over her limit. "How much was the bill?"

"She didn't say. Well. I've got to hurry." He climbed into the van, threw it in gear, and roared away.

With her pulse racing, Charlene slipped inside and shut the door. She stepped in front of the window. John's cloud of exhaust billowed over the road. Within seconds, his van reappeared on the far side of the garage as it barreled east.

Aha. There was another way to town.

He'd lied.

From her bedroom window, she'd never noticed him drive out that way. How amazing what a few feet could add to perspective. "Show us how to do this, Lord," she prayed. "Help us get to the car. Help me think straight."

After counting to thirty, she slipped out the door and edged toward the woods along the right side of the building. She had to find Emily. And fast.

Charlene rounded the corner by the trees and stopped in her tracks. The marigolds, once thriving and beautiful along the back wall, lay broken and trampled among footprints of different sizes. The salty scent of their crushed foliage filled the air.

An Earth Mother Acres nametag, its pin splayed out to the side, lay embedded in a print.

Charlene dug away the soil and stared at the peeling letters. *Cindy.*

She pressed the pin against her slamming heart and raced to Emily's window. Time was running out.

At the window she slipped Cindy's tag in her pocket and slapped at the dusty screen. "Emily," she whispered as loud as she dared. "Emily."

No response. Charlene groaned. Not today, of all days. Where was she?

She shielded her eyes to probe the dimness of the bedroom. Her elbow brushed against paper. She glanced down . Sheets of folded paper stuck out from under the window screen. She yanked them out and scanned the words.

Dog pills and poison?

A bad feeling clutched at her gut. She thrust the letter in her pocket and peered inside the room. Dust from the screen filled her nostrils. Over on the bed, Emily's shape came into view.

In her dream Emily floated face-up, rising and falling on the waves, her arms drifting and useless like kelp in the inky sea. A shriveled brown head hovered nearby, its squid-like eye staring down at her. Scabby lips around a black hole of a mouth expelled hot bands of breath and stinking particles.

"You were found out, weren't you?" it taunted. "They got you, didn't they?"

The creature moved closer. Its nasty lips sought hers.

She kicked and squirmed, trying to get away, laboring for every breath. Her lips refused to move, but she opened her teeth and sent up a feeble prayer, "Jesus, Jesus, help me."

The feeblest groan escaped her throat. "Go! In the name of Jesus."

A sharp blast of air hit her face as the thing howled and swirled away like a punctured balloon, taking the stink with it. She gasped, sucking in a breath of air.

Awake now, she pressed her throbbing head against her fingertips and blinked, straining for a hint of light. *Was it night or day?* Touching her eyes, she discovered them wide open. This was bad. With a throbbing head, she eased into a sitting position with her feet on the rug. What had just happened?

She tottered on the side of the bed as the awful clock ticked. Minutes passed before pinpricks finally sparkled like growing stars over the black curtain.

A distant banging seeped into her consciousness. It was somewhere to her right. It couldn't be Beggar. She reached around for the dog, expecting to connect with his warm, breathing chest. Beneath her palm were stiff cold hairs that did not belong to him. A roaring filled her throat.

It couldn't be.

She traced her fingers down one rigid leg, then over his unbending head, his dry, breathless mouth.

"Beggar." Acid tears burned her eyes.

This stupid place! That stupid witch.

It had to be the chocolate milk.

She pulled Beggar's neck close, and his whole body turned like a cardboard cutout. Pressing her face against his hair, she wept.

The banging increased.

"Beggar, no," she whispered.

The tears had burned away the black curtain, and light flooded in. The pressure of her headache released.

She grimaced, focusing on the dog's small, speckled body. She touched the half-closed eyes on his faithful face. "Beggar." Tears flooded again, dripping onto his now dull coat. The banging grew louder, more insistent. She wiped her eyes with the bed sheet and turned toward the window.

"Mom?"

"Emily. Emily."

She pulled Beggar's head onto her pillow and hobbled to the desk. She tugged at the window but was too weak to raise it.

With Beggar dead, she must have been...

"Hurry, Emily, hurry."

She pulled harder. "I'm trying." She moved the desk, found leverage, and forced the window up.

"Open the screen."

The frame was stuck like before. "It won't budge."

Mom searched the outside edges. "There's a lock out here." She clicked it open.

"What's going on, Mom?"

"Just climb out. Quick. We have to get out of here."

Fine with her. But first—

"Wait." Emily stumbled around the desk.

"Where are you going?" Charlene stuck her head under the screen. "Come on back, Emily, we don't have time."

"My journal."

"Forget it."

Emily plunged her arm between the mattresses for her things and handed them over. Charlene dropped them by her feet and reached for Emily. "Come on, honey," she begged. "They'll catch us." Her voice rose above a whisper. "Climb out the window. Now."

"Your box."

With her strength increasing, Emily reached for the metal box above the closet rod. She stood on tiptoe and worked it to the edge of the shelf with her fingertips.

It tipped and she grabbed for it. Missed. The box crashed to the floor.

Emily snatched it up and noticing Susie's clothes, grabbed them up, too. Careening sideways, she grabbed the window frame.

"Here." She shoved everything into Mom's hands and steadied herself.

"Just come on. Please."

The bedroom door knob rattled.

"What's going on in there?" Maria's voice cut through the door.

Emily froze. "I... I just dropped my book."

The door rattled again. "Are you feeling better?"

"I...My stomach hurts. I think I'm going back to bed again."

Silence filled the room.

Emily tiptoed to the window, and Mom stuck her hand out. "Come on, jump."

Placing a leg over the window sill, Emily slid out. Her feet touched the ground, and she stumbled. "Help me, Mom, I can't walk straight."

"What's wrong with you?" Mom grabbed her things and wrapped an arm around her. They hurried toward the golf cart by the back door.

"The chocolate milk." Emily fought off the tears but couldn't control the waver in her voice. "I only drank a little. But Beggar's dead."

"Poison?" Mom glanced at her face then dragged her up into the golf cart. "Be very quiet. And pray Maria isn't near the back porch." She turned the key, and the cart lurched forward as she let off the pedal.

Mom plopped a straw hat from the cart onto Emily's head. "Here, make like a gardener."

Emily tied the string under her chin as they moved rapidly up the center lane of the garden. The view from the house would be blocked for a good distance. Blackness came and went in her field of vision.

A gardener squatted nearby, shoving young tomato plants into holes next to the picket fence. Mom gasped and touched her pocket.

Her lips formed a thin line as the cart zipped toward the garage at the far end of the property.

"What is it, Mom?"

She shook her head. "It's so good to have you with me." Emily grabbed the dash as they rushed up the lane. "You too, Mom. You, too."

Charlene stopped the golf cart by a power pole on the

other side of the Civic. The garage, its front doors closed, appeared deserted. Forked-tipped Bahia grass surrounded the building, rising nearly as high as the car's hood and bending slightly in the breeze. "Just sit here a second, and I'll look for the keys."

She crept around the side of the car, but found nothing amiss. The car's handle, hot from the late afternoon sun, burned her hand as she touched it. "Locked, doggone it."

Around the building in front of the garage, a doorknob rattled. A door squeaked open. Feet shuffled lightly. For a split second Charlene froze, then dove in front of her car. The garage door slammed shut again. The dull jangle of keys faded into the distance along with the footsteps. Saved by the tall grass. How could she have forgotten about quitting time at the Acres?

She let out a slow breath and crawled around the car. On the other side of the power pole Emily was hunkered down behind the golf cart where she had wedged the hat in the armrest for cover. Emily noticed her glance and gave her a thumbs-up.

"Get down," Charlene motioned. "I have to find the keys, and I think the garage is locked."

Emily nodded.

"Stay behind the cart, I don't want people in those east-side buildings to see you."

Another thumbs-up.

Hang tight, Emily. Charlene crawled to the other side of the Civic and checked to the south. No one. Bending low, she darted toward the side of the building.

Suddenly Emily appeared at her side.

"I told you to keep down."

225

"I want to be with you."

"Then stay here, and don't move. The key is probably inside. You okay?"

Emily nodded. "Just thirsty." She turned on the water spigot behind Charlene and cupped her hand under it. Rusty water ran out of the line. "I have to drink. My mouth is bitter. You be careful, Mom."

"Yeah."

Charlene peered around the corner toward the house. No one in sight. Praying that no one could see her, she stretched her arm around the corner and tried the greasy knob.

Locked.

She returned to Emily. "I'm going around back. You watch the front."

Emily moved to the corner and peered toward the house.

Charlene returned in a few seconds. She pushed aside the vines and tugged at the metal edge of the crank-out window.

The twin panes lifted with a loud creak. She glanced at the woods behind her, but nothing stirred.

Only a sharp tool could lift the screen. She fished out Cindy's bent pin and inserted its point through the mesh to lift it out of its track. Perfect. The screen clattered to the floor inside.

"Thanks, Cindy." She stuck the pin back in her pocket and motioned for Emily to join her.

"I'm not sure I can get in by myself. Do you want to do it?"

"My knees are shaky. But I'll try."

Emily stepped into Charlene's interlaced hands and put one leg through the window. "Gross, it's full of spider webs."

"Webs won't hurt you. Just watch for spiders. We can't go anywhere without the keys."

As Emily touched the concrete, a hot lance of pain pierced her brain. Black ink flooded her vision like before. Gripping the window sill, she waited until the spear subsided and her vision returned. Mom's worried face came into focus.

"I'm okay, Mom," she whispered. "I can do this."

Twenty years' worth of oily dust lined the floors of the garage. The air reeked of gasoline and car engines.

It smelled like *him*.

Emily shuddered, and pushed away Bill's leering image. She scanned the block walls. Under a filmy window on the far side sat a low desk, its dull gray surface grimy with fingerprints.

Emily squinted through the panes.

Uh-oh.

She shaded her eyes and checked again. The blaring sun made it hard to focus through the grimy glass. But a human silhouette marched straight for the garage. And it was shaped just like Maria.

She hurried back to Mom. "It's her." Whispering made her head throb, and she frowned. "She's almost here."

"Stay out of sight, but keep searching. I'll hide."

Emily's legs shook from the exertion. Her heart raced out of control as she wobbled back to the desk, staying out of the light. The metal drawer opened with a loud screech, and she winced. Nothing there but pencils, paper, and some little light bulbs. The drawer on the right slid right open.

Jackpot.

Twenty or 30 key chains lay in a heap. The stretchy pearl bracelet she'd given Mom on Mother's Day lay right on top. How dare they keep her mother's stuff?

She picked up the bracelet. The doorknob rattled.

She scrunched down beside the desk and pressed her back against the wall. Thank goodness someone had locked the door.

Maybe Maria didn't have a key.

Emily glanced behind the desk where thick cobwebs formed little bridges to the wall, and crud packed the corners of the floor. Yuck. She sidled away and pulled her feet against her hips with a shiver. She pinched her nose and tried to keep from sneezing.

Muffled sounds of walkie-talkie static filtered through the door. Maria's voice came through loud and clear. "I don't know. They've just disappeared."

A male voice that could have been John's crackled over a radio, but the only words Emily made out were *shoot on sight* and *check the car.*

"Ten-four."

She prayed Mom was all right, and that Maria didn't notice the open window in the back. At least the screen had fallen to the inside.

Charlene slithered under the car and kicked the trampled blades of grass back in shape. Crusted mud clung above her face like misshapen dirt-dauber nests, and the metal reeked of oil and dirt. No telling what her clothes would look like when she got out.

Only a miracle would keep Maria from finding her.

Radio static reached into her narrow space. Her breath against the muffler made hearing all the worse. She held her breath.

Maria's feet pressed into the grass just inches away from her face. She rattled the door handle. If Maria circled the car, she'd see the flattened grass.

Instead, she stepped away. "I'm checking the perimeter and the woods. Are you on the way back?" A click sounded behind the Civic, followed by the whine of the electric golf cart.

"Ten-four," came a male voice and static.

The sound of the cart faded into the distance. A whole minute passed before Charlene dared to wriggle out from under the car. She brushed a hand across her face and hair. Kept low and craned her neck toward the gardens. Clear. She hurried to the back window. Emily waited inside.

"Here's the key."

"Good job, Emily," said Charlene, helping her out. "Are you feeling okay?"

"I'll be fine as soon as we're out of here. Man, this place is nasty."

"Tell me about it." She brushed at the smudge on Emily's face then peered around the corner. "Come on."

As they hurried to the car, Charlene clicked the remote twice to unlock the doors and slid into the driver's seat. Emily climbed in the other side.

Despite the heat, the burning seat felt good against Charlene's skin. The sunbaked dash smelled like home.

She twisted the key. The engine groaned and fell silent. She gritted her teeth and hit the steering wheel. "No, this can't be happening."

She tried again.

"Pray, Mom."

Charlene nodded. "Lord, please, we need Your help. Please help us get this car started."

Two more tries, and no success. Cold sweat prickled over Charlene's neck.

Lord help us.

She twisted the key again, and the engine turned over. "Thank You, Lord." Her hands shook as she shifted into drive. She pulled into the dirt lane. The same road John had driven down a while ago.

"Mom! Wait." Emily's door flew open.

"What are you doing?"

"Back up."

"What?"

"My stuff."

Emily stumbled toward the electric pole where the cart had been parked. She grabbed her things and lurched back to the car. The clothes, metal box, and journal dropped to the passenger-floor. She pulled the door shut and sank against the gray upholstery. Her hands trembled as she buckled the seatbelt.

"I totally forgot about those." Charlene pressed on the accelerator.

"I hid them on the other side of the electric pole."

"Stroke of genius."

A hundred yards away, the road curved behind the eastern buildings. "I'm pretty sure that's a way out, Emily. But if I'm wrong, we'll have to head back to the cabin and drive around the washout John told me about."

"Washout?" Emily shook her head. "You'll wreck the car. It's this big." She spread her arms apart.

Charlene raised her eyebrow, "Better hope, then."

As they approached the wide stand of oaks, Charlene's jaw dropped. A jagged-edged wall rose high behind the tree line. Its surface, a painted mural of trees, blended in with the surrounding woods.

"I've looked at this end of the property a hundred times and I had no idea this was here. Can you believe it?" She glanced at Emily. "Even close up I couldn't tell it was fake, could you?"

"It's totally camouflaged."

"Clever, very clever." Charlene let off the brake, and they rolled between two parallel walls. A massive open-air packing shed backed up to the wall on the right. Hundreds of packing crates and pallets crowded together on its depot-like platform. Two lines of produce trucks and a couple of semis waited along the right side of the dirt road. "You can't see this from the front."

"Yes, but what is it? What are these trucks?"

"I don't know, but right now, let's worry about how we're going to get out."

The semis advertised *EMA Produce, Organic and Pure* in bold letters, and *Pentalucidity Markets, Atlanta, Georgia* in smaller plain ones. Colored vegetables and fruits flowed from twin-facing cornucopias. A shorter truck sat sideways in front of these. Its headlights stared back at them from under a green hood.

As they drifted past the semis, Charlene blew out a sigh. The workers must have just left. What would have happened if they had come while all the workers were hanging out?

Emily pointed to a gate thirty feet beyond the trucks. The land sloped away on the other side. "A paved road."

The Honda coasted close to the gate. Charlene frowned. "We'll have to break that padlock."

"I'll find a rock."

Jumping out, Emily left the door ajar as she searched around the outside of the Honda.

Charlene peered through the glass. Nothing much around the car but grass and sand. In the trunk she had...

"Mom!" Emily gestured wildly, pointing at a sign beyond the fence. "That's—it's—"

"Oh, my gosh, Highway 98." Only about a mile away, traffic sped by at the bottom of the hill. "We've been this close the whole time. I can't believe it."

As Charlene gazed at the sign, a familiar white van swung off the highway and careened toward them.

"That's John! Get back in. We've got to hide."

Emily slid in and pulled the door shut. "Mom, what are we going to do?"

"I'm parking behind those cabs. He might not see us."

Charlene slammed the car into reverse then twisted around with her arm across the back of Emily's seat. The car zigzagged backwards. "Lord, help us, please, we're so close. Help us. Please, please, please."

The Honda lurched to a stop behind the line of semis, and Charlene jerked the wheel to the right. She pulled up so close to the first cab that their headlights almost touched the horizontal green truck. Its black letters read *Estrella 5 Gourmet Catering, Pentalucidity, Atlanta, Georgia.* Another line of semis boxed them in on the right.

Charlene's pulse raced.

"Mom, we're hemmed in." Tears glistened in Emily's eyes. "All we can do is back up."

"I know."

"Can he see us?"

Charlene pointed at the tall grass beyond the green truck then turned the motor off. "I hope not. But that should help."

Emily nodded.

Charlene touched her finger to her lips and rolled the window partway down. "Listen."

John's van door squeaked. The heavy chain clanged against the galvanized framework and banged against the stop-post. The hum of his engine grew louder. He was inside now, for sure.

Lord, make us invisible.

The van stopped again. John was probably locking the gate.

Voices cloaked in static came through his walkie-talkie as the van pulled closer and stopped. The van door slammed.

"Say that again." John's tone was demanding.

More garble.

"They're still out?"

A pause.

"Have they got the car?" His voice was so loud he must be standing right next to the semi.

"I just went by there. It's still locked by the garage. No sign of them." Maria.

"I'll page Mike and Brian. Come on down. We'll find them. Over."

He radioed again and cursed. "We've got two loose and on foot. Meet me down here by the trucks right away. Bring guns. This stops now. Over."

Emily's eyes grew large as she pointed under the semi's cab. John's legs paced back and forth, and his heavy feet crunched in the sand.

All he had to do was bend over, and he'd see them.

233

Lord, please make him stay put.

Within minutes another vehicle approached. Doors slammed. More heavy feet. "Which way?"

"We don't know," John said. "Here's what we'll do. We'll fan out over the back side of the property here and up into the north woods. Got your silencers? We don't want to disturb the other clients."

"Why don't you call Betty and Donna? Get their help too." The booming voice sounded like Dr. Mike's.

"Good idea. We can take this side and the south woods, and they can meet Maria down front and scout the woods there."

"Here comes Maria now."

The sound of a golf cart whined to a stop.

"I want you to page Betty and Donna," John said.

"They're on the way," Maria said.

"Well, page them again, and meet them up front by the river. You three can fan out west and south."

Boomy-voice responded. "If we don't find them there, then we'll search the next complex. Same plan?"

"Right," agreed John. "It won't be too hard to flush them out. I never let on that there's a road back here. Most likely, they'll head out front, the way they drove in. I already told Charlene there's a big hole up there but maybe she's stupid enough to try anyway." He chuckled. "They won't be able to get their car out."

"They're probably heading southwest through the woods." Maria again.

"All right," John said. "Let's go. Get this over with."

"Think they could be hiding in one of our trucks?" Dr. Mike asked.

"No, they're locked. But check if you want to."

Charlene and Emily traded looks. "Pray, Mom."

"I'm cutting through the middle of the gardens, just in case," Maria said. "They'll show up nice and bright in those pink clothes." The golf cart whined away.

Charlene nudged Emily and pointed under the green truck in front of them. Maria's golf cart zipped past it, flattening a trail through the deep grass. Charlene let out a breath. "That was close."

"Yeah, I saw her leg." Emily wrinkled her nose. "And that ugly skirt."

"Emily, I'm sorry I got you into this mess. I was only trying to help you. After—you know."

"Mom, I know. I forgive you."

"I didn't pray. I should have. It all looked and sounded so good." She leaned her head back. "It fit together perfectly."

One of the men yelled. "There's an open door here."

Charlene jerked her head up.

"Check inside the trucks."

The truck quivered in front of them. Heavy feet clomped through it. "All clear, nothing here."

"Check the other one."

Charlene closed her eyes. "Please, God."

Tears ran down Emily's cheeks. She clutched Charlene's arm and huddled down in the seat, shaking.

"Locked."

"This one's locked, too."

Charlene moved her lips. "Lord, please, make us invisible. We're asking in Jesus' name." She squeezed Emily's hand. "I'm so sorry, sweetheart. I'm so sorry."

"Stop it, Mom. It's all right." Her muffled whisper only added to Charlene's guilt.

The catering truck bounced as the man jumped out. His legs followed the side of the truck on their right. He shouted from the back of the last semi. "We're locked here, too."

Charlene watched through the rearview mirror as he passed behind them and back to John. How could they miss the Civic sitting here in plain view? He had circled them completely.

In less than ten seconds, the engines started, and the vehicles zoomed away.

Safe.

Charlene leaned her head back. *Thank You, Lord.* "We should go now," she whispered.

"Wait sixty seconds, Mom. They might hear us."

"If we wait, and John realizes the car is missing, they'll know we're back here. They'll see the tracks."

"Count to sixty first."

Charlene counted to thirty and turned the key.

No time to lose. She snapped the gear into reverse, threw her arm across the seat behind Emily and pressed the accelerator. They hurtled backwards, clearing the two semis. Back in drive, she yanked the wheel to the left. Swerved onto the road. Her wheels spun in the sand.

Gripping the steering wheel, she raced forward. "We have to get through that gate, Emily. Do you know what a lug wrench is?"

"Yes."

"It's under the floor mat in the trunk. Right side."

"Got it."

At the gate, Charlene stomped the brakes and they jerked forward.

"Fast, now," she hissed. "I'll pull through when the gate opens. You jump back in."

In two seconds, Emily had the lug wrench. She sprinted to the gate. Raised the tool. Smashed it down.

It glanced off the padlock.

"Ohh."

A loud car horn sounded behind them from the direction of the garage. It honked and honked. Someone yelled.

The horn blared louder and louder. The van burst through the blind gate in the wall and around the trucks, barreling, fishtailing toward the gate.

Oh, God, he's right behind us. "Hit it again, Emily!" Charlene yelled, "Hit it hard!"

Emily slammed the padlock. Connection. It sprang free.

Charlene turned the mirror, her heart pounding as John drew closer.

"Hurry, Emily."

Emily yanked the lock out of the link and kicked the gate open. She ducked behind the gate post and tossed the lock on the ground.

Charlene pushed the accelerator. The Honda lurched through the gate and stopped again. She glanced in the rearview mirror.

A cloud of dust boiled over the van as it ground to a stop. John stumbled out, dragging a long rifle off the seat.

"Emily, get in!"

Emily threw in the tool and swung into the floorboard. "Go, Mom!"

A bullet pinged off the gate.

Spinning gravel, the car erupted onto the road, swerving and squealing toward the highway.

Emily pulled the door shut and crouched in the floorboard. "What's he doing?"

Charlene checked the rearview mirror again. "Getting in his van. None of his buddies are there yet."

Pressing harder on the accelerator, she revved the engine, and the Honda sailed toward the highway.

The gate bounced a second time against the stop-post.

John paid little attention to it. He yelled into his walkie-talkie with his rifle still pointed out the window. He pushed on the gas and flew toward the opening.

The gate wobbled in rebound. It hovered between the dirt ruts.

John braked.

Too late.

His grill rammed into the gate and the van stopped cold. Steam boiled up from under the hood.

He cursed and leaped out. With the barrel through the open window, he pulled the trigger anyway.

He squinted. Had he missed? Who could tell with this flippin' fog in the way?

Stumbling over his feet, he circled the steamy cloud, and aimed for the Honda. He blasted again.

More vile words and God's name spewed out of his mouth.

Grabbing the hot gun-barrel with both hands, he slammed it like a bat against the broken grill. The explosion blew a hole through his shirttail and he let go.

He buried his head in his hands and sank to his knees. The car sped away.

Chapter 29

Emily clicked her seatbelt as they merged in with the other traffic. She swiped at the hot tears running down her face and searched the console for a tissue.

"Let's get home," Mom said. "As far away from this place as possible."

"I can't believe he almost shot us, Mom. We ate at his table."

"It's unreal to me, too."

"It's like a horror movie."

"I know. I know." Mom concentrated on the traffic, but patted Emily's knee.

"I'm worried we'll wake up and still be there."

"The nightmare is over, dear. We'll never go back."

The Honda blasted south, eating up the miles as Emily stared out the passenger window. She blotted her eyes and tried to focus on the trees blurring by. The trees of freedom.

"Two hours to Gaskille," Mom said, "and we have a quarter tank of gas."

"I wish we didn't have to stop. Can I call Grandma? Where's the phone?"

"In the metal box on the floor. So's my wallet. We don't have the key, though."

Emily slid her seat back and attacked the box with the lug wrench.

"Be careful you don't break the phone."

"I won't." The lid crumpled, and she pried it open. She waved the phone in front of Mom and smiled. "It's fine.'

She found the charger in the glove compartment. The phone beeped to life as she plugged it in.

"Gas first. Check my wallet, Emily. Should be a hundred dollars in it."

Emily held it open. "Nada."

"Nothing?" Mom's jaw stiffened. "What about credit cards?"

"Nope. They took everything."

"We need gas." Mom pressed her lips together. "Look in my sunglass case over the visor."

"The secret stash." Emily opened the case and squealed. "Yay," she said, pulling out two folded tens.

She sniffed the bills and placed them in the wallet. "Wonderful smell. Thank You, Lord. Can we stop at McDonald's?"

"If you stick to the dollar menu."

"I'll watch for one." Now this was getting back to normal. "Home, sweet home, here we come."

With a McDonald's just ahead, Charlene glanced sideways at Emily's pale, thin face.

How could she have been so stupid as to get them in this mess? The last few weeks had seemed like a lifetime. If she had only prayed. Or listened to her mother.

The McDonald's parking lot abutted the gravelly entrance of a fruit stand. Charlene pulled under the shade of an oak between the two, and they entered the restaurant.

"We should grab some fruit next door," Charlene said after the restroom break.

"Go ahead. I'll order our sandwiches."

"I don't like leaving you all alone."

"I can do it. These people are *normal,* Mom. Okay?"

Charlene hesitated then held out a ten. "Be careful."

The line at McDonald's was long enough to keep Emily busy while she shopped at the fruit stand. Bananas would be perfect. As she passed by the car, she unlocked the doors in case Emily got back before she did.

The chicken-wire structure must have been a huge coop at one time. Baskets of ferns and impatiens hung from the rickety two-by-fours overhead. Inside the corrugated tin walls the attendant straightened a basket of giant tomatoes next to the cash register and smiled at Charlene. "Evenin', honey, can I help you?"

A human. A woman she could talk to without fearing for her life. "Yes, hi. Got any bananas?"

"Next to them apples in the back. Let me know if you need anything else." She turned her attention to a tiny TV hidden discreetly under the counter.

Charlene located two perfect bananas and set them down by the register. She stepped away from the counter and peered over at McDonald's. Emily hadn't come out yet. The line was long, though.

Back at the register, the woman shoved aside a box of tomatoes and rang up the purchase. Charlene's hands trembled as she paid. How ridiculous to get so worked up. It had only been a couple of minutes. Emily was fine.

"You okay?"

"Just a little anxious. Fine, though."

Charlene's eyes drifted to the tomato box as the woman counted out her change. She stifled a gasp when she recognized the label. *EMA Produce, Organic and Pure.*

So much for "food for charity."

❧

Back on the highway, Emily poked a fry in her mouth and picked up the phone. "Let's call now." She hit the buttons with her thumb.

"Charlene?" Grandma's voice sounded so good.

"Hi, Grandma. It's both of us," Emily said. "You're on speaker-phone."

"Oh, I've *missed* you girls. How's Colorado?"

"What are you talking about?"

"Colorado, Charlene. Aren't you in Colorado?"

"We've never—" Mom furrowed her brow. "Did you get a letter saying I was in Colorado?"

"Yes. All about your new job and Emily's school. It's a beautiful house."

Emily frowned. What was Grandma talking about?

"Long story, Mother. I'll explain when we get home. Just passed Highway 320. It should only be an hour now."

"You're coming home? To Gaskille?"

"Yes, Mother. We're coming home."

"Drive careful, Charlene."

"Mother?"

"Yes?"

"I'm sorry. About everything. And thanks."

"Bye, Grandma," Emily said. "I can't wait to see you."

"Here's a kiss for you both. *Mwah.* Bye, now." Grandma's voice sounded teary. And Emily couldn't believe her ears. Mom telling Grandma she was sorry? That was a new twist.

After disconnecting, Mom dropped the phone in the console and blew out a chest full of air. "Emily, I need you to tell me about Maria poisoning you."

242

"Didn't you read my note?"

Mom shifted in the seat and pulled the papers from her pocket.

"No chance to. I guess we both figured out we were in trouble about the same time."

"Beggar died, Mom." Emily choked back tears. "He saved my life."

"Yeah?"

"Maria made me some chocolate milk. I only drank a little and then I spilled it. Beggar licked up all the rest." She bit her lips to keep from all-out crying. "It was poison, Mom. I had figured out the deal with the pills. Every time I took them I got sick. So I quit taking them. Then she tricked me with poisoned chocolate milk."

"And to think I pushed you into this."

Emily dabbed her eyes and blew her nose. "Poor Beggar. I had to leave him on the bed." She pictured his stiff little body and pressed her face into her hands. "I didn't even cover him up."

"I'm sorry, Emily. He was a good dog." Another mile passed. "I think they must have killed Susie, Cindy's daughter."

"Yeah, I found her clothes, too."

"Clothes?"

"I grabbed them on the way out." Emily pulled the striped shorts and shirt out from under the seat. "Maria must have forgotten them. If Susie had been alive, she would have worn them home."

Emily held the shirt by the shoulders. "You know what Maria told me? She said the girl 'graduated,' and I was about to graduate too. Maria looked really happy. I think *graduate* means you *die*."

Mom gave her a sideways glance. "We probably came pretty close."

"I think Susie and I would have been friends."

"Me too, Emily."

Another mile passed in silence.

"I'm pretty sure they killed her mother," Mom said. "I think they would have done the same to me. Once they got through with someone, got all the work out of them, and all their money and child support checks, they killed them. Buried them in the garden." She shuddered. "I wonder how many people are buried at Earth Mother Acres."

"But why?"

"They're thieves. With my driver's license and credit cards, they'd have my identity. Maybe they were going to sell it. If no one knew I was dead, they would keep on getting the child support. The odd thing is, it was such a small amount. We aren't rich."

"But look how many people live and work there."

"Predators. It was a huge scam."

They passed through a small town, and the traffic light turned yellow in front of an old courthouse. Mom slowed to a stop at a red light.

"I hate being used," Emily said.

"At the fruit stand there was a box from Earth Mother Acres. They're selling the produce, not giving it to charity. My clothing boxes ended up with New York labels. It's all for sale. Their place is a glorified sweat shop."

"Selling the clothes?"

The traffic light turned green again. "Oh, yes, they lied," Mom said. "About everything. We've got a lot to tell the law. I'm sure there's going to be a big investigation. But you can be sure, they won't get away with it now."

A train's horn blared, and Emily nearly jumped out of her skin. It raced toward them on a track parallel to the road. "Where are we?

Mom broke her gaze away from the gray asphalt and looked at her. "Sorry, lost in thought. Some little town. I wasn't paying much attention. They all look alike along this stretch."

Emily refolded Susie's clothes on her lap. "What makes you think they killed Susie's mom?

"You know those pink uniforms? I recognized Cindy's from the ink spot on the pocket. The dress was all torn up. Something really violent happened. They brought it to me to fix."

"Susie's mom was named Cindy?"

"Yes."

"The maid's name was Cindy. Toward the end I was doing her jobs."

Mom reached into her pocket and handed a gold object to Emily. "I found her pin."

Emily cradled it in her hands. "Where?"

"Mashed into a footprint under the marigolds."

The puzzle came together in Emily's head, and she widened her eyes. "Mom? I actually might have *seen* it."

"Seen what?"

"One night Beggar woke me up. He was growling. We looked out the window and I saw people carrying things and digging."

"I guess I'm right, then." Mom said. "Know what I think?"
"What?"

"You know the picket fence we saw on the way out?"
"Yeah."

"Cindy said Susie was buried inside the little fence, buried beside the tomatoes. They moved the fence." Mom clamped her lips. "I think they buried Cindy in the new plot. Then planted tomatoes on Susie's grave."

"Tomatoes? And we ate them?" Bile stirred in Emily's stomach. "Stop and let me throw up."

"I hate to say it, but I think they'll plant vegetables on top of Cindy, too."

"Gag, Mom. Gives a new meaning to organic produce, doesn't it?" She folded her arms over her stomach with a groan.

"I doubt anyone gets out of that place alive. It's a miracle we did."

"My head's starting to hurt."

"We'll call the law as soon as we get home."

Another few miles ticked by without a word. Emily kicked off her shoes and propped her heels on the dash. It felt so good to be back in their old car. She studied her toes spread against the glass. "Mom, have you heard of anyone being taken over by the devil?"

"You mean possessed? It's in the Bible."

"Whenever I talked about Jesus to Maria, she would get weird and growl and want me to leave the room. I couldn't even play 'Jesus Loves Me' on the piano. When you were around, she pretended to be nice, but when you weren't there, she hated me. I could tell."

"Honey, I believe you. Maria and John were very evil. It's just God's mercy we got out. If I had it to do over again, I never would have gone. I'm sorry I fell for their scam. Stupid, stupid, stupid."

"You were just trying to help me." Emily stared out the passenger window at the farmhouses and fields passing by. "Mom, do you think they'll try to find us?"

"We're a big threat to them, and they're not idiots. Unfortunately, they know where we live. But we'll talk to the law as soon as we get back."

"I wrote it down in that note, Mom. I don't mind telling everything."

"You're a brave kid, Emily. Then we have to pray. A lot. And keep our eyes open."

When Mom stopped for gas, Emily opened the glove compartment and rummaged through it. She smiled when she found the photograph of her and her friends from their day at the Citra Fish Camp. But that wasn't what she was looking for.

She scrabbled around some more, moving things aside, pulling things out. Finally. The white piece of paper with Tony's number. Right where she'd left it.

Emily grinned and reached for the phone.

Mom slid into the driver's seat. "What are you smiling about?"

"Nothing. I just have to put a number in the phone."

Mom started the engine, and Emily grabbed her arm. "Mom! I just thought of something. You know Maria's twin brother?"

"Yes, she mentioned one."

"He lives in Gaskille. It's Pastor Mario."

Chapter 30

With John on her heels, Maria shut the door of Lucas' special room behind the shop.

"Hello, Maria. John."

She whirled around, her heart leaping at the sound of Lucas' creamy voice. The sound she adored under each full moon beside the sun-fountain and the few occasions in between. She could never get enough of him.

"How did you get here before us? When you told us to wait here, we expected you to be a while."

"Barricade the door, please." Even in the darkness, his white suit and teeth gleamed.

Lucas righted the table that had been lying on its side since the night of the sacrifice then leaned against it. He said nothing.

Maria stepped with confidence toward her precious man while John hung back. The coward.

"Since no one's ever escaped the Acres before," she said, "we knew you would have advice for us. Of all the people in the world, Lucas, we knew you were the one who could figure this out."

She glanced at the throne where he always sat, where he directed them in their bloody rituals after their fountain-dances. She shivered, knowing she was his favorite, of course. He allowed *her*, and *only* her, to massage his smooth olive hands and feet. Even now, in the midst of this disaster, her fingers twitched, yearning to touch his warm skin.

She glanced sideways at John. Silly little man. Of course

he had no idea about her feelings for Lucas. Turning to her dark-eyed lover, she said, "We know you can straighten things out, get us out of this little problem." No problem was too big for Lucas.

Lucas smiled and opened his arms as if to embrace her.

She hurried toward him, eager for his touch, then stopped.

His lips morphed into the scaly lips of a snake, exposing jagged amber teeth. A loud hiss filled the room.

"What's happening?" Without thinking, Maria scrambled backwards. She grabbed John's arm and cowered behind him.

Stringy brown mucous dangled from the creature's mouth. His scaly yellow body stretched tall, revealing a pale chest like the underbelly of a snake. He laughed, swinging the fecal-crusted rags that dangled like pendulums from his shoulders.

Where was the beautiful white suit? His lovely teeth and skin?

A squeak peeped from Maria's throat.

John pushed backward, knocking her off balance. She dug her fingernails into his arm.

Congestion gurgled in John's panicked throat. Seemingly transfixed, he ignored her piercing clutch. He was little help.

The iguana-like skin around Lucas' slanted black eyes glimmered in the faint light as he waggled the loose reptilian *V* below his chin. A breathy "Haaaaah," flew out of his throat. Hot spittle spritzed across their arms throwing a stink over them like dog feces.

They shuffled backward, swiping at the spit on their clothes, and holding their wrists against their noses.

The hiss garbled into a growl and vibrated the walls. "You failed me, you idiots." His rags swayed back and forth as he stared at them with those obsidian eyes. "You have served me poorly, and I have a gift for the stupid."

An egg-noodle of mucous flew out and clung to John's chest.

He dodged and jumped around, trying to get it off, and knocked Maria to the ground. Needles of pain shot through her hip. Stupid man.

John squatted next to the wall, trembling and pulling and shaking his shirt away from his skin.

Maria whimpered. "W-w-we came for your help, your protection. We've always done what you asked."

"Y-you said we're partners." John's voice warbled like an adolescent's. "In this very room, remember?" His face reflected the yellow of the demon's scales.

Maria stared at the thing that wasn't Lucas anymore. A demon, yes. He certainly wasn't human. That illusion of love she'd had for Lucas? Vaporized.

"Help us, Lucas. We need you." Maria rose, panting, her eyes darting about for some way of escape. "We've never crossed you. We've been faithful." She'd always laughed at that demon garbage. And devil stuff. But what else could this be? She glanced at the creature and imagined his scaly lips pressing against hers. She gagged.

"Stupid again." His laugh echoed off the block walls, "I lied! I am the Father of All Lies." He pointed to the sky. "I *am*, I *am*, I *am!*"

Metallic laughter screeched from his throat. The hinges of his mouth opened wide as the sound rose louder and higher until they buried their ears behind their hands. Maria grimaced, hoping her ears would not burst.

Lucas sighed like a tire deflating. "Ahhhh, it feels good to say that."

Swinging around the table, he swung his head near them like a dinosaur, lowering the lids of his billiard-ball eyes. He sweetened his voice. "Did you hear me say that?"

He tipped his face to the side, showing his teeth, "I *am*, I *am*, I *am*."

Maria recoiled, afraid to look away. John trembled against her. Useless man.

"There is no help in me. I don't give. Anything." The creature raised his head up. "I only take." His lids lowered even more. "I take."

His shrieks reverberated in her bones. Pain shot like a machine gun across the inside of her skull. "You are *mine*. So you give, give, give." He waved an arm. "And I'll take mine now."

Maria dug all ten fingernails into John's bicep. He screamed, "Please help us and protect us."

The reptile turned and slunk around the table toward his throne of importance.

Fear gripped Maria's chest so tight that only tiny breaths fit into her lungs.

"Please don't do this," John begged again. With his hair drenched in sweat, John wiped his mouth against his shoulder. "You know we've been faithful."

Maria reeled, suddenly dizzy. Who could help them now?

Lucas stared down at them. Yellow gas, stinking like rotten eggs, swirled up near his feet. A smell from Hell. Something else she'd laughed at. Every breath burned Maria's lungs. John's cheeks ran with tears. She blinked back her own.

Nausea bubbled up in her stomach, and finally she could hold it no longer. She lowered herself like a dog and hurled out the bile. John hit the floor, too, catapulting vomit into their mutual puddle.

251

The creature drew near and gazed at the mess. Sliding the side of his clawed foot into their soup, he flipped it into their faces. "You fool," he hissed. "I come to steal, kill, and destroy." His soiled fringe jerked with the force of his words. "Your faithfulness won't help you. It carries no weight."

Maria eyed the creature. Only a few minutes ago she would have done anything for her beautiful man. Her irresistible king, so full of promises. And none of it counted?

What a liar. If only she'd known the truth.

Lucas swaggered to the throne, his body glowing purple, then yellow again. His arms widened over the familiar table-like altar. He reached to the floor, picked up two steel knives, and placed them on the table.

Maria's breath caught in her throat. The knives glowed as red-hot as blacksmith's iron. How could that be?

The creature stood tall, and a noise like beating sails filled the room.

"Lie down on my table." His voice caressed her ear, patronizing and warm. Another lie. This wasn't him. But his allure caused Maria's insides to leap.

Easing onto the throne, he crossed his reptilian knees and gestured with his thin, lizardy fingers toward the knives.

She must resist. But how could she? Even while he repulsed her, his kindred spirit pulled her like a magnet.

He lowered his head. "Too slow."

Two strong hands grabbed her from behind and slammed her body onto the long table. With a loud crack, her skull connected with the wood, driving her teeth into her tongue. Her mouth flew open with pain. Another blow smacked the top of her head and shot cold needles down her neck. A groan indicated it must have been John's hard head behind her.

A glittery constellation sprayed across her vision. As it faded, an ugly creature came into focus. Something like Lucas, only smaller. Salty blood filled her mouth as his iron hands pressed down on her body and her throat. Copper-tasting blood filled her mouth and spilled over her lips. Her scream only gurgled, spraying blood over her face.

With a sizzle, the creature clamped a red-hot knife into her palm. Her flesh smoked as he clamped her fingers around it. Gnashing her teeth, she inhaled the putrid smell of her own burnt flesh.

He lifted the hot knife, and her world went black.

Laughter rolled form Lucas' belly. He slouched and grinned with his knees apart as he draped his arms over the sides of his throne.

Demons broke loose from the dark corners in a vulgar dance to the beat of voodoo drums. Low waves of combustion rippled over a black lake of fire. Its crests glinted with yellow the color of beaten eggs. The rotten-smelling cauldron roared low over the floor, covering it from wall to wall. It rose like a noisy firestorm, obscuring the decapitated bodies under the ebony waves until they were cooked. Then it disappeared.

The scene lasted only a minute before Lucas and the demons slipped back into their hiding places in the walls, under the door, and into the woods. They left nothing but the burned bodies and the small black area beneath them.

All was still.

Chapter 31

Emily woke as the Honda swung into the driveway in Gaskille. Grandma flew outside with open arms.

"Charlene. Emily!"

"Mother!"

"Grandma! It's so good to see you."

After bear hugs in the front yard, Mom placed her hand on Emily's head. "You were so right, Mother. Forget the therapy."

"This grandbaby just needs her grandma, don't you, honey?" Grandma said, pulling Emily her to her side.

Emily grinned. How great to hear them getting along.

"And something else," Mom added. "I *know* you've been praying. There's no way we could have survived without your prayers." She squeezed Grandma tight. "Thanks."

Emily raced up the steps. When she reached the porch, she turned back. "Wait till you hear everything, Grandma."

"Are y'all hungry?"

"For chocolate chip cookies!"

Grandma laughed. "Like I suspected."

"Business first, though," Mom said.

"Yeah," said Emily, opening the door. "We need to call the cops."

Mom and Emily huddled with the two sheriff's detectives at the dining table, talking and drawing diagrams of the Acres for them. Grandma hung around, trying not to intrude, but looking worried about what she was overhearing.

Emily glanced out the window as the questions dragged on and on. Night swallowed the sunset. All she wanted was to curl up in her cozy bed.

After awhile, the deputies stepped outside, casting long shadows away from the porch light. Night bugs circled as they talked, but they kept their voices too low to hear.

The taller deputy's phone rang, and Emily read one thing from his lips. FBI.

He reappeared inside to speak to Mom. "An agent needs to pick you and Emily up tomorrow at six. To revisit the crime scene."

It hardly seemed fair. They'd barely escaped the place.

"Won't they shoot us?" Emily said.

"Agents are already there. You'll be safe."

Emily groaned. She'd just gotten home.

At Earth Mother Acres, Emily leaned against the agent's car where it was parked across the cracked sidewalk in the backyard. Law people swarmed across the gardens, digging, writing, photographing. The way they were acting, it must be pretty bad. Yet all around the place, birds sang and flitted in and out of the trees as if nothing bad had ever happened.

Drop-dead tired from walking around and talking with the agent, Emily scowled and sprawled her arms across the agent's trunk. He'd driven them over most of the area, but she'd had enough. Time. To. Go.

"You tired, young lady?"

"Maybe Emily should sit down," Mom said, fanning herself. "She's been pretty sick."

"Sorry, young lady. Have a seat in the car." The agent,

melting with perspiration, opened the door for her. He probably wished he could yank that hot suit off.

"No trace of the other suspects yet," he said to Mom.

Emily stuck her head back out the door. She pointed toward the south. "Did you check the church? It's a drive, though."

"We'll do that." He gave his keys a twirl. "And speaking of driving, are you ready to drive back to Gaskille?"

Emily grinned. "You bet we are."

At McDonald's in Starke, the agent bought them lunch at the drive-through.

He spoke into his cell phone as the food came through the window. The crinkling bags obscured his words, but Emily picked out one. *Holocaust.* "How many bodies so far?" He passed a bag and a drink over the seat. "Unbelievable."

Emily exchanged glances with Mom in the passenger seat.

He held up a finger as he listened to his ear bud. "Four? You picked 'em up in the church?"

Emily grabbed Mom's arm. "You think I actually helped them?"

"What about the other two?" The agent shook his head and peered at Emily in the rear view mirror. "Burned?"

He spoke again. "So how did their killer get out if it's locked from the inside?"

In Gaskille, a hand nudged Emily out of her exhausted sleep.

"More news." Mom's voice.

"Mmm?"

"They arrested the bad guys from Gaskille."

Emily opened one eye.

"Pastor Mario, the psychiatrist... and some people out in Colorado and California. An identity-theft ring."

"Nobody's going to hurt us, then?"

"They're all in jail."

Emily closed her eyes.

Home was so good.

Tomorrow she'd call Tony. Then life would really be back to normal.

Epilogue

Emily reached for a yellow rope in the bottom of the fishing boat then tossed it over a snag on the ancient log. This was definitely the place. Same snag and all. She looped the rope around the broken branch where she'd found Susie's picture ten years ago. Old cypress logs must last forever.

Black water slapped against the boat's aluminum hull, and a water lettuce twirled along its side. Her fiancé crawled onto the log above her head gripping the pale wood, exactly as Emily had done so long ago.

She flopped onto the seat in the bow of the boat and waited while he satiated his curiosity.

He'd cajoled her until she'd finally agreed to show him the place.

For two minutes. Against her better judgment.

Fine that he wanted to check the place out. And sweet that he wanted to share this part of her life and all.

But with the memories that still haunted her, especially this time of year, her cushion in the bow of the boat was as close as she wanted to be to the riverbank. She wrapped her hands around her knee and stretched her shoulders.

Behind her, across the river, the sun backlit the tops of the cypress trees, transforming their tips into a brilliant lime green. And yet, something hung in the air, dark and heavy, as real as the current tugging at their boat. She shivered and turned back to him, noticing his shoeless feet.

"Don't fall," she said. "I'm not diving in that black water."

Her own toes combed through the hair of the sleeping

Australian shepherd at her feet. Even his markings looked like—

"Roof's still there."

Without thinking, she glanced toward the woods where he pointed. The log blocked her view. "They should have burned the place down years ago."

For the longest time, Emily gazed at her beloved's features, poised like a statue in the sunlight. Probably thinking about the stories she'd told him. Imagining the bell. Fitting things into the scene.

Instead of the bell's ugly sound, which she didn't want to recall, the cicadas' loud rasping filled her ears.

She was glad that he came and saw this. Shared it with her.

Emily couldn't help herself. She steadied her feet in the bottom of the boat and stood, needing to see what drew his attention.

"Reach down here and help me," she said.

He crept back and took her hands, pulling her up beside him. She straddled the log's bleached surface once again, and pressed her hands around its smooth grain. He lowered himself to the log behind her, bringing with him the smell of summer sun on his skin. He wrapped his arms around her waist.

Through the woods, only a fraction of the building remained visible. At least from this angle. The rusted metal of the cabin's roof seemed to have collapsed over its front porch.

She leaned back against the steady beat of his heart.

"Thank you, Emily," he whispered, his face against her hair. "I know this is hard."

They stayed this way a long minute, without speaking.

"See, there's nobody there." He turned her chin. "They can't hurt you now."

She blinked away the burn in her eyes and nodded.

He kept her from turning away and touched his warm lips against hers. Ten years ago she wouldn't have imagined this scene on the log.

The dog's noise interrupted them. The shepherd yawned and stretched, rocking the boat as he sat up.

They needed to get going.

"We'll make our own memories," he said with a sparkle in his eye. "Fade the old ones out."

She grinned and slid into the boat. "Your two minutes are up, by the way."

The boat joggled dangerously as he leaped in next to the motor. "Why don't we find some fried fish up at the boat ramp?"

"Food, always food."

Owls echoed across the water, sending a shiver up her spine as she unknotted the rope.

She shoved her hand against the log as he cranked the motor. Smoke billowed behind them as it sputtered to life.

From his place in the floor of the boat, the dog raised his nose and sniffed.

She smelled something too. Cigar smoke. "You smell that?" As they circled the log, she scanned the elephant ears and cypress knees near its base.

Her fiancé shook his head.

Maybe it was her imagination.

The engine kicked up another notch, and Emily's end of the boat rose from the water.

Her hair whipped against her face. She gathered it into a ponytail as the motor gained full speed. Lifting them toward the curve of the river, its noise overpowered the racket of the woods.

Beyond the boat's frothing wake the pale log grew smaller and smaller, and finally disappeared around the curve of the Black Suwannee.

Acknowledgments

Wheelbarrows full of flowers to all those who helped with *Summer on the Black Suwannee* over the years. Thank you, first, to the Lord for entrusting me with the project, and Pastor Ricky Roberts who recognized it and told me right up front that God didn't give me this idea to pass on to some another author. He gave it to me.

Well! That set off a string of hustling. Where to begin?

Peggy Masino, my dear friend and writer saw me stranded and gave me the first big push. She became my first beta reader. She steered me toward writing-methods books and writing groups I should be a part of. Yes, Peggy, I followed all your excellent advice. Thank you.

Cynthia McFarland, Cathy Clark, and Sonja Lonadier, you saw the beginning of the project, and encouraged me on despite its (blush) earliest renderings. And my dear beta readers Danny Odom, Cheryll Cannon, Mickey Cruey, Alicia Gilligan, Mark Mynheir, Janene Teeters, and Abby Lonadier.

Word Weavers International, how marvelous when I hit the jackpot by discovering your writers conference at Lake Yale. What a difference you made, what a wealth of wisdom and opportunities you offer! It changed my writing life forever! And my fellow Word Weavers in Ocala, I could never name you all, but special thanks to Delores and Chuck Kight, Marian Rizzo, Lois Lin, Shirley McCoy, Linda Bellig, Doris Hoover, Tom Paonessa, Vicki Uridel, Lorilyn Roberts, Karen Skirpan, Mary Busha, Leah Taylor, Jane Cardoso, Elsie Bowman, Robin Collison, Yeny Rowley, Diane Kitts, and Jen Cason.

And thank you all my joyful little second graders who through the years knew their teacher was working on some kind of book, and one day they'd get to read it.

Thank you my wonderful editors Johnnie Alexander Donnelly, and Fay Lamb, for your advice and expert knowledge, (God bless you for not running the other way). I was never alone.

Extra thanks to my loving family that was always behind me, always patient, and always full of encouragement. Thank you, Danny, Jeremy, and Gabbie. Kisses to you all.

A very special thanks to everyone at WordCrafts Press, especially my very gifted Publisher, Mike Parker. He is an angel in disguise. And many thanks to his very apt and talented artist, David Warren, who knocked it out of the park on my cover. I love it.

And I love and thank you all.

About the Author

J ennifer Odom, 2003 Teacher of the Year, is a 40-year veteran teacher of elementary education. She has taught kindergarten through fifth grades in all subjects. For the last ten years she has incorporated video-production for her magnet school students at Dr. N.H. Jones Elementary, leading them to win many local, state and international video awards, as well as those in writing, and technology.

Jennifer writes human interest stories for her local newspaper, *The Ocala Star Banner,* and has also been published in such national magazines as *Splickety* and *Clubhouse Jr.* In 2015 she was honored to be named the Florida Christian Writers Conference's Writer of the Year.

Her award-winning Young Adult novel, *Summer on the Black Suwannee,* is the first in a new series.

Connect with Jennifer online at:

www.jenniferodom.com

And now, a sneak peek at:

HEADS
Book II of the Black Series

Two dark presences drifted along the train tracks near Paradise Trailer Park. The twin demons, Callous and Tyrant, followed Vinnie the teen. His big sneakers crunched over the gravelly cross-ties that lay underneath the rusty train rails. If fact, they'd clung to Vinnie's family and kept them company for at least six generations.

Callous nudged the teen from behind. Vinnie stumbled on a cross-tie. *Get going.*

Behind them traipsed the girls, ages 10 and nine, and the boy, barely six, followed at a distance by their own imps.

Callous' tongue flicked out in anticipation and he licked his beady golden eyeballs. This assignment promised to be fun.

The demons' toad-like bodies slipped along unseen. They blended well with the verdant gloom of the park's thick growth of hickories and the shady orange groves beyond.

Callous snorted. People could hardly ever discern the demons. Those who could, mostly belonged to Him. Mostly. But not all.

The discerners might glimpse a shadow or fleeting presence, hear a noise—or feel creeped out, but hardly ever witnessed their form.

And others—Callous almost stopped to laugh and slap his knee, but glided on instead—others just thought of them as fairy tales. *How idiotic.* His tongue flicked out again and licked his eye.

Tyrant, as toady and ugly as Callous, slithered in place beside him. He lifted a fist and slammed Callous on the top of his head like a sledgehammer, then went right back to drumming his padded fingertips together. Drool drained from one side of his wide smile.

Callous hissed. "You're ugly, bub."

"Shut up, squirt. Keep movin'." Tyrant couldn't help but be himself. Yet he, too, seemed eager to get started on their long-term assignment.

Callous and Tyrant raised their warty lips and grinned at each other. Sulfurous breath rolled from between their short amber teeth.

Callous tipped his head over his shoulder. "Here come the inferiors."

Behind the young kids, and further back on the track, Subjugation, another demon, followed. Two friends slunk along with them. Not friends, actually. They all hated each other. Callous hissed.

Tyrant had to say something. "Step back, you scum inferior. You're not allowed up here with the likes of us."

Subjugation, as pale and milky as a glob of glue, cowed and stepped back.

Callous cackled. "You ugly pasty-face, red-dotted, jiggly albinos. Just stay back and don't feel welcome." He wiped the drool off his own lips. Slither on, you cowardly things, slither on.

Tyrant slammed his fist down on his head again and Callous returned his attention to the teen.

Those trailer park mothers had no idea who they'd

entrusted their kids to—to walk them across the highway.

He licked his eye again.

Three ducklings with a fox.

HEADS

Book II of the Black series

by

Jennifer Odom

Coming this Fall

from

WordCrafts Press

Also Available From

WORDCRAFTS PRESS

Believe
by Abby Rosser

Home
by Eleni McKnight

Tears of Min Brock
by J.E. Lowder

The Awakening of Leeowyn Blake
by Mary Garner

You've Got It, Baby!
By Mike Carmichael

www.WordCrafts.net

Made in the
USA
Columbia, SC